THE TRUTH THE DEAD KNOW

A Novel by

R.W. Kennedy

ISBN: 1542683122
ISBN 13: 9781542683128
Library of Congress Control Number: 2017900983
CreateSpace Independent Publishing Platform
North Charleston, South Carolina

For my mother, the Kennedy's, Chanyeon, Malesra and Weisser; keep rowing.

{Dramatis Personae] (Principal Characters)

Michael Gilbey	Expatriate teacher, son of Herman
James Eckhart	Expatriate teacher from Wisconsin
Herman Gilbey	Degenerate gambler
Richard Wallace	Criminal Kingpin
Goran Perisic	Wallace's right-hand man
Chantal Wallace	Richard Wallace's teenage daughter
Yazmin Hechevarria	Prostitute
Mike Powell	Associate of Herman, gambler
Seraj Mukhtari	Expatriate teacher
Saeed Mukhtari	Seraj's father, dishwasher
Thomas Beck	Bookmaker
Dae-su Jung	CEO of Goldmoon
Rim "Jacob" Jung	Dae-su's only son & heir, academy owner
Woo-jin Han	Detective (Male)
Hye-jeong Kim	Detective (Female)
Tae-woo Kim	Motel Clerk
Agent Owens	FBI Agent
Jin-hee Jee	Young handsome tea farmer
Bo-kyung	Rim's wife
Ji-soo Shim	Jin-hee's mother
In-jo Seung	Family Attorney
Jong-suk Jee	Elder of the Jee clan
Na-ra Jang	Bo-kyung's aunt
Shore & King	Floridian detectives
Se-ra Choi	Jin-hee's intended
White Mantis	Caucasian leader of an Asian gang.

CHAPTER 1
THE DISTANT STRAINS
OF TRIUMPH

"Bright and early for their daily races
Going nowhere, going nowhere"

- ("Mad World") Tears for Fears

Under sweltering heat, Herman Gilbey sat wedged in with the opening day crowd, waiting for the steeds to burst nobly out of the gate. He tried to wipe the mustard stain from his brown polo but was not availed, so he adjusted his Yates fedora and looked down at his apprentice and son, Michael Gilbey, and assured the young lad that he had studied these horses all summer and that the wild appaloosa, What a Feeling, was bound to shock many race cards. The program guide disrespectfully described the youthful horse as being "overmatched by the field." Well, Herman had been a track-rat when the odds-makers were still in diapers, and he knew precisely which horses possessed a competitive fire, and which horses had been whipped and strung along to parade around the track. What a Feeling was of the former variety, and he would take the flag that day.

Nothing filled Herman with excitement quite like the races. He loved the sport for what it was, and loved it in spite of the corruption, greed, and cheating that garnered many detractors. It mattered not how hideous the underbelly of the sport of kings became. Herman was eternally in love with the gilded veneer, the heraldic trumpet, the buzz that ushered the horses forth for that glorious prize. Above all, he loved to win, but not just win, to watch the horses he had chosen waltz brilliantly ahead of the pack and glide to an easy finish.

He grew to love the gritty character of the sport and the atmosphere surrounding it: 115 pound jockeys, grown men who in speech sounded as though they had filled their lungs with helium, men undeterred by the prospect of a broken collarbone, 57 year old women with blackened lungs hooked up to oxygen machines going through a jar of quarters at the slots, handlers and physios secretly trying to give their runners an illegal handicap, men like himself who were willing to risk their paycheck for greater glory. The track was the only home he had ever known. The Kentucky Derby could keep their financiers with their ridiculous hats and mint juleps. Herman Gilbey belonged to Suffolk Downs, and it with all of its hollowed lonely patrons belonged to him.

As one might expect from a track rat gambling junkie, Herman was not the handsomest of folks. His paunch jiggled when it popped out of the shirts that were a good fit twenty years and twenty pounds ago. Cigarettes and whiskey had made his skin leathery and stained his teeth yellow, but a charming jolly spirit always shone through.

The horses were off, galloping forward like enraged ghosts. As the odds predicted, I Saw the Light could not keep pace with the rest of the pack, but the eyes of the crowd quickly moved away from that shameful sight if they stumbled upon it at all. The focus was on What a Feeling, who had charged out of the gate with steadfast fury. He was half a nose length ahead of Pouring Rain. Even though his horse was in front, Herman worried that he had spent too much of his energy gaining an advantage, and wouldn't have enough juice in the final stretch. What a Feeling was a young appaloosa, and Herman hoped that his youth would carry him through. With clenched fists, Herman prayed for his horse to keep its lead. On the final turn, the heavy favorite for this mile began to turn the turf into a blaze of dust, passing ahead of the field by a few yards with his elegant stride as though he had velvet hooves.

Herman had lost. For a moment, he looked up into the fierce yellow orb that was the sun, then turned toward his losing race card and tore it into confetti.

A look askance greeted the boiling Herman when he had turned to look behind him at the rather large clock fastened to the tower. The man holding the glare was leaning against the handrail, vociferously chewing a piece of red bubble gum that had lost its flavor. The scar cut diagonally across the whole of his face stood out prominently in the minds of those he encountered. It was an irrevocable token of something he had suffered long ago. His name was Goran Perisic and he had a score to settle with Mr. Gilbey.

⇌ ⇋

Richard Wallace sat in a rocking chair in a dark room beside his teenage daughter's bed. After the horrific acid attack, he found it difficult to look directly at her. To stare at her freakish countenance was to be at once repulsed and in that contorted visage were tiny pieces, small reminders of her ruptured beauty and the glorious life that she was slated for. Now, her face was shrouded by a protective plastic mask like Lon Chaney in *Phantom of the Opera*.

Counselors and doctors urged her to get out of her room, but it was easy for them to speak; they weren't met with instant revulsion everywhere they went. At all costs, Richard Wallace vowed to bring the perpetrator of the acid attack to prolonged torture, to make him beg for death over and over again. However, about eight years had passed since the masked man jumped out of his sedan and threw sulfuric acid in her face, and a lead hadn't been found. Business went on as usual but Richard Wallace would forever hold a firm place in his heart for vengeance until it had been exacted.

"I bought you something. Do you want to see it?" Chantal wriggled under the sheets and turned the other way. Richard took out the doll and placed it on the bed. It was ordinary and not a fitting gift for an adolescent girl. She reached back for it, and held it close to her, wishing that she could fall back into sleep.

"Hey babe, maybe we can go to The Cape this weekend. Some peace, quiet and fresh air will do you some good. I hope you can still ride your bike like the wind. "

Her raspy voice was lifted unintelligibly in response.

The door opened a crack, enough to let a sliver of light in. Richard turned around in the wooden chair; his wife's head was visible through the aperture.

"Honey, Herman is here to see you."

"Fucking degenerate. Just a second, Babe." Richard turned his attention back to his forlorn daughter. "I'll be back soon." He brushed his daughter's hair with his long thin freckled hand and kissed the piece of plastic over her forehead. To ease her misery, Richard put a record player in her room, and every time he left the room, he would put an old record on. This time it was the Beatles' *Let it be*, and the needle touched down on the grooves of "The Long and Winding Road."

The wino was in the kitchen, at the Formica roundtable, drinking a glass of wine that Mrs. Wallace had prepared. The Sagrantino in the Schott Zwiesel Clasico glass didn't look right in his chubby hands, but he didn't care; he'd drink vodka from a sippy cup if he had to. When Mrs. Wallace left, he quit his attempt to feign a couth manner and started to drink straight from the bottle. He hummed a song from his youth as he drank.

Mr. Wallace walked into the kitchen, looked disappointingly at Herman and grabbed a seat. Herman immediately launched into his pitch with visible anxiety:

"The fix is in my friend." Wallace tightened his lips and looked down.

"The fix was in last time and your 'boy' magnificently pulled away from the pack. I would have been better off doing the exact opposite of what you told me to do."

"This is different though. Turns out John Murphy has a superior gambling problem, not unlike my own, and he's already agreed to throw the race in order to keep those brutish debt collectors – men in your camp, I suppose – from knocking his teeth out."

"Where'd you get this information from?" Herman seemed incredulous at the implication that his sources were less than credible.

"Whaddaya mean, where? I practically live at that fucking track. I know all the underhanded dealings."

"What's your fucking source?"

"Buccellati, strapping fucking greasy ginzo, part of the new muscle for Turin."

"It doesn't sound very reliable, certainly not something to stake a lot of money on."

"I'm telling you Dick: this guy is at the gym every day. He's part of that crew, and he's 100 percent certain that this thing is going down. You know I wouldn't push the thing so hard, 'cept I'm kind of short on capital, and seeing as you've been doing well for a while, I figure that we could help each other out. I get out of debt and you increase your already abundant savings. Shit, what the fuck you got to lose?"

"It's the principle of the matter. You and I go way back, but if the word gets out that some degenerate gambler walked off with ten grand of my money...Hey, a spade's a spade. Look, fact of the matter is that I can't look weak. I'm going to give you an advance, but if you fuck this one up, it'll be just like anyone else fucked up." Richard breathed a heavy sigh, disappeared for a moment, and came back with a thick brown envelope.

"Here it is." Richard announced these words as a magician might, and Herman resented that this sum, which would have been almost nothing to Mr. Wallace, had to be so prudently accounted for by a man (Herman), to whom it meant everything.

"Also, since you owe me more than a couple, I'm going to need quite a hefty favor from you."

"Sure anything."

⊫ ⊨

Down at Sal's diner in Randolph, Herman Gilbey squeezed the sliced lemon over his fried scallop roll, and watched his son do the same, but Michael somehow managed to get the citrus in his eye.

"Fuck that stings."

"You're unbelievable Michael. Next time you should eat with goggles" Herman roared with mirth, his cratered face jiggling in the process. Michael wasn't enjoying himself; the caustic sting had failed to subside. "More adventures in dining, oh man. I remember when your mother and I paid for cotillion – bigger fuckin' waste of money than a three-legged horse. You refused to dance, ate the food with your fingers, all that shit. We never taught you etiquette, I suppose that's on us. Still, I was always amazed how much food you got on yourself. You actually managed to get ketchup behind your ears. I mean, that takes talent."

"Yeah, I'm a regular ninth wonder of the world."

"You're just not careful is all. You have to take pride in your appearance. All successful men have a well-kempt appearance. Unless you want to end up like me, you're going to have to get acquainted with a mirror. Aren't you interested in girls? Dammit, this Pepsi is flat. I remember when I was your age, I would have given my friggin left nut to put my hand up a girl's blouse, but you seem content on wasting your youth on video games. Come on, you should be out there pumping iron, wooing the broads, doin' the curls for all the pretty girls. Go get 'em tiger. The world is yours, but you gotta keep your head on a swivel and work for it.

"By the way, how is my favorite fat broad doing, besides sucking the air out of my wallet with alimony?" Herman grinned bitterly, revealing his crooked yellow front teeth and the glossy film covering them. The sting in Michael's right eye began to subside.

"She's alright."

"Is she still with that Bill guy?"

"Unfortunately, yeah."

"Yo, if there's a problem, I can come over there and straighten him out."

"Yeah, don't worry about it. Mom's just using him for money. Like the last couple of guys, he won't be around for very long."

"You need any money for yourself?"

"Nah, I'm good."

"I don't know who taught you to hate money, but it wasn't me. Here, take something for yourself. I can't use it. I'll just blow it on another bum horse. I'm in a slump, but don't worry, I'll get the juju flowing again." Herman produced an envelope much smaller in volume than that produced by Wallace. "Jesus Christ, it wouldn't hurt for this place to have an air conditioner, would it? I feel like I've already gone to hell but I don't see your mother anywhere in the vicinity, so I must be alright." Herman handed the envelope to his son, who was grateful for whatever the contents were, knowing that they would not disappoint. Michael touched his fingers to the encrusted remnants of the fried scallops, swirled it in the ketchup and sucked his finger.

"Michael, this is exactly what I mean. When are you going to start acting like a gentleman? Would you do that on a date?"

"It depends on the kind of woman I'm with." His dad chuckled a bit, then fell back on his lingering disappointment but Michael remained in a state between dejection and complacency.

"How's the car holding up?"

"I hate this piece of shit. The side mirrors suck. There's a shitty back-view as well. When I go on the highway and change lanes, I have to pray first."

"Well, no one likes their starter car. Just try to stay in one piece. Do you want to drive up to the track next weekend?"

"I have to see what my plans are, but I might have homework."

Michael departed the restaurant. His father stayed behind, looming over his losses, softening them by perusing the back of the sports page. With a full contented belly, he got up to leave the restaurant, and looked shiftily towards the last stragglers occupying the far booth. He gave a cheerful wave to the woman in the apron behind the counter; she waved back disinterestedly. A bell rang as the door closed behind him.

CHAPTER 2

DANCE RIGHT THROUGH YOUR LIFE

But he's the only one who knows—
And he's the man who fights the bull.

-Domingo Ortega

June 22nd had come, and Herman Gilbey sat reposefully against the bleacher behind him. It was a picture perfect day with a high of eighty-four. The feverish crowd was ranked in rows, and a few of the regulars howled at the trotting horses, while some of the more curious folk stayed put and chatted with one another over a couple of drinks, failing to examine the horses.

Herman sat on the last white bench, sharing it with a disheveled man and his more composed girlfriend. He finished his last nip, which was eyed enviously by the disheveled man, and analyzed his race card with intense focus, as though he had hoped to find a secret Kabbalistic message scrawled somewhere on it. Recognizing

Herman Gilbey as a regular, the disheveled man asked for a tip, nudging him on the shoulder playfully. He replied that Ants Marching would have a big day but said it with no conviction.

The race horses trotted to the gate. Herman nervously rubbed the race card in his hand and looked over the jockey who had three red dots forming a diagonal pattern across his chest. How motivated could Percy Peyroux be by the prospect of the humble purse given to winners at this dilapidated track that was on the course of closure? But Percy rode that winged appaloosa, What a Feeling, and Herman decided that if he was going to lose the last nickel he owned, and get his throat slashed as a result, it mine as well be on the behalf of this spotted darling.

The day's races began uneventfully. Herman had picked the first three horses correctly, but he was less than excited because he wasn't even halfway there. One loss on the streak to victory and all would be lost. With each win, that intense hope lingered, but the threat of potential failure was almost too much to bear.

"What if?" Herman muttered under his breath, and he continued to dwell in that manner until he got to the final race.

"Having a good day?" The disheveled man asked.

"Potentially" Herman answered, fixated on the card that was one win away from what would be one of the luckiest cards in the history of the track.

I been unlucky all my life. My father used to beat me, and my mom didn't give a fuck. The other kids used to tease me, and I was never given the chance to become anything, only a disrespected fool. Things never crumbled my way. Is today my day?

As he meditated upon this, the whole of his life lay before him, all of it hinging on the final race, on one horse, What a Feeling, outmuscling and outmaneuvering all the others. Winning the accumulator bet had only once been achieved in the track's 118 year history, in 1946, and a mafia conspiracy likely played a pivotal role in authoring this rare winning ticket.

The dust kicked up and the rapid clattering of hooves reached Herman's ears like a massive machine cycling – the only symphony he ever cherished. His muscles tightened as he watched the horses gallop. The maiden Informer struggled its way to the pack before losing steam and dropping off behind for another inevitable dead last finish. At the head of the pack, the favorite, Tesseract, was on the silver heels of a first place finish. However, Percy Peyroux was guiding What a Feeling out to the right wing and he charged with hellish fury past the striving contenders, till he was neck and neck with Tesseract, but the thoroughbred with the venerated pedigree was no match for What a Feeling's burst. Herman's horse had won by four lengths.

Peyroux patted What a Feeling after the finish and ambled over to receive his banner, which he used to adorn the horse. Herman Gilbey took his shirt off in the stands, and did an old disco dance, his belly jiggling to the amusement of the regulars. A muscular dude in a tank top raised a playful fist in the air to congratulate Herman.

"Got the trifecta?" he asked.

"Not fucking even. With What a Feeling I've just won the impossible, the accumulator bet!" He continued to dance and began to sing Irene Cara's "Flashdance...What a Feeling" like a football anthem and much to his surprise, the regulars, who had grown to regard the man as a local legend, if not a local fixture, joined in as he sang the chorus. Eventually, the security guard, a personal friend of Herman, had to hush everyone down, but the old weathered man still somehow beamed with youthful exuberance.

Herman Gilbey cashed out and promised that he was done with high stakes gambling. He would bet small for the rest of his life, so he wouldn't owe sharks like Richard Wallace large bundles of money. That was it. He was out of it. It was time to go straight, except he had one last errand to run.

In order to celebrate this momentous occasion, Herman rented a motel room, bought a couple of bottles of bubbly champagne, called his sometimes girlfriend [Yazmin] over and had the time of his life. By the end of the night, the bed had been covered in Dorito fragments, cigarette ash and spilt alcohol. Yazmin asked if she could stay by saying that it was the perfect day for arrunches, whatever that meant, to which Herman replied that this was of course impossible because he couldn't trust a woman in a room with large stacks of money.

"I'll go to bed rich and wake up poor again." He gave her enough money for a taxi and an Italian club sandwich, which he figured to be more than generous.

"You're a piece of shit" she said snarling.

"Yeah, but if that's the case, how come I smell like roses." He sang the chorus to "Flashdance...What a Feeling" again. "Seriously Yazmin, you need to go."

"Will you call me?"

"I can't promise anything, but I suppose I'll get bored sometime in the near future"

Yazmin cried as she gathered her belongings, pulled her sweater down over her flabby torso, gave her tired face a look in the mirror, and scampered off in tears.

"Are you honestly crying?" She looked back at him blank eyed, like a cat fearing punishment from its owner. "Jesus Christ, I thought we had a good time. Why are you acting like we're married or some shit? Alright, just leave, and if you want to have a good time again, you know who to call."

"By the way, you got a small dick and are a lousy lay."

"Likewise." The half-naked smiling Herman found a Dorito remnant wedged under his flabby right pectoral, put it in his mouth and chewed it, washing it down with the dregs of the last Champagne bottle. "Cheers princess Jasmine. I wish you a glorious future. However, until that glorious future arrives, I imagine that you'll have to spend that meantime cleaning motel rooms like this one." Still full of song, Herman sang a parodic version of "A Whole New World" from Aladdin, and then digressed back toward "What a Feeling."

Old Sandwich Road wound like a serpentine nave under a canopy of arched boughs. The firmly rooted noble pines swayed about in the early autumnal wind. It was along that road in an hour unholy that Michael and his father made their exchange.

Though he had been sitting on hundreds of thousands of crisp bills, Herman Gilbey kept the same decrepit red Ford Focus with roll-up windows. He would get a new car when he was long gone from this place. Along with his son, he studied the majestic mountainous green bundles of cash in the trunk of that very Ford Focus. He seemed begrudged to part with his winnings, but knew that it had to be done, so he coolly placed the bills into a suitcase with Michael looking on in awe.

The son opened the trunk of his own Chrysler Sebring, which also had its fair share of miles to it, and put the suitcase inside. His father stuffed some of the bundles in the belly of the car, where the spare is often stored, then cut the seats open with a razor blade and stored the rest of the greenbacks in there.

"That's all of it" Herman said, looking at the purplish glow on the horizon over the tall pines. He looked back toward his son, his face partially illuminated by the headlights of his sedan. Still, Michael could see now that his father looked as a bloodhound might, the whole of his chubby face sliding down to his chin. Suddenly, Herman appeared ghastly and grotesque to his own son. The fedora crowning him belonged to a past that Michael could not see into. The appalling figure reached out it his hand so that his son could embrace one last time. They shook hands, and parted into the darkness, going forthwith to their own destiny.

Mike Powell snacked on a hefty chicken parm sandwich in the passenger seat of Herman Gilbey's Ford Focus. They were cruising around the crowded streets of Chelsea in an attempt to find a parking space near Powell's apartment.

"Can you not get that on the upholstery?" Herman requested. Powell looked around at the beat up car incredulously.

"Are you kidding me? The last thing you gotta worry about with this shit box is some tomato sauce stain on the seats. When are you gonna get a new ride anyway? You won the fucking accumulator. I heard that all these billionaires like Warren Buffett live in the same houses that they had when they were school teachers and book keepers. Is that what this is?"

"Look, Mike, it's the principle of the matter. I don't want you to get in the habit of eating food in my car when I get my fat Cadillac and roll around these streets like a star." Herman showed a manufactured smile.

"That's what I'm talking about, Gilb. It's time for us to live large again." Mike was filled with excitement as the prospect of the return of the freewheelin' days was kindled.

"Us?"

"Was I not integral to your success?"

"Are you taking credit for the accumulator?"

"Explicitly no. Implicitly yes. We developed our system together. I know for a fact I played a role in this sweeping win. You should start showing me some money. Not a whole lot. It was your luck, but…"

"It was our faulty system that drove us deep into debt" Herman coolly spoke these words as he parallel parked in a tight space on Clark Avenue.

"Eh, we had a good thing going" Powell responded. "I admit we should have diversified and that we should have never placed such a life-altering wager on Cydonia, but that steed seemed indestructible, like he came out of Camelot just to run around our rinky-dink track.

"Anyway, we're all paid up now. I got a new system now. Real mathematical. It's a formula I developed based on past performances, imposts, jockey weight, weather, and the breed of the horse. I'm ready to test it out this Saturday. They've got this new stallion, Lateralus, racing. Looks like one of those wraith horses from *Lord of the Rings*. What's the point of having all this cash if you're not going to have a little fun with it?" Herman rolled his eyes, even though he could appreciate the sentiments of this gambling junkie, for he often shared them. There was a time when Herman couldn't watch two mice scurrying along the wall of his garage without expressing the desire to wager a sum on which one would be the first to obscure itself in the crevice of the wall. He had hoped that the accumulator would be the victory to end all victories, that this would making gambling dull for him.

"Sorry, Mike, but I'm done hardcore gambling. I'll play the Keno while I'm waiting for my steak and cheese and Coors to come out, but this money is meant to be held onto. If I go back to the track, that part of my brain that got my ass into trouble will start firing with renewed interest. Think about it: this racetrack shit nearly killed both of us a dozen times. There has to be an end-game, right? And for me, the accumulator payout was that very endgame"

"So then let me hold something. Shit, what is five grand to you, now that you're six figures in the black?" Powell looked away as he spoke. Herman adopted a more somber tone.

"See the thing is I am not entirely paid up on my debt to Richard Wallace. He needs me to do one more errand for him. Then I'm free of that weasel, at least as far as I know."

"Shit, I won't get in the way of whatever errand you need to run. Hell, I'll do it for you if you let me hold four-thou for Saturday's races." Herman sighed and held the bridge of his nose with his thumb and forefinger.

"I doubt you'd oblige if you knew what it was."

"Try me, Herm. I used to run with Doyle 'The Mohel' before the Hamblin crew performed a vengeful bris of their own. I don't have as much piss and vinegar in me as when I needed it, but I've still got enough of a mean streak to collect or shake someone down if that's what's required."

"You're a lost child, Mike. Just take a look in the glove compartment." Powell opened the glove compartment door and saw a silver revolver with a black grip resting on the registration. He raised his eyebrows and tilted his head.

"Oh shit you get the dainty Derringer along with you. He didn't ask you to…?"

"You know I only carry the snub when I fear for my life. I never thought I would be forced to…" The two men looked at each other, trying to gauge what the other was thinking, and assuming that it probably was the same thing.

"But if you've never done this kind of dirt. I mean, Herm, is there any way out of this? I mean, do you really want this on your conscience? Who is it? A debtor?" Herman listened to the inquiry and licked the canker on the inside of his lip.

"Yes, in a manner of speaking."

"So, you gonna do this? Do you know who it is?"

"Mike, the target is you. They want you dead."

16

"Me?! Jesus Christ! What for?"

"He didn't say. I assumed it was because you still owed him."

"I promise you I'm all paid up. What the fuck!"

"Hate to play devil's advocate, but you ain't actin' like a man who's settled all his debts. You look like a cash hungry gambling junkie if my eyes don't deceive me." Mike Powell breathed a deep sigh and lay back against the passenger seat.

"You don't think he knows about the thing from way back?" Powell asked.

"The thing! God no! If that was the case, he wouldn't send me out to snuff you. He'd put his pro, Goran, up to it, and we'd be hogtied in a warehouse somewhere begging for our lives with our balls hooked up to a car battery."

"Well, I appreciate you not doing me dirty."

"So, now you owe me one, and this is what has to happen. I bought you a 28 dollar bus ticket to Buffalo, and I'm going to give you a little something to hold you over, some of that money you wanted me to *show* you, just because I'm a nice guy. If you come back here, they'll kill you. I won't fucking be here. I'm getting far away from this mess in case Mr. Wallace and his associates have a change of heart."

"Where you headed?" Herman refused to answer. Instead, he looked at the lush elm trees unbowed at the top of the hill.

"I see. Well this is where we part ways, then."

"It is indeed." Herman handed his longtime friend the bus ticket and a paper bag filled with cash. The two shook hands. For a moment, Herman thought about reneging. There was only one way to make sure Mike Powell would never come back to Boston, and that way was through the barrel of a snub nose. But, Herman thought it a cruel thing to do, to promise a man life, and give him death instead, even a degenerate like Mike Powell, so the elder Gilbey watched his friend exit the car, give a halfhearted salute and walk up the steps of the duplex.

For about twenty minutes, Herman Gilbey just sat there with the engine off, the lights on, and the radio booming. He had abandoned the classic rock station for public radio. The station was broadcasting Mahler's seventh symphony, but Herman didn't know the composer or the symphony; he merely enjoyed the absence of some rich guy proclaiming his unconditional love with instrumental accompaniment. To relax himself, he concentrated on the rattle of the tambourine, the rising and falling of the brass, and the shrill of the mollifying violins that were once again interrupted by suddenly erupting brass.

'This is life' he told himself, 'constant rising and falling, reaching out to touch the flame and falling right back into place.' With Mahler filling his ears, Herman turned the engine back on, and drove back to his house to sort some things out before he was to cut through the night, down 95, to his new sanctuary under the Floridian sun.

CHAPTER 3

THERE ON THE SAD HEIGHT

**"I felt all flushed with fever, embarrassed
by the crowd"**

- ("Killing me softly with his song") Roberta Flack

In the center of Tanbang-Dong, across from the mall, there
stands an apartment complex, High Plus. The apartments within, though tiny, are considered choice cells but the foreigners who
are placed there by their companies know not why. The exterior
of the giant vertical rectangle is more window than steel, which is
consistent with the southern sphere of the Chosun Kingdom, the
most windowy region in the world. Light does not merely squeak
through; it pours in from a teapot with the rays of the rising sun or
deep night neon glow. Unlike Rome, the whole structure appears
like it could have been built in a day but above the square cells,
which aesthetically give you nothing more than you something you
would find at Cedar Junction Correctional Institution, there is a
rooftop garden that belongs to the fourteenth floor. In Korea, so

many miserable souls commit suicide, it must be considered an impolite impediment to prevent people from putting an end to their misery by free falling to the cigarette laden pavement below.

The plants comprising the garden were a motley mixture of geraniums, hibiscuses and the occasional Bonsai. I guess it gave jumpers something to look at in the waiting room of their final moments.

With peals of thunder rolling in, Eckhart had ventured forth to the roof of High Plus to watch lightning assail the sky. Standing in the rain, he amusingly watched his friend cower as the night sky was illumined by violent flashes that brilliantly tinted it mauve. The cigarette in his mouth had been whittled down to almost nothing, so he took one last drag, and tossed the dying light into a pot of earth holding a single wilted geranium.

"Come up close to see the show, Michael Gilbey! We have but a few winters on this earth. 'Tis better to go out with the hail and plagues of a burning sky than to perish like that geranium. Why should we rot out of existence like a bum tooth?"

"You're fucking crazy, James. Why don't you come in from the rain?"

"Tell me dear friend. What else is there, but moments like these, moments wherein eternity can be felt in the hollow of one's bones? Celebrate the darkness with me, the chaos of lightning flashing menacingly across the night sky in a foreign land. Look at the devil show his wolfish teeth. One can only love this madness, this sudden onrush of passion."

Eckhart held his unconsecrated hands to the sky and prayed in secret. After waiting a bit, Gilbey crept out to join him, but was not so bold as to lift his hands to the rupturing heavens. They had celebrated the sadness that enveloped them in their own particular way, Gilbey by suffering under the weight of sorrow like wretched Atlas, and Eckhart by futilely raging against it.

When one looked at James Eckhart with his country corn-fed constitution, one would never suspect that he harbored feelings of existential dread. Even in the midst of his ruminations, he merely looked absent, as though he were between moments of vulgar joy rediscovered. Clad in his work attire and crimson suspenders, he slouched back in his chair and put the ceramic cup to his lips as both men glanced through the large glass windows of the restaurant at the familiar yet unwelcome landscape, which they had collectively nicknamed "Neon Hell." The streets of Daejeon, South Korea were littered with drunk old businessmen at this hour, men who staggered along with great difficulty as their willing and thankless servants of a younger age buoyed them up along the way.

"What were you doing out in that storm?" Gilbey asked, as he peered into an empty metallic cup. "Do you have some sort of death wish?" The ajumma bustled about paying little heed to the white men and their discourse, which was unintelligible to her ears.

Eckhart moved his eyes from the window, and looked rather pensively at the dish containing gochujang (red pepper paste).

It was during a melancholic exchange that Jimmy Whelan walked in. Whelan was the lone New Zealander in the expatriate crowd. Not only was he soft spoken, he was difficult to understand because of the idiosyncrasies of his accent. One could not listen to Jimmy Whelan's speech in its whole; one had to pick out words and phrases from his thickly coated mumble.

After Whelan had sat down to join them, despite the fact that they were almost finished, they inferred from his incoherence that he intended to hit the bar scene later that night in order to continue his quest of acquainting himself with the local females. Jimmy Whelan was by no means a good-looking guy. If anything, he was a scrawny little lad who reeked of cigarette smoke and cheap rum. Yet somehow, this selfsame haggard individual managed to bring home a different girl every night. Apparently, that night, Whelan had sought to employ his mates as fellow "pussy hunters." Gilbey was more than reluctant while Eckhart found that the proposition had piqued his interest. He had been on these scavenger hunts before, and he had come up roses each time, more so even than the scruffy Whelan. Honestly, with Eckhart's polished dress, irresistible charm, and robust Midwestern face, pussy hunting was too easy, for which of these helpless miniskirt clad girls could deny him?

"So, whaddaya say, Gilbey, come along and we'll throw you some scraps" Eckhart joked.

"I don't know; I'm kinda tired."

"Well...What you got an important meeting in the morning?" Eckhart asked. We only have a few winters on this earth."

"Yeah, I remember, *coach*, but been there, done that."

"Oh, sorry, I didn't know that you were a regular Casanova" Eckhart said. "You've done everything there is to do with women. Maybe you could write a book for the rest of us. We are all interested in hearing about the fabled tales from the great legend."

The tension was not relieved by Whelan, who just kind of sat there disinterested in the spirited banter. However, another unexpected guest, Jefferson Prescott, waltzed into the joint beaming with intention and ambition, which was characteristic of him, palliating the angst between the growing rivals.

"You ladies ready to hit the town and impregnate some natives?" he announced to the world. Some of the patrons turned their heads to the sound, but did not possess the requisite English to make heads or tails of his words. Eckhart laughed loudest, while Whelan could only muster an appreciative sonorous grunt. Consciously, Gilbey refused to laugh, instead turning his attention to the muscular calves of the ajumma, who was still full of vigor despite the fact that she had been on her feet all day.

"Unfortunately, Gilbey here has no intention of celebrating his youth" said Eckhart. "He would rather go back to his cell in High Plus than loose himself upon the night"

Lifting his fist triumphantly, Jefferson Prescott proclaimed that he would make a man of Gilbey yet, though the latter youth did not seem to share in his triumph. Prescott prodded further.

"Whaddaya say Gilbey? When are you going to take part in the rituals of manhood, plunge yourself into that stench-filled sarlacc pit and drink of that tangy fish juice?"

Gilbey winced, and the three other souls had all at once spurned the naive boy once they collectively came upon the realization that their colleague had no intention of getting his "dick wet" along with them.

As Prescott and Whelan gathered their money to pay for their more than satisfactory meals, Gilbey, who by this time had become the butt of the jokes among the group, inquired as to what the three amigos were planning to do for brunch. Jefferson sighed, and after paying the vigorous ajumma, left with the other two gallivants, leaving Gilbey to stew. Gilbey would have stayed longer, but he didn't want to ruminate any longer, watching the thoughtless throngs rush to and fro, so he walked along the slick pavement through the thick air and longed for home.

⇥ ⇤

Gilbey should have known better than to struggle with an arcade game while intoxicated in the wee hours of the morning, but he was desperate to prove that he could defeat Xelthor in the final level with his last remaining coins.

When he had spent the last of his 500 won pieces getting annihilated by Xelthor, Gilbey cursed the screen and vociferated a complaint about Commander Slash, a virtually unblockable special move that drains half of your life bar.

"I never got this far." Eckhart complimented him while drinking "Captain Q," a cask matured premium rum of questionable quality, refined by a process used since the days of the early Korean empire. It was made from dark chocolate, pepper and brown sugar. "I always die when Boghzar throws those magical rocks at you."

"Boghzar's tough, but you just need to time it right. After that move, he's really vulnerable. This game is fucking rigged to take all your money anyway."

The two friends disappeared down the long avenue littered with used cups, cigarettes and flyers advertising the next big raves. Every morning without fail, ahjussis (older men) managed to carefully remove the streets of their excess trash. Neon lights were flashing. Loud K-pop music boomed from outdoor speakers. Drivers struggled their way over the discarded paper and plastic, honking to get the remaining hordes out of the road.

"You done for the night?" Eckhart asked. "You look totally shitfaced."

"I'm not doing this again" Gilbey replied staggering over to a wall so that he could lean against it. "Tomorrow morning is going to punish me. By the way, don't you think we have an obligation to say something?"

"What do you mean?" Eckhart closed the cap of the Captain Q bottle. He did not want to get wasted tonight. Rather, he knew he would enjoy watching his chubby friend in an intoxicated state while remaining somewhat sober.

"C'mon bro. You saw Seraj in there with Bo-kyung. If they're not fucking, I'm Bard Pitt, Brad Pitt I mean. No, I'm Grad Pitt. That's Brad Pitt with a diploma." Gilbey laughed rather obnoxiously at his own joke. "Yo, this bitch is supposed to be getting married in a month, and they're tonguing in broad ass daylight."

"It's two in the morning." Eckhart gestured to the large clock looming over Dunsan-dong. Above it, spangled in gold was the word "TimeWorld."

"Are you saying I should just let it go" Gilbey protested.

"No. I'm saying that it's two in the morning, which is not broad ass daylight."

"Bro, you know what I mean, not literal daylight. I mean they're doing their shit out in the open, and no one is calling them on their bullshit."

"What's it to you? Bro, if you had one of these cute chicks to blow a load onto or into… "

"James, we can save someone, albeit a boring square, from a horrible train wreck of a marriage. Let's just send him a letter or drop an anonymous phone call or text, something. Right?"

Eckhart stroked the smooth flesh on his neck and chin and looked up toward the clock.

"I just feel that we don't owe Jacob anything. Live and let live, but I'm not gonna stop you."

"This Seraj dude, is he your friend?" Gilbey staggered a bit and caught his balance once more against the wall.

"Yes and no, more of an acquaintance really. My thing is: this isn't our barbecue. If Bo-kyung doesn't play this corporate sucker, some other girl will, and probably worse. There ain't a chick on this wretched peninsula, north or south, who isn't some succubus waiting to suck the life out of her husband. I think you're drunk and unable to see what throwing a ginormous monkey wrench into the mix will do a month before a wedding. It's your call; I just don't want to get dragged into some crazy shit.

"Come on, let's get a cab. We'll talk it over with some hangover food tomorrow."

Herman Gilbey had watched the races at Gulf Stream Park with the interest of an academic. Just before the final race, he got the attention of an elderly man hooked up to an oxygen tank, and tried to explain to the brittle man that he should bet on Anything You

Can Do because he was sired by Killing Them Softly, an Anglo-Arab who had his future glory cut short when he shattered his carpus rounding a turn on a damp track. The old man gave back an empty stare with his translucent eyes as though he were looking through Herman.

"By the time Mel gets down to the ticket window to place his bet, the only horses he'll be seeing are the four horseman of the apocalypse" a voice called from the bleacher behind. The old man scowled, and then reconvened his blank staring. Herman looked back at the man who ridiculed Mel and listened to the man glowing from the sun speak,

"Anything You Can Do has a good pedigree but Ginseng Sullivan is a descendant of Love Me Darling and has a better track record in tropical climates. Up in Saratoga, Anything was chewing up the competition, then they brought him down to the swamps of Louisiana, where his best finish was fifth. I got Anything You Can Do finishing second, and I've got Burning Rain rounding out my trifecta." Herman dismissed this valid reasoning with a singular wave.

"Say, do I know you? You look awfully familiar" the man continued.

"I've got one of those faces I guess." Herman Gilbey turned red in the face and looked back to the man hooked up to the oxygen tank; he was sleeping now.

"Hey, I saw you on the news! You're the guy from Boston, the one who won the accumulator. Say, how much did that pay out?" Herman glumly gazed at the reflecting pool located in the center of the track lawn.

"Almost nothing after taxes."

"That's right, Uncle Sam wins every race in the end. So, you retired down here, eh? Me too, from Sherman, Illinois originally. I collected my government pension and up and went to the land of the wrinkled, where every day is a wrinkle in time." The man expected Herman to roar in laughter. Instead, he seemed rather resigned, fixing his eyes on the high rises planted over the horizon.

"I have to go" Herman announced sullenly. He got up to leave, and the man behind him asked if he had been offensive in some way, to which Herman replied,

"Of course not, I have something I have to take care of before sundown."

"But, you're going to miss my trifecta."

"I won the accumulator with my own mind. What the fuck do I need to see a trifecta for?"

Without making haste, Herman got in his Cadillac XTS and sped toward his studio apartment in Biscayne. He rushed inside the apartment that he failed to furnish and packed full the two mega-suitcases that he had been living out of. It took all of twenty minutes. Through his bedroom window, he leered at an old woman walking her two rodent-sized dogs and wondered whether he should stay here and let his fate be decided in the land of glorious sunshine.

Under the spell of desperation, Herman called one Thomas Beck, a bookmaker who had just finished serving a ten year stint for "trumped up" charges. The district attorney's office was vigorous in their pursuit of Beck, not because of his crimes, but because he refused to finger Wallace, and disavowed any possible relationship that might be established between his enterprise and that of the aforementioned crime boss.

"Beck, this is Herm" was the rough greeting that awaited the bookmaker. The slovenly answerer chuckled with hoarse laughter.

"You lowlife piece of shit. I thought Wallace chopped you up and discarded your remains. Why you gotta go calling me when everyone thinks you're dead? Are you back in Mass?"

"Every Sunday on my knees."

"Cute. I figured even you weren't dumb enough to come back. I like you Herm. I'm glad you left before they got to you. What they did to Mike Powell, man...Grisly shit is part of the business but that shit was beyond business. I wouldn't do to my worst enemy what they did to that dude. Whatever he was in life, whatever evil he's done, he's paid for it ten times over in flesh and blood."

"Did anything happen to Paterlini?"

"That fucking Ginzo. I figured the two of them had to be connected. For weeks, all of New England was in a frenzy talking about serial killer. I says to myself two criminals from Revere wind up corpses on opposite ends of the state, two guys that I knew, ain't no fucking killer behind this besides Richard Wallace.

"Well, unlike Powell, Paterlini's head was still attached to his body when they found him. Unfortunately for him, they cut his dick off and shoved it in his mouth, some Doyle "The Mohel" shit. I'm sure you remember that guy from the old days. They also found sulfuric acid in his eyes, and I got to wondering why these two brutal murders and sadistic dismemberments happened so suddenly, especially with it no longer being the way of the criminal world to flash your violence on display for everyone to stand and take notice. I almost forgot Wallace had a daughter; can you believe that? That reclusive girl who wears that Mike Myers mask because she had acid thrown in her face like some raghead bitch from Kabul, poor kid. Then, it all made sense. Powell is a fucking talker, and when facing the business end of a gun, he's even more of a talker. Powell knew that Paterlini was responsible for the acid attack, and in the hour of need, he just spilled his heart out."

"Oh shit, so that's who did it. I wonder what would possess Paterlini to go do a thing like that. I always knew that they were such close friends, so I was wondering how the Guinea would take to it. Fuck, well no wonder those bodies got brutalized." Herman could hear Beck munching on the other line, smacking his lips as loudly as possible. Somehow, he knew that it was greasy oriental noodles that were being devoured. Silence lingered on the line for nearly half a minute. With nothing left to say, both men said their farewells and offered what blessings they could.

Herman sat in his car, stuck for some moments on the sight of the freakish Atlantic. He put a palm to his clenched fist and like the great pioneers of the frontier, lit out for the west.

CHAPTER 4

APPOINTMENT IN POHANG

The jealous God, when we profane his fires,
Those restless passions in revenge inspires;

- ("Eloisa to Abelard") Alexander Pope

A forest of black umbrellas was pitched under a kaleidoscope of bright neon hues in a frenzy of disjointed movement. Adorned in black business attire and his trademark red suspenders, Eckhart recalled the first time he realized that Korean people used umbrellas in the snow. Other foreigners explained to him that it was necessary to guard against the acid present in precipitation. Out of principle, he thought an umbrella was for "faggots" and should only be found in chick drinks, unless of course it actually was raining. More often than not, he felt that the Chosun Kingdom would somehow spell his end. If acidic snow didn't kill him, a freewheeling motorcyclist late for his delivery, blazing over the sidewalk, would.

Rather ironically, Eckhart had been seated for quite some time under the cover of a large yellow patio umbrella outside of a "Buy the Way" convenient store, smoking his favorite cigarettes, Marlboro Blacks. He loved to tell people that he loved this cigarette because it wasn't sold inside the continental United States due to its strength. However, this was simply not true. His breath was lifted into the night, enveloping the cigarette fumes, smoke within smoke.

Ascending the concrete stairs to the platform upon which Eckhart smoked was a dogged Michael Gilbey. He sat down in the plastic chair and watched as his colleague's vapors and fumes rose and vanished. A rare classic song was playing, "Daejeon Blues." It was a welcome departure from the flashy assault that was K-Pop. The proprietor of this particular "Buy the Way," was the wife of a wealthy tech magnate, and he had bought this business for her in order to give her something to do. She never closed out a single month in the black, but that was really of no consequence, since her husband always footed the bill for the deficit. The single saving feature of this operation was the aforementioned musical selection. Classic ballads were heard, not tinny K-Pop songs.

Gilbey began not with a greeting, but with a question,

"So, how did we make our way over to this part of the world anyway?"

Eckhart gave it some thought, took his last drag, and extinguished his butt in the tray on the table, then breathed out the last withheld cloud of smoke through his nose.

"Money I suppose."

"Yeah, but that's never the ostensible reason. 'I wanted to experience another culture, or I wanted to help children' is what people always claim. This culture is just a jazzed up extremist version of our own and we ain't helping these children. We're just turning the cogs to make money for these academy pigs, and taking away these motherfuckers normal childhood." Eckhart folded his hands in contentment like a Midwestern Buddha:

"That's why these kids are so awking fuckward socially" Eckhart continued. Truth is all the transplants here are running from something. Usually, it's a fucked up family situation. Look at Golden Boy Brad Couples. He might be as unthinking and as unliving as the dead, but from the time he was eighteen, his parents basically issued the edict that upon his 18th birthday, he could never go home again. So he completed the necessary credits for his bachelor's degree and shipped off to this wonder of the world. It's a good place for a good-looking all-American boy like Brad, who just wants to fuck every girl with a nice pair of gams, but once you start dwelling on the dark things, this place starts eroding sanity. You realize you are trapped in a neon hell where everything conforms to cuteness."

"So, what's your story?" Gilbey asked. "If you hate this place so much, why do you linger? Why not go somewhere else?"

"Better to rule in hell than serve in heaven. I'm a fucking king here. I make twice the median income. In America, I'd be getting twelve bucks an hour to stock shelves at Target or Walmart. I'm just better off here than at home. What about you? You're not the prototypical foreigner. I mean, you don't strike me as someone who's in it for the money, and you certainly don't strike me as someone who's in it for the pussy, so what's your deal?"

"Nowhere else to go I guess." Eckhart nodded in confirmation. "Couldn't get a job in the United Greats of America."

"Same here, and the longer I stay here, the harder it is to go back. I gotta fucked up family situation myself to be honest. I wanted to return home as soon as I got here, and was planning to do just that, but my rents split up two weeks after I got there."

"Shit...waited to get you out of the picture before they made the move. So, who was it on, your mom or your dad?"

"Both, to be honest. They're shitty people and it was a long time coming. But, I can never go back to that mess. In fact, I tried to.

My mom was with some douche named Del, a fucking mail carrier, but she's one of these bitches that defines codependence. I booked my flight, had a heartfelt farewell and found myself under Del's roof, with him questioning why I wasn't gainfully employed within two days of being back. I was still jetlagged as a motherfucker. So, I ended up staying at a Days Inn until I could get my visa in order so that I could come back to this extraordinary company." Eckhart air-jerked an imaginary giant penis.

"By the way, how is their continental breakfast?" Both men laughed.

"About what you would expect. The muffins are miniature sweetened travesties and their coffee is burnt. Anyway, I ended up staying there, looking for jobs and shit, but after a couple of weeks, I realized it was costing me a fortune."

"Didn't your mom try to reach out and be like 'this is fucked up that you have to go live in a motel?'"

"She obeys the man that she's with and somehow finds a way to make herself into the martyr every time."

"Damn, your mom is a cunt."

"Tell me about it. So, I called Jimmy, and he said that certainly they could find a couple of classes for me, and so I booked my flight and was back here within another couple of weeks. You never know, man. Your parents might get real used to you being away. Hell, they might be fucking in your bed right now with your stuffed animals still on it. Bobo might catch one in the eye." Both men roared in laughter.

"See that's the thing. My own rents, ain't still together, and this new guy is in her ear an awful lot and might be giving her new ideas" Gilbey said.

"Oh no doubt. If he ain't your biological father, he doesn't want you around. Even your own biological dad probably doesn't want you around. How long have they been together?"

"Two years."

"Yeah, he definitely doesn't want you in the picture. Truth is though that I don't think that they'll throw you to the dogs. I could have stayed under this cocksucker's roof. It would've been hell, but I could have done it if I absolutely had to, but I've got a lot of pride. I've now been here for the better part of four years, and in that time, I've taken care of myself and I alone. I couldn't go back to relying on the patronage of some mailman with an iron skull. Just do your time here. The contract is for a year. They can't expect for you to give them any more than that, even though your step dad is going to want that. Just tell them that the contract is up and you need to come home, even though there's a good shot that you can renew without being an exceptional teacher, which you aren't, obviously." Gilbey breathed a deep sigh, and tears welled up in his eyes.

"I haven't been entirely honest with you, Eckhart. That's not the entirety of my situation. The reality of it is that my father is a degenerate gambler who either owes a lot of bad people a lot of money or did something else fucked up to make him a hunted man. Well, if they can't get to him, they can get to me, so I graduated from college, just like Brad, and shipped up to Neon Hell as we have come to call it. I remember the first night I landed in Incheon, and the long bus ride to Seoul, and looking through the filthy window at the factories and the Han River. I thought I could die, and I remembering wandering Gangnam, which felt like the loneliest streets in the world. I was hoping to fix my eyes on some sudden saving sight, but instead I met the indifferent gaze of those who passed me in the street.

"I was told by my father to avoid all contact with the United States for the next year or so and probably well beyond, so I have no idea how any of my friends or family are doing. I just do a google search every now and again. So far, nobody, including my father has turned up missing. I worry about my mom because she refuses to move, but I think that whoever is after my father must know how much my father hates my mom because there hasn't even been a sniff of a threat – knock on wood."

"Forgive the suggestion, but it seems like relating this story, if it is in fact true, isn't necessarily the smartest thing in the world. I mean, like I said, I'm not sure I believe you. How far reaching are the men who after your father? Do you have any idea? I guess I should feel honored that you trusted me enough to tell me. My dad didn't do a whole lot for me but one gem he left me with was 'DTA: Don't Trust Anybody.'"

"Your dad is Stone Cold Steve Austin?" Eckhart smirked and briefly wondered why a Baptist minister would share an aphorism with a pro wrestler who used to pour beers on himself and the surrounding crowd. "My dad grew up in a scuzzy part of Boston, and he never really overcame the circumstances of his childhood. He had regular jobs here and there, but he always tried to supplement his income by gambling on horses, scratching lottery tickets and playing Keno. I'm guessing he lost more money than he won. That's why we never moved on up out of our duplex. My dad said it was because of tax reasons but he always owed this person or that person. I'm guessing that one of his creditors grew restless with his antics but murder for debt seems a little extreme to me. Every now and then my dad would come home with serious injuries because he bet on one bum horse or another, but I never sensed that his life was in danger. I guess times have changed."

⇌ ⇌

Above the humble mountainous landscape in the distance, dark pregnant clouds rested over a golden crowning cast by the setting sun. Gilbey sat on a bench located on a subway platform in Daejeon station and watched the slow commuter train struggle its way toward Gwangju. On another platform, the sleek KTX bulleted along to Seoul, but Gilbey had no interest in either train. He had an appointment that night in Pohang.

At 17:46, the commuter train to Pohang slouched onto Gilbey's platform. The roly-poly foreigner reached into his polo pocket and produced a couple of Korean banknotes, making sure he had enough money for the journey. He then concentrated on a folded piece of notebook with six digits on it. Following the queue of people, Gilbey filed onto the train, but was unable to find a seat, so he sat on the steel steps and looked through the door-window as night came on. He fingered the piece of paper again as though he were afraid it would spontaneously vanish into thin air.

A young man approached him and began to speak of his desire to learn English and become a famous Korean poet. He mentioned something about moving to San Francisco, but Gilbey's concentration was fixed on the silhouetted mountains lit only by a half-moon. Far beyond them lay Pohang, and that treacherous appointment that awaited him there. There was nothing Gilbey could do but ruminate now while the train slithered toward the sea. Nothing could hinder its inexorable progress.

Finally, the train rolled into Pohang station. Gilbey thanked the aspiring poet for buying him a beer. They shook hands and parted ways. Compelled, Gilbey felt once more for the paper. He rejoiced when he felt the frayed edges of it against his thumb. A wry smile managed to emerge on his lips. Disappearing into the night amidst the throngs, Gilbey pulled his hat down lower.

There was a great freedom in his step as he moved about the crowds departing from the station. A light drizzle could be felt now. He wound his way through the streets as if they were his own, going farther and farther from the center of things, till he reached a commonplace high-rise surrounded by other high-rises.

Trails of paper lanterns were strung over the sidewalks. Fireworks meeker than what Gilbey was accustomed to, struggled to rise and held their fizzing glow before guttering from the sky.

The Waygook (foreigner) hustled along the harbor-walk, merging into the night as well as a foreigner was capable of. Many locals had turned out for the festive occasion, and stood shivering along the riverbank gazing up as brilliant colors burst over the bridge in various shapes.

Past the reeds, and the quiet awe-inspired huddled masses, Gilbey walked on towards the address he knew by heart, Whangsil Apartments, building #4, Apartment #44, the residence of one Seraj Mukhtari, the vile libertine who was unleashing himself on the night 169 miles away in the capital.

To be safe, Gilbey took the stairs, tucking his face into his jacket to better shroud himself for any passersby who may take notice of the stealthy man in question. He punched in the code written on the piece of paper, Mukhtari's birthday and lo' and behold, it offered him passage into the apartment. Gilbey remarked immediately that he wished that his own Hagwon had picked out for him such a spacious room on the outskirts of his town. Instead, they believed that pampered foreigners needed a residence at the very center of things, where the music blared the loudest and the neon lights shone the brightest. Of course, no Waygook officetel (that's what the Koreans called the miniature sham studio apartments that they wedged foreigners into) was complete without large panes of glass to make these awful cells absorb greater the nocturnal cacophonies and sleep-depriving lights that they were beset by. This peninsula, however, sucked into its gut those who could tolerate sleeping on ceramic tiles, and it spat out the barren seeds that withered under such penetrating light and noise.

Gilbey breathed deep and surveyed the apartment, noting the rather vast pockets of empty space as well as the piles of dirty clothes that missed the laundry bin. Nothing was out of the ordinary. It was your typical careless bachelor's pad. Gilbey found some space on the stairs to the claustrophobic loft above. He sat upon them and reflected on what he should do next. A couple of ideas were mulled over but were mostly met with intense dissatisfaction.

The poor lad had spent the last couple of months plotting a break-in and though he succeeded with relative ease, he put no thought into an endgame. He merely figured that it would be enough to trespass, to break the seal of someone's sacred space. Leaving some puzzle behind briefly appealed to him, but Gilbey had nothing of import to leave on the bed of the libertine. There wasn't enough menace in Gilbey to engineer anything beyond his clever trespass so he set his mind to his egress so that he could wreak true havoc on a day when his actions were guided by more foresight.

The next KTX train to Daejeon departed in just twenty minutes, and Gilbey hoped to be on it, so that he could make a cameo at some late night convivial affair in TimeWorld, amidst the slobbering fools, pounding music and pervasive light. Then again, Gilbey was never expected at any affair, and never made his presence a common sight. Guests loathed him, his negativity and incessant probing of questions that they thought had no place in the light; he was a buzzkill.

Before making his final departure from this dwelling, Gilbey's bloodshot eyes fixed themselves on a thick packet that was wrinkled, water-stained and partially buried under Seraj's dirty boxers. Out of disordered Gehenna, Gilbey pulled the papers. The title page boasted something in Hangul with the English translation beside it, "Hanwha Life Insurance Co." Red and orange interlocking circles accompanied the prestigious name, and immediately Gilbey was hooked. What was Seraj of all people doing with a detailed life insurance policy in a tongue completely foreign to his own? Gilbey gave a cursory glance to the contents of the paper but its indecipherability led him to gather up the papers surreptitiously and make his exit.

CHAPTER 5
THE PETER PRINCIPLE

"All I ever wanted was to pick apart the day
Swallow up the pieces
Spit 'em at your species
Reachin' the city of lost barnacles and leeches
Nightlight got me when the daylight went to evening."

- ("Night Light") Aesop Rock

The Gubongsan Mountains in the distance were covered by a smoggy haze. Eckhart created his own plume with the slow drags of his beloved Marlboro blacks. Across from him, sat his companion, Gilbey, who was shooing the secondhand smoke away from his orifices.

"I was ready to slam Hyunnie last night or I should say, she was ready to slam me," Eckhart said.

"Ah, my dream girl...won't give me the time of day, but two words from that soot-filled chimney of a mouth of yours, and she's spread eagle on your futon ready to receive it with her shapely thighs. What the fuck am I doing wrong in this life?"

"Knock off about ten kilos, give yourself some confidence and girls like Hyunnie will be starting you off with rim-jobs in no time. What, do you expect bitches to love *you* for who you are? How many mediocre chicks are you attracted to because you love who *they* are?"

"Some. There's some chubby chicks or not so pretty chicks that I would like to get to know. Anyway, so what happened with Hyunnie? I have to say, I'm really glad you didn't smash that. I mean we'd still be friends, but I would just resent you, my life, Hyunnie and life in general after that."

"Tommo Chang cock blocked me."

"It makes sense. That dude wants your cock all to himself."

"Don't remind me. The dude insists he's not gay, but I've had to resist more than a few come-ons. In fact, come-on is exactly what he would like to do to me." After some laughter, Eckhart continued his story: "Hyunnie was ready to come home with me, but Tommo stopped her. She looked like a dog in heat, my friend."

"How come I can never get that?"

"Because the night unleashes the succubus. You need to stay up past 10:30 for once."

"Forget it; it's not worth it."

"Why won't you just come out with us? You just go to the love motels. What do you do there, beat your dick?"

"Sometimes. I just like to wind down."

"But, a little fun, every once in a while?"

"It's just not my speed...Hey, how do you feel about your hero, Seraj?"

"My hero?" We go gallivanting together and pick up chicks together. I would hardly call him my hero."

"Can you keep a secret?"

"It depends."

"Now, you're being no fun... Fine. Geez, some people want everything...So I went snooping around Seraj's apartment."

"You did what?!"

"Stop acting so damn surprised. I'm a voyeur. That's what we do. That's how I spent my Lunar New Year."

"I thought you were staying in?"

"Part of my ruse."

"Shit, living a secret life, so what did you find, some dirty panties that you put in a plastic bag to sniff later on down the road?"

"I understand that I'm a laughingstock and I'm over it. I found an insurance policy for Jacob Jung with Bo-kyung as the beneficiary."

"In Seraj's place?" Eckhart asked. "How? You can't even read Korean. This is some invented bullshit like your mob stories"

"I had David Kim read it."

"That's a lot of trust."

"My curiosity was too great to forget this thing altogether. I figured it was worth the risk."

"Well, there may be an explanation for Seraj having this document," Eckhart said, "but one cannot justify your breaking and entering, but hey, since we're chronicling our trespasses here, I'm fucking BK too."

"Good Lord, does any foreigner keep their dick dry in this country at any time. I'm getting pretty darn sick of this life. All I ever wanted was for somebody to love, and all I ever got was rejection…"

"You never tried."

"That's beside the point. Let me finish:, and all of you swashbuckling motherfuckers like Seraj and like you, are basically throwing away pussy like it's two week old chicken. It ain't right. What do you guys have that I'm lacking?"

"Game."

"Yeah, I never really understood that, but I'm not about to abase myself and violate my code in the hopes that someone is going to fuck me."

"I'm not going to say that it works on every female, but you have to make them feel that you are special and that they have a small window of opportunity to claim you as a mysterious conquest. You have to break them down to build them up. Joke with them. Insult them. Be confident. Show them that you have the leader-of-the-pride character and mentality because for most women, that's what they want. They don't want to control the thing. They want to control the thing that controls the thing; ya understand?

"Many would write me and my cronies off as misogynists but I don't hate women. Au contraire, I love them. I love their soft skin, their gentle manner, the way they can come onto you like a dog in heat. I like seeing a change in them, when you've won them over in spite of themselves. For me, that is greater than the sex itself. Before you get any ideas, I'm not a lousy lay, but the orgasm as a climax is only four or five seconds. It's bound to lead to disappointment. Getting her on her knees or on her back is the fun part and then, my only concern is to give her the experience of a lifetime."

"If your ego were any bigger, it would actually be at the point where it's eating itself."

"It's big for a reason. It's big because I'm big if you know what I mean."

"Yeah, yeah, yeah."

"But hey, my ego is big because of success. I've figured them out, females that is. That's all I ever wanted. When I was a nerdy teen playing World of Warcraft in Wisconsin, women were part of this big mysterious world. Now, I've unraveled the mystery. Like I said, the orgasm is short lived. The French call it 'The Little Death' for a reason. Ever try Vicodin or OxyContin? Once you get past that initial nauseating barrier, you feel like you're floating on a cloud."

"Yeah, I had that with Toradol. I had it in the hospital when I had a kidney stone. It's used as a less addictive substitute for morphine. I remember just lying there. I was in heaven, too."

"Probably more powerful than the prescription painkillers if they delivered it via an IV. Fucking is healthier though, as long as you don't do it raw. No one gains a higher sense of self-esteem through excess drug use."

"But you can fuck your way to happiness?"

"Yes and no. You can feel better about yourself, even from a primal level, if you can bed chicks. Start with mediocre chicks. Slam some chick with a glass eye or missing teeth, then work your way up like the Peter Principle."

"The Peter Principle?"

"Yeah. There's a certain level of chick who isn't going to want to suck your Johnson, plain and simple. Shit, even on my best night, I couldn't nail a Swedish Supermodel. I'd be lucky if she gave me the time of day. My level of incompetence is a 7 or an 8; after 8, the game becomes too complex for my skill. Some girls are dirty as fuck, so maybe you can land a seven or an eight. Think about that chubby bitch at the GS25. She thinks you're cute and she's Asian and somewhat unattractive, so you know she'll work hard to get you off.

"In the very beginning, it's going to be work. Being naked with another person is awkward as fuck, but just like anything else, it gets easier each time you do it. You're better off with a fat chick or an ugly chick or both is even better. Two pumps into a Victoria Secret Supermodel and you've already gone to it. With a big fat cavernous bitch, you'll be up all night. You'll feel like a regal Lion, so long as you don't bump into her cervix."

"So, let's put all of my sexual frustration aside for a moment. We've got this document burning a hole in our figurative file drawer. What are we going to do about it?"

"If it's really that big of a deal to you, I say contact the police. I sound like a broken record."

"You didn't want to do anything when Seraj was going hard and sloppy in Bo-kyung on the low. Why the sudden change of heart?"

"I'm looking out for myself, always. I didn't want trouble then and I don't want trouble now. I'm not being a fool. I just don't want to spend the rest of my existence confined to a narrow cell because you had what you thought was a good idea."

"Where is the man that I saw on the rooftops, the man who felt bound to death?"

"I might be ready to die but I ain't ready for a fiasco like the one you're concocting. I do have a death wish but I want to die in peace, not while trying to unfuck myself because of you."

Eckhart and Seraj sauntered through the plush aisles of the Galleria of TimeWorld while looking at expensive items they would never buy and shooting the shit about female workers at the school whom they would love to knock boots with. After trying on some fancy fedoras and striking some poses that belonged in *Vogue*, Seraj was beginning to upset the floor people at the large department store.

"I think she loves me" Seraj said out of the blue.

"Who? Bo-kyung?"

"Yeah dude. I know my dick is special, but she can't get enough of my loving. She's gone and left some three times now."

"How do you feel about her getting married?"

"It's bogus, dude."

"I doubt you can keep this up. Are you going to change your ways?"

"You mean stop plugging her? Hell no. That pussy is too sweet."

"What if you get caught?"

"What's that faggot Jacob going to do? I'll kick his ass for walking in on us and ruining my climax. I don't work there anymore. He's powerless."

"You know it's a crime here to fuck a married woman? I'm just saying: be careful. He's got the kind of weight to leverage the legal system against you."

"True, true, true. Ugh, I just can't let that pussy go. You should see the way she looks at me when I'm about to cum. Her face and the tips of her ears turn rosy red. We're in sync, dude. She's just marrying this dude for money, but he won't be around for very long."

"What do you mean?"

"Shit, isn't it obvious? She can take that little worm so many times before she starts missing the gooey venom that gets spewed out of the monstrous Mumbai mamba."

"So, do you think she's going to give up all those diamonds and pearls, a suite up in the Legacy Towers and a blank check for this fucking galleria at Time World to be with you? She might fuck you on the side, but I know Bo, she's too smart and too much of a woman to fuck this up for herself."

"Don't be so sure, bro. We're in love. This is just temporary. You'll see. Fuck, all this is bothering me. You ready to get smashed?"

Day turns night. Seraj and Eckhart were joined by latecomers Jimmy Whelan and a new Welsh arrival, Gareth Ramsey. The latter man was an expert in getting his colleagues to drink far more than they could hold. Tonight, he robustly sang a few Welsh drinking songs, which nobody else knew. He waved his trembling hairy finger at the two Americans (Seraj and Eckhart),

"It's a shame your people have no drinking songs. Only Americans choose to drink in silence."

"I can't drink another" said Seraj, who hitherto had always been equal to the challenge. This surprised the gathered who always believed that Seraj would never declare that he was actually done. He was only done when he passed out in a pool of his own urine in some filthy alleyway.

"You're barely beyond buzzed" commented Whelan, even though Seraj was far beyond sobriety.

"I'm on the verge of my windfall" slurred Seraj.

"Did you just say 'windfall?'" Eckhart asked. "You got fired. You work for ABC English. You're the brokest person in this bar."

"Take a good look at me now because this phoenix is going to rise from the ashes. Me and my girl will be up in the towers of Richville, sipping heavenly champagne without a care in the world."

"With what money?" Eckhart asked sardonically.

"Let the boy dream" Ramsey exclaimed.

"I don't need money or a plan. God's got my back, that's my plan."

"Did you dream of a pig?" Whelan asked gleefully. "I heard that's good luck here."

"I'm dreaming of a stuck pig." None knew what to make of the statement, so they just paused and carried on and Ramsey mumbled a few more lines.

⇥+ +⇤

Seraj and Bo-kyung had saturated themselves in the afterglow of another coital tryst. Dawn had come up several hours ago but the couple was content to lie there until either body stirred itself to rise. Broken shafts of lights funneled through the windows and the blinds, creating an unobtrusive gleaming. Bo-kyung held Seraj's tanned face in her hands as they cuddled away what remained of the morning. But, suddenly a voice called out with plenty of gravel and very little timber,

"Ah, such tenderness. Men have sailed the seven seas to know this love." The lovers whipped their necks to look over at the source of the sound. A rotund figure occupied the chair, his whole figure not entirely visible. The beer bottle in his hand refracted the light.

"Who?!" Seraj inquired. He got up, naked as he was, and walked over to get a better look. "Gilbey! What the fuck are you doing here?" With Seraj's shlong hanging down and flapping around, he walked over to the reclining Gilbey and stood over him in order to intimidate him. Gilbey would not be moved, though he admired the way the fractured rays of light complimented his well-sculpted physique. Gilbey grabbed Seraj's genitals and gave them a firm squeeze, prompting revulsion and horror from the Muslim.

"Wha...?" Seraj took a swing and landed his hook right on Gilbey's chin, but it was only hard enough to stun the man. He removed his hands from Seraj's testicles and stood up, suggesting that he may walk out, but instead, he took the beer bottle and smashed it against Seraj's chin, knocking him out. His leg bent backwards and the stress of his fall came upon his bent left knee.

Gilbey admired his handiwork but noticed that he sliced part of his hand in addition to Seraj's face. He licked the wound and smiled sickeningly at Bo-kyung, who was now sitting up, covering the intimate parts of her body with a sheet as ladies are wont to do.

"You did well not to scream" Gilbey said.

"What the fuck do you want, creep?" she asked.

"A woman with a head about her. Now I see what all the rage is about, why on the very eve of your wedding, men will be clamoring to spread those thighs and go headlong into it. What do I want? The answer to that is quite simple. I want in."

"I would never touch a pervert like you."

"Don't reach for that phone or you'll end up like that home-wrecker there. I don't want a slice of your Kimchi pie. Let me spell it out for you. I'm not asking for a fuck. I know I am not intriguing enough, good-looking enough or rich enough to get a shout from you.

"I know about the insurance scam. This is not my first time in Pohang or this apartment. I have meditated for long hours with Seraj gone, wondering whether your boy-toy would come in here and put his fury on me. Never did."

"How...?" she asked.

"That's not important. What is important is that I haven't yet gone to the police?"

"Does anyone else know?" she asked.

"Eckhart. And I have to tell you that he is seriously pondering phoning the police, though I think he has refrained thus far. What does the indemnity pay out?"

"Indemnity?" she asked.

"How much money are you and this struggling motherfucker going to make when you kill your husband?"

"You're crazy!" Gilbey tossed the insurance packet on the bed and opened the blinds. As soon as Bo-kyung saw the Hanwha seal, she knew what it was, but ever the self-preserving actress, she displayed a confounded look, as though a worldwide conspiracy had suddenly been cast against her.

"Are you going to deny this?" Gilbey asked.

"What is this?" She leafed through the pages with childish wonder, pretending to be reading the document for the first time. "Why do you have a copy of my husband's life insurance policy?"

"Because it's a scam!" Gilbey yelled. "And you know it. I'm tired of these games. I actually thought the two of you would be forthright. I certainly didn't expect to have a ding-a-ling waved in my face. I put my phone number on the packet. You have one hour to call me. If you don't, or if you decide to phone the police about your fuck buddy getting roughed up, Jacob and the police will know within moments about your little scheme. Yeah, soon we'll see if you're so innocent." Gilbey stepped over the unconscious body of Seraj and left.

CHAPTER 6

THAT WINTER THE WIND BLEW

**"And what of the dead? They lie without shoes
in their stone boats. They are more like stone
than the sea would be if it stopped. They refuse
to be blessed, throat, eye and knucklebone.**

- ("The Truth the Dead Know") Anne Sexton

At the modest pinnacle of the Hanbat Arboretum and surrounded by snow covered shrubs, Eckhart and Gilbey watched the last flurry linger in the form of dust on the single-tiered pagoda that stood just beyond the snowy river. The straining friends conversed with their cold gloved hands tucked in their pockets. Eckhart opened the bidding.

"You smashed him in the face with a bottle, you savage."

"He punched me in the face. I need to defend myself."

"Use your hands. Let them do the talking, not a fucking weapon. You realize you might get hauled off to jail. Police might be waiting for you in Daejeon as we speak. What if the insurance policy was bought legitimately? Isn't there a better way?"

"There's very little chance that they're going to the police. They don't want it known that they're fucking and most of all it would spoil their plans for a payout."

"You know that when Seraj sees you, he's going to demolish you." Just then, Gilbey's flip phone vibrated. He answered it. Bo-kyung was on the other line.

"Meet us at Bukbu beach as soon as you can. Is Eckhart with you?"

"Sure is."

"Bring him with you."

"Eckhart, we've got another appointment in Pohang. Do you have Colleen's car?"

"I guess I can borrow it. It's a shoddy Hyundai. The brake pads and lining are shot to shit but I suppose it's good for one more adventure.

The moon hung over Bukbu; crickets wept far from the neon buzz over the water. Facing one another like druids in a circle, Eckhart, Bo-kyung, Seraj and Gilbey found a remote spot on the pier. Celebratory voices echoed over the water from a nearby cafe. Amateurs were setting off their pathetic fireworks, Seraj gave a weak wave to Eckhart and looked at Gilbey with menace out of the corner of his eye. He was all stitched up now under the chin.

"You keep all your teeth?" Gilbey asked, goading the Muslim. Seraj stepped to him and even under the poor illumination, Gilbey could see the sea of muscle ripple and the neck vein bulge.

"Alright, let's calm down." Eckhart was quick to be the peace-maker. "We are all under strain here. I'm just trying to get a sense of what's going on."

"How innocent?" Gilbey protested. Eckhart rolled his eyes, resenting the interruption.

"So, just put it to us straight, Seraj" Eckhart requested. "Are you going to off this dude?"

"Are you seriously entertaining this crackpot's delusions?" Seraj protested. He already broke into my apartment, interrupted us, and knocked me out cold with a beer bottle."

"Why haven't you contacted the police?" Eckhart asked, pointing to the gruesome wound all stitched up. A long silence was held.

"We will...We..."

"Gilbey already showed me the document. You really plan on killing this man." Eckhart's tone turned to genuine disbelief.

"It's just my husband's insurance policy" Bo-kyung chimed in.

"What the fuck was it doing in Seraj's care?" Eckhart demanded.

"Your psycho friend probably stole it from Jung" Bo-kyung replied. Eckhart stroked his chin.

"Well, I guess there's only one way to settle this" Gilbey said gleefully. "Let's ask Jacob." Another silence fell over the four. "Ah, you two don't want to go down that road because if Jacob found out that you were fucking, well, it all comes down after that." There was a long silence. The wind fell in like stones from the neonhearted water. They all stood as stiff as cowboys wondering who would draw first.

"You each get 100,000, no more, no less" Bo-kyung suddenly declared.

"Well, there's the admission of guilt from our buttercup that I've been awaiting" Gilbey said with a menacing smile flashing across his face. "And, how do you mean to do the deed?"

"Don't you worry about it" Bo-kyung said stoically, evaporating Gilbey's smile. "All you have to do is wait, and when the insurance money comes in, you'll both get your cut in small installments. We wouldn't want the authorities finding out that a new widow is giving large sums of money to her friends for no apparent reason."

Eckhart was disconsolate. This cute girl, seemingly superficial and naive, had risen to show her wickedness. He made love to her as others had done before and after and he thought nothing of it but now he felt dirty, as though he entered some unhallowed ground whose stench he could never clean from his shoes.

Alone together now, Eckhart and Gilbey walked together some ways along Bukbu beach and now stood face to face in solitude on the splintered planks of the pier.

"Why don't we pound some sojus?" Gilbey suggested. "There's nothing but neon for miles." Eckhart was irate.

"We have just sentenced an innocent man to die and you want to celebrate?"

"Who said it had to be a celebration? I thought you drank in all moods and seasons."

"Have you no heart?"

"At any point during that meeting, you could have protested, walked away and gone to the police. There's nothing we could do, except try to physically restrain you. I think we all know how well that would have worked. No, you wanted to know what it was all about. You want those six-figures. There's a part of you that's resisting all of this, but Eckhart, my sweet friend, I think you are intrigued by all of this. You can't have your money and clean white hands so wash yourself in the blood"

"I don't know if I can do this."

"That's the beauty, baby. We don't have to do anything. Those two worthless scumbuckets are going to do all the work. All we have to do is wait."

"Murder money."

"Yeah, you keep saying that, but what has Jacob ever done to deserve life, or any of us for that matter? Are you going to teach third-graders the difference between 'will' and 'going to' for the rest of your natural born existence while some rich asshole like Jacob presides over the whole affair? Fills his pockets with silver? C'mon bro, you don't think he's sucking and fucking supple side chicks his damn self? And, the whole time, we are the cogs churning this sick fucking machine that is bleeding to death. If your Jacob Jung could enslave foreigners for the sake of the bottom line, he and the rest of those greasy bandits would have no fucking problem. Now, here you are acting like the second coming. It's kill or be killed. Do you know what happens if I go back to Boston? I get a fucking bullet in my brain base, so what the fuck do I care if some millionaire or almost millionaire gets blasted and ends up face down in a gutter?" Eckhart seriously pondered what was said and had no decent rebuttal. *Was Gilbey right? Was this no more than what Jacob deserved?*

⊷⊷ ⊶⊶

Claims investigator Hur sat at his modest desk and looked over the report that just came his way, the accidental death of one Jacob Jung, 32 years of age.

"Ji Young, over here, please!" he called to his assistant, a chubby mid-twenty something, who was the laughingstock of her peers because of her heftiness, which is rather uncommon in Korea. Hur hired her because he didn't want his pretty wife to grow jealous or suspicious of his secretary. With Thunder Thighs storming through the halls, how could she be?

"Yes?" she called, ready to receive her order.

"We've got a pineapple." Immediately, Ji Young put her manila folders on a vacant chair and joined Hur on his side of the desk.

"How much?" she asked.

"One Billion Won."

"That's higher than I've ever seen."

"Sure, and would you look at this: the ink is still fresh on this application. It's still January and the date on this application is mid-November." Ji-Young looked confused or didn't know what to say. "Do you have any idea how rare this is? In five years, I've never seen a case like this." Ji Young remained silent and looked down and away, perhaps to suggest that five years was not that long to be in the industry. He ignored her passive aggressive body language and continued on with his inquiry, hoping to find concurrence:

"Also, it's a bit odd. I usually get claims from ahjussis who have spent their whole lives paying premiums. Why isn't this on Dongwhan's desk? I'm going to run this by him, see what the veteran says."

Dongwhan, the senior claims adjuster, a skinny old man, had the look of constipation when he examined insurance documents, and so that strained look defined his countenance for at least eight hours a day.

He looked up at Hur, who was just entering the bright yellow room through the heavy glass double doors and tried to adjust his eyes as one does when one suddenly goes from darkness to light or vice versa.

"Yes?" Dongwhan inquired, irritated by the distraction.

"I have a claim."

"We are all inundated with claims, including myself. What makes you special?"

"Sorry sir, I don't mean to take up your valuable time."

"Then don't."

"Yes, of course. Normally, I wouldn't take up your time but I think this case merits special attention."

"Leave it on my desk. I'll get back to you before the end of the day."

"How was Grumpy?" Ji Young asked while she sent out messages through her computer.

"Same as usual" Hur said. "He could have walked out of here with his pension several years ago, but he wouldn't know what to do with himself if he weren't making others miserable through his terseness. There's a dude who's going to croak the night after he retires or the day before his term policy ends."

"You shouldn't talk disparagingly about your elders. He's been a rock for this company, even if he is aggravating."

"Of course. I just...Well, you called him grumpy." Just then, Dongwhan marched through the doors, chewing on the last of his moon pie. He didn't look at anybody, only the withering fern across the room.

"The only action to take is to deny the claim on the grounds that you suspect foul play of some sort. More often than not, we are forced to pay the indemnity, but if you can make a case for suicide, you might be able to stall the payments to the beneficiary. I would be remiss if I didn't warn you that his father is a high-ranking executive at Goldmoon; it pays to use the extracurricular databases. I know his dad a little bit from hanging in the background of some elaborate Hweyshiks over the years." Dongwhan took a sip of Vita500, a Vitamin C drink, to wash down the moon pie and continued,

"These kinds of police reports are why I have health problems. The Daejeon police don't want to investigate anything, unless it's to find out who threw the first punch in some meaningless bar scrap. With Jung Senior's influence, I think we're going to get a much different police report, one that is the result of a far more thorough and transparent investigation. One can hope anyway. What type of business executive goes mountain climbing alone in January anyway?"

Police Captain Byung-hyun Lee worked diligently with his chopsticks, attacking his tuna gimbap with the right amount of ferocity.

The ringing phone bothered him, but he always felt obligated to answer with his line of work being what it was, so he licked his lips and wiped the corners of his mouth with a napkin before picking up the polished black receiver.

When greeting the caller, he was surprised to hear that it was Dae-su Jung, the father of Jacob Jung, on the other line. He wished the secretary had forewarned him; he would scold her as soon as this call finished. In the meantime, he became flustered by his underlings for failing to inform him that they just investigated a high-profile case and instantaneously deemed it an accident. The scolding of his cute secretary and the sight of her perky breasts would have to wait.

Lee felt like a punching bag as the Goldmoon executive told him in plain and furious words that his son's death was no suicide or accident. The detective tried to explain that the original decla-ration of "accidental death" was only a preliminary decision until more evidence was gathered. Byung-hyun Lee suffered so many insults, curse words and threats that it all just blended together into one wrathful sound in his mind's eye. When he got himself together, after the berating stopped, he vowed to see the investiga-tion through and get justice for the Jung family.

The tuna-filled dumplings, which were slated to be the high-light of Lee's day, had to be put aside and the two detectives who worked the case were called upon immediately. Lee remained seat-ed as he ripped into his inferiors, who stood attentive, their hands respectively remaining pinned behind their back.

"Sir" Woo implored. "Early signs showed that Jacob skidded on the slippery surface of the mountain and fell to his death."

Captain Lee let his furious eyes fall on Woo-jin with concen-trated ire.

"That's what killers do. We need to find..." The phone rang. Lee asked his secretary who it was and if she could hold the call. When she told him that it was claims investigator, Hur, and that it was about the mysterious death of Jacob Jung, he took the call in the presence of the two detectives. Captain Lee and Hur exchanged greetings. The latter man inquired as to whether this death was ruled a suicide.

"Early indications are that Mr. Jung slipped on the terrain and fell to his death."

"Who goes to the mountains in January, anyway?" There was a long pause.

"We're investigating the matter, but that's what we're ruling for now."

"Ok. Thank you." Hur winced as he hung up the phone.

"It looks like we're going to have pay out that claim after all." Jung just thought harder and harder, churning those ever-turning wheels of the mind. "Not yet."

CHAPTER 7

WHERE BEFORE MANY MORE HAVE GONE

"Jealousy, turning saints into the sea
Swimming through sick lullabies
Choking on your alibis."

- ("Mr. Brightside") The Killers

Down in the cold cold morgue, Woo-jin and Hye-jeong listened to Dr. Yoon, a middle-aged sort of woman with owl-like spectacles explain the cause of death for one Jacob Jung.

"When a person receives trauma to the head, especially in the case of multiple blows, the brain tends to swell, pushing it up against the skull. Sometimes, it is necessary open the skull, so the pressure can be relieved. Otherwise, one is likely to suffer a brain hemorrhage, which can lead to massive brain damage, a coma and above all, death. This happens to boxers who often receive multiple heavy blows in a twelve-round bout."

"Is it possible that he could have sustained these blows falling down the mountain?" Woo-jin asked

"Possible, but highly unlikely. The blows suffered to the head are far more frequent and severe in nature than the rest of the anatomy."

"Even if he dove head first?"

"I don't know who has the will for that but the skull shows repeated blows with something hard like a stone. Could he have bashed his head seven times against the side of the cliff on the way down? I suppose, but I certainly wouldn't rule out foul play." The detectives thanked the coroner for her report and walked back to their office.

"Fuck" Woo Jin exclaimed. "Captain Lee was right. We've got a murder to clear. Let's start with those closest to him."

"You totally have the hots for Doctor Yoon" Hye-jeong said.

"Plea...Hey, she's a doctor. She's got her own money, a good job, must come from a good family. What's not to like?"

"You already asked her out, didn't you?"

"Flat out rejected. She's cute but I know that she's not cute enough to be batting guys away. I figured I had a shot."

"She probably wants someone from a more educated family and you are not exactly the hottest guy ever."

"Ouch."

"What ever happened to Ye-Jin?"

"She worked at the Lotteria and danced on a platform for the grand opening of furniture stores. It was never meant to be taken far or long."

"You're a man. You're supposed to take care of her in the end. It doesn't matter what job she has. She'll quit it to take care of the kids."

"That's my fear, that she'll want to. Look at your sister. Her husband is a doctor but she is a dentist. She didn't just quit her job when your nieces popped out."

"How romantic? You're a police officer, Woo-jin. Let's face it, you're not in the upper crust of society. Getting someone like Dr. Yoon is a reach for you. I believe in love. I'm a woman after all. I'm still with Yun-seok because I don't have to be with the man of my dreams to be happy. He works as a chef, but he's sweet."

"He puts too much gel in his hair. He looks like a K-Pop star without the money. Are you sure you're not just afraid to be alone?"

"It's a good thing everyone doesn't think like you. You're a loner. You need to find a good woman and settle down. You should see if Ye-Jin is still hanging around."

"She's getting married."

"Really? To whom?"

"Some computer programmer."

"Well, I guess that ship has sailed, unless of course you're up for crashing a wedding."

"I'm hardly beside myself."

Woo-jin and Hye-jeong went to Legacy Towers, the residence of the deceased, where the widow still resided. Bo-kyung let the detectives in and Woo-jin was awed by the sheer size of the place. His partner remained composed.

"I could upgrade to this" he said, forgetting his manners and that he was talking to a fresh widow. "I'm sorry for your loss" he apologized. Bo-kyung was clad in a smart black dress with a matching beret, making the pearls around her neck shine brighter.

"Can I get you anything?" she asked meekly. Woo-jin hesitated, pondering what this rich woman might have that he couldn't have on a daily basis. He knew his partner would give him shit if he asked for some special kind of tea, even though there was plenty of help to prepare it; it's not like she had to lift a finger.

"We're all set, thank you." Hye-jeong spoke for both detectives. "We understand that this is a difficult time for you and your family. I can only imagine how difficult it is to lose a husband so soon after a wedding. Still, we have a couple of questions for you, so we can get to the bottom of this and mete out justice if any is to be had."

"Do you think he was murdered?"

"Please, let us ask the questions, but let me just say, we're looking at all possibilities at the moment. What can you tell us about January 4th, the night your husband fell off of Gyeorydong Mountain?" Two terriers pranced over to Woo-jin, who wanted to shoo the dogs away, but to exact the limited politeness he had, put his hand out to be sniffed.

"I was in Seoul, in Gangnam to be exact." Bo-kyung answered meekly. Apparently, she was so aggrieved that even simple matters of discussion were rather burdensome.

"Shopping I presume?" Woo-jin asked. "That's not a judgment." It was too late to backtrack successfully.

"Yes, of course. I have expensive taste or so said my husband."

"Can anyone corroborate that story?" Hye-jeong asked. "We believe you. We just...."

"Of course. Ye-rin, my old high school friend, was with me."

"Can you provide her contact information?" Woo Jin asked.

"Yes." Bo-kyung scrawled the information on a piece of paper.

"This may be uncomfortable," Hye-jeong informed, "but we have to ask: are you in any way responsible for the death of Jacob Jung?" Bo-kyung looked up at Woo-jin incredulously. "Sorry, we gotta ask."

"No."

"This investigation is still in its infancy" said Hye-Jin. "We haven't even ruled yet whether this is a murder, suicide or accidental death, but we will be in contact with you one way or another." When Hye-jeong and Woo-jin passed to the outside, the female inquisitively gazed toward her partner so as to chide him for his boorish behavior.

"She's a pretty girl with a nice place, eh?" Woo-jin only managed a meek forced smile in response. "So when do you move in?

Are you still waiting for the casket to cool...Do I need to remind you that her beauty doesn't make her innocent?"

"How patronizing. We'll drill her harder if our investigation leads us down that alley. But, to be honest with you, I'm ready to move on yesterday. Her refrigerator dispenser makes ice. I've always wanted a fancy fridge and that massive TV is perfect for sports. You think she might be willing to catch a guy like me on the rebound?"

"You're not in her league and you should not be inclined to be on her side. Everyone's a suspect."

"Yeah, but when I win the lottery, and I have 7.8 billion won to my name, she won't be in *my* league."

"Keep dreaming."

Passing in and out of sleep, Hur tried to remain focused on the Winter Olympics broadcast. Yuna Kim, the heavy favorite and Korean champion, was competing for gold in Vancouver, and she was moving flawlessly through her routine with excited commentators relishing her every flourish. A gargled cheer came from Hur as he watched his compatriot perform a gravity-defying butterfly jump. His desk phone rang and he wondered who could be calling at such an hour.

"Claims investigator Hur" he announced still half asleep.

"Yes, how are you?" The enthusiasm and cheer caught Hur by surprise.

"Fine. Who is this?"

"This is Youngbo from PL Group, life insurance division."

"You guys have a life insurance division?"

"It's new, but yes, we've gotten in the game." The voice on the other end, though spritely, sounded old and ready for lighter workloads.

"Well, how can I help you?"

"I was just checking the insurance consortium database, ClaimSwift, and I have noticed that recently deceased Jacob Jung had several large policies taken out from several companies before his death. We may have a case of wholesale fraud."

"Well, he just got married. Could just be a case of bad luck."

"You must be new to the game. We don't pay claims out like this until a judge bangs a gavel down and orders us to."

"I see. We fight the good fight as well. I really appreciate the call and if you're instinct is to defer the claim until a proper trial is conducted, then we will stand with you."

"*Stand* with us? We're not the fucking girl scouts. Jesus. Very well then. If I can give you some advice young man…"

"Yes sir."

"The path to success in this business is not paved with good intentions. The insured don't have them either."

"I understand, sir."

"Very well. I'll send the list of the claims requested under the deceased's name."

"Much appreciated, sir."

For the last seven years, Tae-woo Kim had manned the desk at the Gallery Motel. It was rare that occupants were privileged enough to get a glance of his face, only his chubby hands exchanging the money and keys. He preferred it that way, little contact with family and having little to console him, save for the contrived television dramas he watched and instant noodles he ate while on duty. The legs of comely females caught his eye and he observed in silence, judging whom she might be with. Eventually, he got used to it and just made a mental note every time a passing woman grabbed the attention of his eager eye. But, he was always discreet.

In the cycle of his days, he had no more ambition than to live out his final ones as the guardian of the keys at the Gallery Motel. At the very least, he did not expect two members of the Korean police force to press their badges against the Plexiglas window. He didn't panic though. He just came out of his little office, as though he were an actor breaking the fourth wall. To Woo-jin, he looked like an inquisitive chimp, but he and his partner gave the clerk the benefit of the doubt.

Rather than drag the clerk back to the old station down the road, Woo-jin and Hye-jeong accommodated Tae-woo by meeting him in his little hovel of an office. The suspect was not nervous nor was he friendly. He sat comfortably in his worn executive chair and heard them out.

"Do you know why we're here?" Woo-jin asked. The suspect only cast his eyes downward in disappointment. Even the prospect of criminal accusation couldn't pull him out of his rut.

"I suppose you guys don't want to rent a room." Hye-jeong was taken aback and Woo-jin was ready to slap the clerk, but he thought the better of it. "Sorry, I couldn't resist. I imagine you're wondering if I've seen a certain person of interest in the last couple of days. You can give the picture here."

"Have you ever heard of Jacob Jung?" Hye-jeong asked. Immediately, Tae-woo perked up.

"Who? No."

"Now, you're not in trouble yet, Tae-woo," Hye-jeong replied, "but trust me, it's in your best interest to tell us your side of the story. If you perpetrated a crime for any reason and aided other menaces, now is your chance to cooperate. You don't want the masterminds of this thing to get away because you had some code of silence."

"Masterminds of what thing? What happened?!"

"Let us ask the questions" Woo-jin said, spinning the plastic container of half-eaten Buldalk Bokkeummyeon with the chopsticks still stuck in the middle. Do you know who Bo-kyung Lee is?"

"No."

"Have you ever seen this woman?" Hye-jeong asked as she slid the photo into his path. He thought long and hard, casting suspicion on himself.

"Did she stay at this hotel?"

"You tell us" Woo-jin said snappily.

"No, I've never seen her. Dozens of guests come in here on a daily basis. How do you expect me to remember?"

"Show him, Hye-jeong. We need to expedite this crap. I'm tired of these stall tactics." Hye-jeong handed Tae-woo a manila envelope. "Are the contents of this package familiar to you?" Without examining the majority of the contents, Tae-woo tried to call their bluff:

"Congratulations, you have a picture of me, just like my mother."

"You're mom has a picture of me" Woo-jin rebutted. "Keeps it by her nightstand every night." This visibly upset Tae-woo and so Woo-jin played on his rush of emotion. "Well, let me explain what's going to happen if you say nothing. You can live the oncoming days in relative peace, watch your romantic dramas, see if Jan-Di can win the heart of that spoiled brat in *Boys over Flowers*. But then, soon enough, you'll be in a real life drama, trying to save your own life from imprisonment because when this insured for murder scam comes to life, you're going to be looking at a long time in jail. If there's a murder, and you hide details from us, why wouldn't we believe that you played an integral part?

"The photo in here – I mean, why is some bum like you dressed in a fine Italian business suit. I'm going to bet that once we get a warrant for your ass, the signatures on Jacob Jung's life insurance policy will match yours. We're going over all this shit with a fine-toothed comb. But hey, if you speak now, you can get out of this relatively unharmed...only if you speak though." Woo-jin made his pitch and was ready to walk out of the door unedified, but he held his gaze for a moment, reading the planes of Tae-woo's face, hoping for a sudden revealing twitch. Tae-woo leaned back, scratched his patchy stubble and breathed a deep sigh,

"Ok" he uttered reluctantly. "I was approached by two peculiar guests. Immediately, I wondered what such a fine lady was doing with a "Waygook." They all come to this country to sleep with our women and live a playboy lifestyle."

"They're living your fantasy I suppose." Hye-jeong shushed him. "Sorry. Continue."

"Even though I figured something was out of order, it's not my job to investigate. I thought they would just ask for some towels and be on their way. Just like y'all, she demanded a conference in here, while that Waygook, who I assume is her lover, waited in the room."

"What did she ask from you?" Hye-jeong asked. Woo-jin took notes furiously.

"She told me right off the bat that the request would be strange but that it was important not to panic. I could refuse the offer; I just needed to hear her out. I noticed that she had an elaborate wedding band on. It was big. I imagine it was expensive. I didn't think that that Waygook was her husband, so I became enraged. Who was this man to defile one of our women? Then, I started thinking that even though she was gorgeous, she might be one of those freaky-deeky sex addicts. I thought she was going to ask me for a ménage a trois; she didn't. But, it did turn out that she was my type...You see, our lady was an opportunist. I try not to be seen. I don't hang around here, except on my numerous cigarette breaks in that parking lot. They must have seen me on their way in here. Most couples, especially the adulterous ones, look away in shame. Apparently though, my resemblance to her husband, even in this ol' jumper, is uncanny. I get the feeling that she noted this resemblance, rented a room, had a fuck session with the Waygook, and then thought about how she could use this resemblance to her advantage. That's when she came back down to request an audience with me, his holiness, the Pope of the Gallery Motel."

"Ok, Your Holiness, can you state what she asked for?" Woo-jin asked.

"Just some medical tests and a meeting with the insurance agent. How came you guys to find me?" The detectives refused to answer, but if the reader must know, Tae-woo was a huge card player and was busted for violation of article 247, helping to open and operate a gambling place for profit. In truth, he had agreed to take the fall for a high-ranking *Chil Sung Pa* (Seven Star Mob) member. In exchange, he was taken care of in prison and was given a job upon his release. As a result of this criminal charge, Tae-woo's fingerprints and DNA were in the system and when myriad insurance companies grew skeptical, they tested Jacob's fingerprints against the criminal database and found a match in Tae-woo.

"*We* ask the questions. You're doing a very good job. We're almost home. Do you have any idea what happened or what was to happen to Jacob Jung?"

"I have no idea. I was just told that he was a very serious business man, that he didn't have time to go to the hospital and that he didn't have time to meet with the insurance agent."

"You must have heard what happened since."

"No, what happened?" Tae-woo's voice remained flat.

"You don't have television?"

"I don't watch the news. Did this guy die?" He did a poor job of feigning surprise.

"How much did you get in exchange for your time and risk?" Hye-jeong asked, almost begging for the answer.

"Four million won"(4,000$ US, roughly).

"Do you have any idea what the claims are slated to pay out?" Woo-jin asked. Tae-woo shrugged. "A billion won, and now you're wrapped up in an insured for murder scam. You could be looking at life, and what did you get for your risk, a working man's monthly salary."

"What can I say? She was kind to me. And she was beautiful and she needed help."

"A man is dead" Woo-jin said "and soon the warrants will be issued and the doors will be kicked in."

Hye-jeong handed her card to Tae-woo. She politely asked him to come in.

CHAPTER 8

THE HEART OF SATURDAY NIGHT

**"Rain, midnight rain, nothing but the wild rain
On this bleak hut, and solitude, and me
Remembering again that I shall die
And neither hear the rain nor give it thanks
For washing me cleaner than I have been
Since I was born into solitude."**

- ("Rain") Edward Thomas

The crack of pool balls greeted Tae-woo upon his entrance into the billiards hall. *Dangu* (four ball) ace, In-seong Jo, was being watched by several serious men wearing tailored suits and dark glasses. They all turned their head when the scruffy motel clerk entered. One of them put his hand up to indicate that he recognized the interloper, so the other men just turned back around to watch the artist at work. The man whose hand was raised walked over to

Tae-woo, greeted him and ushered him into his office. Tae-woo expected something more regal than the hole in the wall that awaited him. It was all too familiar to the motel office. At least this office had a view to go along with some beat-up cabinets and a mini-fridge.

"I have to be honest with you" the man said, sitting comfortably at the corner of his desk, sipping on a glass of makgeolli, sweet Korean rice wine. "Oh, how rude of me! Would you like something to drink? I know one O'clock is not the normal drinking hour for most folks." The cordiality and politeness of the gangster surprised him; Tae-woo politely refused. "Suit yourself. Where was I? Oh, that's right: I don't appreciate you coming here because those three guys you just saw start to wonder what a made man like me is doing with a square like you."

"I'm not a square. I make 800 Won an hour to watch TV and hand out keys."

"You're not a gangster either. You had a chance to walk the made path but you didn't want to do dirt and so now you're here begging for money."

"Not money."

"Not money?"

"Legal counsel."

"Do I look like an attorney? Look, we can't be giving our attorneys over to every Joe off the street who needs a favor. I appreciate what you did for us last century, but you didn't have much of a choice. It was either you get pinched for me or you'd be floating down the Geum River into the Pacific.

"My father died in the Pacific during the war. It would be above your honor to be buried in the same ocean. That's neither here nor there. Maybe you came here thinking you were an honorable man in my eyes because you never switched. Now that's worth something, but there's gangsters and everyone else and you ain't a fucking gangster. Since money grows on trees, I can give you a couple of C notes for whatever, but it ain't 'cause I like you."

"I'm involved in an insured for murder scam." The man licked the flavorful wine off his teeth, tilted his head back pensively and peered into Tae-woo's eyes.

"So you're a killer now, is that it? And, you're looking to me for hiding, even though you ain't done a damn thing for me in years. It's always a good policy to ask from favors to those indebted, not the creditors of the world. In fact, you wearing a wire?"

"Come on, dude."

"Stand up and face the wall."

"They already checked me." Tae-woo reluctantly did as he was told. The search yielded nothing. The man took a stack of bills secured by a currency strap and handed them to Tae-woo. "Don't come back here and good luck with your murder charge." Disappointed, Tae-woo walked out into the cold feeling despondent. The only thing stopping him from drowning himself in the river was the freshly procured two million Won and the intrigue of being involved.

Immediately, the lowly man conjured up images of himself as the Korean Houdini, brilliantly weaving himself out of sure calamity. Yes, he would outdo the Korean mob and the police and return to his little shelter a victorious survivor. Why get legal counsel at all? He felt able enough to outwit any prosecutor. The only reason he was down in his little hole in the Gallery Motel is that he never got chances like the dead and stiffened Jacob Jung.

Out past Dorydong Bridge, just outside Science Exposition Park (which ran out of funding at the turn of the millennium), there is a drive-in theater that shows mostly Korean flicks. Beyond that, there is a shabby amusement park that stores its gigantic props of cartoon characters in an adjacent lot. It was in that adjacent lot that a dyspeptic Gilbey sat leaning, listening to his friend kvetch about the circumstances that Gilbey had steered them into. It all felt so very surreal with a five foot toothbrush wedged in between two giant replicated incisors.

"Thanks to you, we gotta make the old 'midnight run'" Eckhart said.

"Like our fellow expat rejects before us. Beats going to jail though."

"I'm just curious: how much did you get from this venture?"

"Not a cent, but it was a tremendous opportunity and seeing as what's happening to the prime movers, I'm happy to escape still breathing. We were all set up but I couldn't take a dime from Bo-kyung now. It's officially blood money. So, you're going back to South Dakota after this?"

"Do I have a choice?"

"Do you mind if I join you? I mean, do you have an extra room to dwell in? You made it sound spacious."

"You ruined everything for me and now you're asking for shit. I'm not responsible for Jacob and I'm not going to be responsible for you. If you die, it will be a certain justice for the world."

"We all die, James. You drive a hard bargain and I don't need to stay with you, but I've got another proposal for you. I may not be as needy as I've been letting on."

"Just shut the fuck up. Whatever you're thinking, just keep it between your ears. I'm sure it's perilous and not worth it and will be unsuccessful in the end."

"No crimes this time, at least no risk on your end. I've got six-figures stacked in a storage bin in Rhode Island."

"Bullshit. You're a fraud. Why don't you use that fortune to rent out a room somewhere else? You don't want to get through a South Dakota winter anyhow. I'm done with you and your scams man. I built a life here. I got promoted. I was primed for glory, a University job. Now, I have to start from the beginning in rural freezing-ass uninhabitable South Dakota."

"Don't the Chinese use the same word for crisis and opportunity?"

"You're something else."

"This is a special relationship. We are too star-crossed not to meet again my friend. I look forward to meeting you and your family in South Dakota."

"Man, if I ever see you again…"

"What?" Gilbey laughed. "I've got people back where I'm from who want to erase my whole bloodline. I will find you, Eckhart. Even if I should die in a plane crash on my way back, get immolated in a cruel structure of metal that meets its end in the vast Pacific, my ghost shall perplex you for all of your days."

"You're like a tick that I can't burn off."

"More like an STD that just keeps coming back. Isn't it funny how joy flees but pain comes running back? From the moment we're thrown into this world, we're fated to bring each other nothing but pain and misery. I don't want to torture you James, but sadly, you're all I have."

"Why don't you just throw yourself in the Han River and leave me be?"

"Our fates are tied together. To die alone would be to apostatize. We're going to die together like Bonnie and Clyde like Butch Cassidy and the Sundance Kid."

"God, I should get a restraining order. But, it would do you no good. It would only accelerate our end. Did you eat paint chips as a kid?"

"Something like that. I don't know if it makes a difference if you're born crazy or if this world makes you crazy. Personally, I think the latter is true for me, but I suppose there is something valuable in being cognizant of your own psychosis. I'm slipping away James. I'm watching everything that I cherish slip through my hands. My mind is going, bro. Don't you understand that this insurance thing was never about money? I needed to feel alive again."

"Women can do that for you. I find that a fine romance is healthier than murder schemes."

"I bet. But, tell me, who would look my way? Those who have an easy time with women, like you, think it must be just as easy for everyone else. I am poor in love."

"Do you think I like pumping iron and spending my free time grooming, but that's what you have to do. If you want money, you have to work hard. If you want love, you have to work hard for love. I wasn't born with more pheromones or some bullshit like that. I worked hard and built myself up to not be alone as you are now."

"And yet here we are level."

"Level? We are not level in any way! The worst of it is that you look at me and see what you could have been. Yes, it's true, it's true; ladies love cool James Eckhart. And, now you want to drag me down with you to prove some crackpot theory about the universe. You want to prove – what's your mantra again?"

"It just ain't worth it; can put that shit on my tombstone if you like."

"Well, I'm here to fragment your world view. I'm here to tell you that there were and there are things worth fighting for. I know because I tasted that nectar. You're not some starving kid living in Aleppo, hoping to end his misery by running into mortars. You could have been somebody.

"Good speech, but James, we all end up in a fucking pine box in the end and there's no eternal flower, just some withered old tulips that your great aunt made you plant that ended up getting dug up by hungry rodents. I don't work out and I don't build myself in this world because everything tends towards decay. What's the point? Given time, every tooth you have will rot out of your head. Not only that, you will go mad and blind and become incontinent. Even for the chosen few, life eventually becomes a nightmare from which we must awake. Don't you understand, friend: there is no balm in Gilead. Feel the gyre, brother, as I feel it, as it turns and fixes its cold lifeless eyes upon you. You should have thrown yourself from that roof if for no other reason than to be free of the decay that has already sunk its teeth into the very fiber of your being. See you soon, brother."

⇒⊹ ⊹⇐

Winter in Korea doesn't go out fighting the way it does where Eckhart is from, Sassoon, Wisconsin, where the broken reeds remain still and stiff, so he didn't mind waiting outside at a bus station at 3 AM, to catch the overnight shuttle to Incheon airport. Somehow he longed for the company of that deranged treasure hunter, Gilbey. The more rational part of him allowed for disdain and revulsion at the character of his colleague. Still, churning and churning through the eye of the mind was the question of whether they would ever meet again and if they never did, could Eckhart shut out the experience of being in the exotic neon-littered East? What could he do back home to kill the beckoning of the hills penitent? Would he have to self-terminate to stop the whistling of the trolls within the snow-covered valley as some of his relatives had done?

The bus pulled up and Eckhart got on. He could not sleep and wondered if the cause was the excitement of escape but he hardly aroused any suspicion; the police had not come knocking on *his* door. The Korean police had who they wanted in their sights and the forced contrition was about to begin, starting with the widow. Seeing her reflection in the guillotine, would she snitch on Gilbey and Eckhart? Of course she would but what power did she have? People will say anything with their neck in the noose. Just four hours stood between him and the skies over the pacific.

Panic set in.

If Gilbey and I both make the run, will the police suspect us in Jung's murder? I can't go back now. This bus is pulling me like an anchor on wheels, away from everything I fostered in the last couple of years. All that I built here...All that I loved here. Goodbye to neon buzzing lullabies.

There at Incheon airport, the world's finest, Eckhart stopped and stared at all the bodies moving to and fro. He gathered himself and told himself that all of this, good and bad, would be behind him in 48 hours. It was impossible to say goodbye.

⚒ ⚒

Eckhart merely had to present the ticket agent with the ticket and walk through his gate to freedom in the heartland of America. But, he didn't want to forfeit all that he gained with a midnight run, so he turned and walked back to the bus terminal and slept until the next outbound bus arrived.

Instead of returning to slumber on the bus, Eckhart looked far off at the construction cranes beginning their work. There was something strangely mesmerizing and the desolate scene of expanding fog somehow uplifted his spirit. He would go to the Daejeon Police Station and see this thing through even if it meant spending the rest of his life in a jail cell. It was more important for this principled Midwesterner to free his soul of the guilt that plagued it.

⚒ ⚒

"Why the fuck are you still here?" Gilbey asked Eckhart. "I thought you were making the run. What happened to that ticket that you purchased?"

"Must have lost it" Eckhart replied sarcastically. "Funny, I remember you saying that you weren't too far behind. Quite a dangerous game for a killer to linger at the scene, don't you think?"

"Killer? I'm no more or less a killer than you. Is that the play then? If you stay, then I stay. We fight this thing together."

"Why are you so certain I'm not going to rat you out? I've got my own skin to look after, after all."

"Because you can't prove anything or make any accusation without implicating yourself."

And just like that, Eckhart found himself a prisoner of Gilbey's logic. Even though it was the same logic that put Eckhart in this predicament, he could not fight it, so he kept his mouth shut and his head down.

Of course, the detectives came knocking once they obtained Bo-kyung's phone records and saw a string of curious text messages back and forth between Bo and Gilbey.

The chubby expat fidgeted in his chair until Woo-jin and Hye-jeong entered. He was uncuffed so he stood and greeted them with a smile and urgently forced a handshake upon Woo-jin. They entreated him to return to his cold hard seat and Woo-jin was struck by the smoothness of Gilbey's hands.

'These are not the hands of a killer' Woo-jin thought but the inquest proceeded.

"You were friends with Mr. Jung?" Woo-jin asked.

"I was cordial with him. After all, he owned and operated the academy where I work. From a personal standpoint, he represented all that I detest about Hagwon owners. He was another slick, rich womanizer. I didn't do nothing but I'm not going to sit here and pretend like I'm sad he's gone."

"So, you're saying you had motive?" Hye-jeong asked.

"I'm a man of peace and hate to see any man fall before his time but some deaths are more tragic than others."

"Let's talk about these text messages and phone calls you received and sent to Bo-kyung and Jacob."

"It's quite simple. Being the godly man that I am, I merely warned Mr. Jung about his wife and her skeezing ways."

"Skeezing?" Woo-jin asked. "Also, did you just call yourself a God?"

"No, I said 'godly.'" Gilbey played with the rims of the lens-less prop glasses he had recently purchased. "It's an old word that means righteous, good or religious. And skeezer is a newer word for those dirty girls who are without loyalty."

"We also have a record of some phone calls with Bo-kyung" Hye-jeong said.

"If she's such a skeezer" Woo-jin said, "or whatever the word is, then why did you meet with her in Pohang several weeks before the death of Jacob Jung? Did *you* also?"

"Please, I already told you that I am a godly man."

"And that means religious, right?" Hye-jeong asked.

"Right" Gilbey confirmed. "No, we merely met in Pohang for some drinks. It was nothing special. Eckhart came with me."

"Where were you the day Jacob Jung died?" Hye-jeong asked.

"Nowhere special, I imagine."

"You imagine?" an incredulous Woo-jin asked. "It was February 3rd."

"The days all kind of blend together. Usually, I watch a show called *Flashpoint* on XTM. It's pretty cool; it's about hostage situations and the cute pink Power Ranger is in it. Then, I wander the streets of this city, take some photographs, and eat once I get hungry enough."

"So, you're not sure?" Hye-jeong inquired.

"Probably wandering like I said. That's what I do every weekend."

"What about Eckhart?" Hye-jeong asked.

"What about him? I don't know where the fuck he was. Why don't you ask him?"

"We will" Hye-jeong said, "but you sound awfully defensive. Is something wrong? Is there something you haven't told us?"

"Yeah, there is something." The detectives practically had their ears to Gilbey's mouth. "I'm about to miss *Flashpoint.*"

Eckhart's interview passed as uneventfully as Gilbey's had, though the Midwesterner had the decency to show some respect for investigators and so, the Daejeon police decided to focus their investigation solely on the widow and her lover.

Once they obtained a warrant, Pohang police assisted by their counterparts in Daejeon, searched Seraj's apartment for incriminating evidence and hidden behind a wooden panel that could be removed to access the circuit breaker was a bloody stone. A collections specialist retrieved the stone and placed it in the evidence bag.

Had the rock gone straight to the lab, Seraj's case would have been cleared and he would be free to live his life out of captivity. But, the rock did not go straight to the lab. It sat in an evidence locker for three days and in that time, it remained in the custody of some vengeful officers, who damn near ordered that the tests be shown to be inconclusive once it was determined that the blood on the rock did not belong to Jacob Jung. When the results clearly showed that the blood did not belong to Jung or any other human, the cowardly scientist did as she was told and even went one step further and reported that the blood belonged to Jacob Jung through a careful and brilliant doctoring of the report.

With the proverbial smoking gun found in Seraj's hand, or apartment rather, the conviction was easy. Mr. Mukhtari's attorney wanting to put to rest this hideous case, put together a sloppy defense and when it was over, the all-Korean jury needed just two hours to convict Seraj Mukhtari to life imprisonment without the possibility of parole for first degree murder.

Bo-kyung was allowed to plead to lesser charges that had almost nothing to do with the murder. I speculate that it had little to do with the lack of physical evidence linking Bo-kyung to the murder. Korean people simply didn't want to see something so beautiful wither to death in a cage. So, while her lover rotted away in Cheonan prison, condemned to breathe his last breaths there, Bo-kyung would be freed in less than one calendar year.

⊨+ +⊨

Wandering along the Gapcheon River, Eckhart and Gilbey stopped on a bench and watched a group of young boys skip stones on the water.

"I won" Gilbey said with an amused snarl. "The sleek ones are rotting away with nothing but push-ups and crunches to occupy their time but we both sit here as free as a bird." Eckhart looked downward and shook his head. "They said 'Michael Gilbey can't stand up to pressure. They say I have no composure but boy did we handle our business."

"So, that's why you did this to these people, to prove some point to yourself?"

"I'm jealous no more and by God, Eckhart, didn't you enjoy the thrill?"

"No! The guilt of it all. I think I shall never sleep again."

"Trust me. Soon we'll be far from here and we'll be no different than these little kids. I should think though that you might need my companionship when you go back to the Black Hills."

CHAPTER 9
SAD BUT TRUE

"All we wanted was peace and to be left alone."

-Crazy Horse

Under the inky firmament, Eckhart trudged through the Black Hills of Custer, South Dakota, up 385. Stars blotted the sky, and when one looked upward, one instantly knew why the Sioux held this land to be sacred. The ruddy orange glow emanating over the mountains made Gilbey feel as though he were entering the very edge of the universe into something too mysterious altogether. Eckhart lamented the fact that despite a thousand protests, Gilbey had managed to finagle his way back into his life.

"This is where man goes to find himself" Eckhart said, "across these diamond-studded highways of the Dakotas. There's nothing but stars and road for miles, and the further you get out here, the more inward you go. I used to cleanse myself out here."

"Why'd you leave?" Gilbey asked.

"I grew restless and tired of peace. I wanted to go slay some dragons. I told myself I'd never come back here."

"Why, if you found it so therapeutic?"

"There is something wild in these hills, some baleful force that wants to seize you. You have to fight with all of your inborn strength against it. I can't tell you how many relatives parked along the side of the road, contemplating blowing their brains out, even on the very brink of redemption. Out here, it's darkness within darkness, and the same power that redeems can also destroy. Quite simply, this place is the gateway to all understanding.

"Man, what we did back in Korea, I've been thinking on it...."

"The important thing is that we got out of it and we're still alive" Gilbey replied.

"But, Seraj is going to spend the rest of his life in Cheonan for something he didn't do."

"Just because he's a victim, doesn't make him innocent. What would he have done with his freedom? Sin upon sin upon sin. Now that he is confined to a cell, he can reflect on his past and repent for what he's done."

"What did he do that was so earth-shattering? Fuck girls and re-cycle them? How many saints did that in the profligacy of youth?"

"And now that his soul has been put to the fire, he can more readily be made a saint."

"I've been thinking about paying him a visit."

"I don't think he would welcome your presence."

"If anything, he's lonely."

"We framed him for a murder and testified against him, and you want to pay thousands of dollars of your own money and countless hours as well to see a swollen demon stare at you through Plexiglas.

"I appreciate you inviting me out here. It really was therapeutic as you say, but hey, let's not dwell too much on the past. Find some-thing to do, Eckhart: paint murals, run a restaurant, sell used cars for all I care. Just stop acting like you owe something to the past. It's the past that owes *us...*

"I have to go and find my father."

━━╪╪━━

Herman Gilbey examined his Keno Card and cursed himself for not playing the eights. Every time he played the eights, the screen was chock full of fours and every time he played the fours the screen was chock full of eights.

"Sometimes I think that this machine is telepathic" Herman said aloud. Just then, the old steel door of the Winston Tavern swung in like an iron gate, letting the hard whistling winter wind play its bitter tune inside. Herman looked over toward the un-invited sound and standing in the threshold was his son, who had just politely removed his ski mask, gloves and hat. Herman sat stupefied for a moment and then emphatically waved his son over.

Gilbey spotted the motion of the arm waving in the afterlight and stepped toward it, while some of the bar patrons examined this out of place youthful character before returning to their shallow glasses.

Herman stood up and greeted his son with open arms with the expectation of a hug. Gilbey reluctantly embraced his father, but made sure to at least give him a few half-hearted taps on the back.

"My boy" Herman announced jovially. "Here, let's go into the corner." He took his drink and ordered two more pilsners, one for his son and a refill for himself, along with a shot of gin. Michael was swiftly ushered into a corner booth by his double-fisted father. The boy looked down at the leather upholstery which had taken a beating over the years and popped a squat.

"There was a day when I thought I'd never see you again" Herman exclaimed gleefully. Michael glimpsed at the mirror over the bar. In it he could see his own reflection and just how haggard he had become. He meditated on the reddish bags beneath his eyes and the tough sallow scruff of his father.

"Are you with me, boy?" he asked, before pausing. "It's good to see you too dad" Herman said mockingly. "Is that a new scar?" he then, asked pointing to the tiny blemish above Gilbey's lip.

"It's a long story, Dad."

"Well, I got time. I've been stuck in shit towns like this for the last year or so. I might get into the fracking game, since I have no income outside of gambling."

"I thought you were going to quit when you won the accumulator."

"I was, but a man starts to worry when the money is only travelling in one direction. I gave you some of the winnings and I've been burning through the rest. I can't register for anything. The last apartment I was able to lease was in Florida, but I put my name to the records and a PI is going to find me, and if a PI finds me, then Richard Wallace will and my last days on this earth will be as painful as any that ever were, except I have a plan.

"You see this hat?" Herman asked. He took the withered fedora from off of his head and laid it on the table.

"Yeah, it's the same ugly fedora you've had forever."

"It's my lucky charm."

"Well: heart, stars, rainbows, horseshoes and balloons, but what's your point, Dad?" Herman handed the hat to his son.

"Look at the lining" Herman said.

"Looks raggedy" Michael said, handing it back after a disinterested glance.

"Look closer." Michael heeded the command but sighed as he felt around the sweat stained lining until a lump protruded out from the smooth cardboard.

"Are you talking about this piece of plastic?"

"It's a cyanide capsule." Michael immediately tossed the hat back to his father.

"If this capsule breaks, the poison will seep into your skin and kill you."

"That's the point, Michael. If Tricky Dick Wallace gets his hand on me, I'm going to make sure – what is this pussy music? They just played "Sweet Emotion" and "Paradise City." This ain't a classy enough joint for that mellow Starbucks eight dollar latte shit.

"Where was I? Sorry, yeah, just like a CIA operative, I pop one of these things in my mouth and I go to sleep forever. There are some things worse than death, Michael. I spend a lot of lonely nights shivering under thin semen stained motel blankets with a bottle in one hand and the remote in the other."

"I've been there dad" his son answered with self-pity. "The streets of Seoul, Daejeon and Pohang are some of the loneliest streets in the world. I ran the motel circuit because my apartment/cell became a worm infested nightmare."

"I'm sorry to hear that, but it sounds like you're blaming me for your woes. I had a hard life, Mike. If you've seen some of the things I went through, you might not find shelter and a shower so bad. I ran away from home when I was eighteen and tried to join the Marines. That didn't work out. I was never one for taking orders."

"If your life was so bad, why did you have a child?"

"I was trying to save my marriage. We (your mother and I) thought that this would change us. I guess it did but not enough. If you're feeling a little blue, you can't blame me for your misery. Very few of us have the parents we want. I tried my damndest Michael, but I'm only human. All this will be in your taillights soon. You have a college education. I never got that. Once all this is over, you can get a good job in publishing or something."

"I don't think you understand everything that happened in Korea. Eckhart and I will never be the same again. We became men."

"I don't know what you did, Michael, but you're a good kid. You're not racetrack scum like me. I've probably done a lot worse than you could ever dream of."

"Dad, I orchestrated a murder. I wanted to be a romantic provocateur, so I let some woman and her lover kill a man when I easily could have put a stop to it. This wasn't enough. I was so happy to be a puppet master, to orchestrate events. I thought prison was imminent." Tears welled up in Gilbey's eyes. "I'm tired of being trapped in this pathetic mind. There is no escape from the nightmares. Eckhart wants to go back to Korea to talk to Seraj, but I told him we need to move on, but we're just like flies circling around a steaming pile of dog shit." Herman understood, and so he held out his withered hand and covered the back of Michael's hand with his pudgy calloused fingers.

"I understand completely, Michael. I'm proud of you. You made a lot of stupid errors, but here, you thought your way out a very tricky situation. When death becomes easy, you cease to be human. That's what happened to Wallace's Croat with the scar. Must've grown up in war torn Kosovo or some shit. Death and killing became like paying his auto insurance bill. And, now he's hunting me." Herman shook his head and looked inside his pub glass, which now had more beer than foam.

"I suppose you're wondering what I did to become wanted by such men of means like Richard Wallace and his Slav."

"I am because if it's a gambling debt, surely you could have paid it."

"You were always quicker than your mother gave you credit for. You have your head in the clouds but you're a thinker; I respect that. I'm going to need to take a shot to tell this one. This is hard. Just like your story, no-no, much worse, this is awfully hard." Herman Gilbey downed his shot of whiskey like it was water and regretted not ordering another.

"I did have a gambling debt, starting back from when you weren't much taller than one of those stools. As much as Richard Wallace doesn't mind hooking up jumper cables to a guy's scrotum, he never really laid a hand on me because we had grown up together and I think he always wanted to be faithful to that world of our youth. I guess even killers have sacred places in their minds, even if it is next to the porn stash.

"Anyhow, shit got to the point where Wallace was done lending me money. If I was going to be a clown at the track, and he wasn't going to punish me, then I had to do it on someone else's dime. So, I did the unthinkable. I did a favor for a rival crew in exchange for twenty big ones. Dumbest shit ever.

"Just what that favor was has haunted my dreams every night ever since. I hope there's no heaven and hell, Michael, because if they exist, I'm going to burn like kerosene. I don't deserve life. I should be tortured to death by those awful men…

"I acquired sulfuric acid. It was easy. My friend was working as a janitor at Chelsea High at the time and we just took a nip full from the Chemistry lab. Of course no one noticed that it went missing, and that is the reason why that delightful girl, Chantal, now wears a mask."

"You were the one!? You threw acid at a girl's face!"

"Keep it down, Michael. Jesus!"

"You are a horrible human being. I knew I came from tainted blood but this is…"

"I'm not justifying what I did. When you're addicted to something like I was gambling, you'll do anything for money. I would've sucked a dick for a chance to make a wager on the superfecta."

"Yeah, well that would be a lot better than permanently ruining the face of the pretty young girl of a fucking mob boss!"

"I told you to settle your voice down. I'm pouring my heart out here. What we don't need are any unwelcome visitors…

"So that's my story. I thought it was important that I tell you that."

"Thanks, I guess."

"Aren't you going to ask me my plan?"

"I assume it involves cyanide."

"This is important, Michael. Can you not be cynical for once? This is important. Don't you understand if you come back to Boston, they will torture you and kill you?"

"Like they did my mother!"

"Hey, that is not my fault. I warned her and her lover. That's not fair."

"Well, I'm sure they appreciated the warning before their throats were cut."

"I'm here because I love you and to state the facts. This may be the last time I see you. This isn't a confession, where I seek absolution. If you want to stay in here and cry and shake your fists at me, I suppose I deserve that. I'm just telling you that this nightmare is over. I love you son. Now, just remember to stay the fuck out of Boston, unless you are instructed to do otherwise."

Ray Charles' rendition of "Georgia on my Mind" came on over the speaker system and Herman thought that the song echoed his sentiments exactly. Father and son sat in silence. They gulped down one more pilsner each and prepared for the cold.

"I wonder what these fuckers do when January comes if it's just above zero in mid-November. I thought New England was bad. Here, you actually *can* freeze your balls off. Did you drive here?"

"Eckhart's picking me up."

"He's from here?"

"Yes."

"I hope we'll meet again one day, Michael, but I wouldn't count on it. I hope you can appreciate that this may be the last time you see me." Herman slid a piece of a paper across the table. Gilbey examined it. It was the magic ticket, the card that won Herman the accumulator bet. "Keep it for good luck, Michael, 'cause we're I'm going luck ain't a factor."

Herman basked in the smoky darkness of his room at the Comfort Inn. An early 90's movie with Tom Cruise was playing on the old analog television. The volume was turned down low and the picture was grainy. Herman suddenly decided to add to the totem of holes scattered over the wool blanket. Then, he washed down the tobacco with a couple of good swigs of Vodka.

For once, I ain't gotta plan, no strategy on horses to pick, no way to weasel my way out of a debt. Thomas Beck was right to tell him never to come back, but Herman had always thought that he was one horse away from escaping the problems that had plagued him since his youth. There were no horses left to run at the track. This, he felt, was his final chapter, so he looked at the peeled paint on the ceiling and the floral patterns on the wall. He would have called his son but he had no number, his ex-wife, but she was dead. Verily, the elder Gilbey was alone.

"Ain't no shame in ending it this way, with my balls still attached to my body." Herman took a pear knife from out his pocket and carved the lining of his hat open. He dug through the aperture he created with his fatty fingers and found the object he was seeking, a tiny pill given to him way back in Florida. With contempt, Herman examined the tiny white capsule, incredulous that something so miniscule could undo a man completely. Briefly, he thought of God and of middle school crushes. Then, he meditated on why the accumulator should fall on him. Finally, he wondered if there were in fact a way out this predicament. He waited twenty minutes for a divine intervention or some sign from God, but nothing came, so Herman popped the capsule in his mouth and closed his eyes with the intention of never opening them again.

He was lying supine when he woke twenty minutes later and thought himself a ghost until he looked down at his Johnson and saw that he had a raging boner.

I might actually believe that I'm in heaven; I'm just missing 72 virgins. It dawned on Herman that the cyanide pill was in fact a Viagra capsule, so he did what came natural: he rung up his old booty call, Yazmin and explained the situation.

"Are you serious, Herman?!" she asked angrily in a heavy Latin accent. "You became rich, fucked me, and leave me poor. Now you want me again because you're lonely."

"It's not because I'm lonely. It's because I took Viagra and have an insatiable erection."

"You've got some huevos, Herman. You know what happened to your friend, Richard Powell? You shouldn't be here in Boston. Maybe I'll tell Richard Wallace that you're back in Boston. I can make some money that way."

"I have money for you if you help me."

"Help you do what, get your penis wet?"

"Not only that. Let me *esplain*" Herman said, mocking her accent. "Listen Yazmin, this is very important. You will get the remainder of my fortune if you would only do a couple of favors for me."

"You're a liar."

"I'll give you half of the cash up front. You won't have to give your body to another man for some time."

"Where are you, Herman? If you're lying to me, you won't have to worry about Richard Wallace because I'll cut your balls off."

"Alright now. I'm at the Motel Six on Newbury Street in Danvers, room #14. Come alone, and then we'll come together."

Herman waited in room seven of the Comfort Inn, his snub nose in his lap, his boner still raging. A green civic pulled into a space across the way and Herman recognized it as Yazmin's mode of transportation. She was alone, and there didn't seem to be anyone tailing her. He let her come to the door of room four and when she knocked, he came out of room seven and grabbed the unexpected woman by surprise, using his limited strength to haul Yazmin inside; a struggle ensued.

She kept trying to grab inside her purse but Herman prevented her from doing so. He wondered why she didn't scream for help.

When he separated her from the pocket book, he looked inside and found a derringer smaller than his own.

"So, this is what you were reaching for" he said. She was sitting on the ground, wondering what he was going to do next. He had her gun in his hand; he left his own on the bathroom sink. "Jesus, Yazmin, you don't have to extort me for the money!" She looked fiercely at the bulge in his khakis. "Yeah, I told you I can't get rid of this erection. You think you could help me shoot one off 'fore we talk a little business." Yazmin froze up and looked disappointingly back at Herman.

"Fine, I'll finish myself off in the bathroom."

"No need to be a martyr, Herman. You can present it, but you're just getting a hand job, nothing more and no cuddling."

"Yeah, whatever."

Herman zipped up his pants and thanked Yazmin for her handiwork.

"You have no idea how badly I needed that. Let's get down to business" he said. "He took thick rolls of twenties and handed them to her. "This is your day's pay but it's for more than a measly hand job. I need Goran Perisic dead."

"You want me to kill him? That's nuts. That guy is super dangerous. I had him once; he was very rough. I'll never be with him again."

"That's ten thousand in your hand. There's more where that came from if you oblige; just hear me out. Setup a meeting with him." Just then, her phone vibrated. She looked toward the phone and then back at Herman with shifty eyes.

"What should I...?" she started before being interrupted.

"Who was that?"

"Nothing important"

"I didn't ask what it was. I asked who it was." The two locked distrustful eyes for a moment. Yazmin's eyes moved toward the gun on top of the television. Herman's eyes followed them there. They both rushed toward the gun. Yazmin had a slight head start but like an inferior sprinter in a quarter horse race, she was quickly overcome. Herman pointed the gun at her and demanded that she answer the question. She rushed to the phone, which was in her purse, but Herman drew back the hammer, stopping her immediately in her tracks. He casually walked over to the phone to check the call log.

A big black Ford Explorer suddenly made its way into the barren parking lot.

"Say a word and we both die here" Herman said sternly. "Keep your mouth shut and you walk away with ten thousand." Four gladiatorial men stepped out of the SUV, one of which was Goran Perisic, looking markedly older. He led the way, the diagonal scar across his face as arresting as ever. Goran's three associates stood around room four keeping an eye out for witnesses while their leader knocked loudly at the door.

A Hispanic man in his mid-thirties answered the door in his boxers.

"Can I help you?" he asked. "I think you have the wrong room." Goran and his associates barged in and took out their pistols.

"Where is he?!" one of them demanded.

"I'm alone" the man said. "I'm not a gangster. I'm a plastic liner salesman." Goran's associates gave a quick look around the house and confirmed what the man had said. They pistol-whipped him for good measure anyway. Goran called Yazmin one more time, but there was no answer, so they left abruptly licking their wounds.

"How am I going to explain this to Goran?" Yazmin asked as she and Herman watched the Explorer pull away.

"Just say that I lied about my location; I did. You betrayed me, Yazmin."

"You abandoned me." The woman was beginning to cry.

"Not this again. At least, I didn't try to have you killed for money. I can't trust you, not after this episode."

"But you're still going to let me go with the ten-thousand, right?"

"For a hand job? Fork it over, slut." Herman thought about a quick murder-suicide. He could rid the earth of two miserable weevils with one instrument, but Herman was beginning to feel false confidence like he could win this just as he had the accumulator. He took back the rolls and disrespectfully tossed a couple of bills at the sitting woman.

"Keep the change you filthy animal." He threw her about five more twenty's and told her it was for the gun.

Now, he was back in the dark smoky silence with the curtains drawn. There was still more gin to drink and Herman was grateful that his legendary erection had subsided.

What's the play now? She's going to alert them that I'm in room seven as soon as she can. If I wait any longer, they're going to torture and kill me. Herman emptied his snub nose revolver save for one bullet. He left it in the cylinder and rotated the cylinder. *Should I leave my fate to chance and if this bullet ends me, let my fate end here? I'm tired of running...No not like this, I've got a second chance at life. The accumulator, the fake pill, it was all meant to be.*

CHAPTER 10

WILD HORSES

"And when he finished speakin'
He turned back toward the window
Crushed out his cigarette
And faded off to sleep
And somewhere in the darkness
The gambler he broke even."

- ("The Gambler") Kenny Rogers

A dark shroud lay over the yuletide season for the Wallace
family ever since its youngest member had her face disfig-
ured five years prior. Yes, the evergreen conifer lay spangled with
the finest ornaments and lights and a cherub stood guard atop it.
Presents were scattered along the base of this tree. A Christmas
wreath was fastened to the door and the hearth crackled.

Chantal came down the bedecked stairs gracelessly, veiled by
her protective mask. Before the attack, she was a social butterfly
who enjoyed doing a jig for her grandmother. Now, she enjoyed

the solitary space that she was afforded when her parents had ventured out of the homestead. On this day, she hadn't yet decided whether she would play the piano or paint.

Before she was to do anything, it was essential that she turn to the fridge to get her daily nourishment. With sorrow in her bones, this nourishment had become the meager stuff of true penitents. Today, it was oatmeal and fruit, and as she strove to pull the milk from the back of the fridge, she heard the infamous click of a gun's hammer being cocked back. Instinctively, she pivoted to the sight of distress and there she saw the jaded face of Herman Gilbey.

"Where is he?" the track rat demanded. He expected a tremulous voice to utter a plaintive response, but instead she answered monotonically,

"I assume you mean my father. My mom's away on vacation, so the bastard is out with a mistress or call girl. Maybe you can try to come back another time."

"I have a gun you know. In fact, I have two."

"Is that supposed to impress me?" She groped Herman's genitals. "You've got some shriveled balls. Do you want to fuck?" Herman was taken aback.

"I'm pointing the gun at you. Can't you see that through the mask?"

"Yes, now, are you going to fuck me? Chances are that it's been forty or fifty fears since you've pounded a pussy this tight...You look like you've seen a monster." Chantal giggled.

"This is highly inappropriate."

"So isn't breaking into a person's house. C'mon geezer, I've never felt a man before, and won't have many chances, not since they took my face away. Do you want to see it? What they did to me? Do you want to see it?"

"No."

"It's too much for you. I must live with it, but you won't even look at me." She removed the mask. Herman beheld the scarred face, the monstrosity of his own doing. He trembled like a child in the cold and then stumbled backward, pursued by Chantal, who was able to catch the old man by the arm and keep him from fleeing. She grabbed the snub nose firmly by the barrel so that the gun had simultaneous possessors; Herman was frozen now. Chantal inched her head close to the barrel and rubbed her head against it as a cat might in order to show affection.

"Can you do it, old man? Can you release me?" Despondent, Herman slipped his pointer through the trigger guard and stroked the thin black trigger.

Mercy.

Herman swallowed air and pulled the trigger. The bullet went into Chantal's skull and blood sprayed out of the back of her head onto the kitchen cabinets and floor. Her lifeless body dropped to the floor and her body shape assumed an unnatural pose.

Revolted by his own work, Herman remained still for a few moments, his gun still pointed outwardly. He then bolted to his car and sped off to anywhere.

From a local junkyard, Herman rescued his red Ford Focus.

I thought for sure they'd scrap this thing and salvage what parts they could. Elena is just as I remember her, rusty and filthy but willing to thrust her nose forward for one more ride. I guess I'll be granted my dying of wish of leaving this world with my bitch by my side. Lord knows it was never going to be Sara.

Herman had worked his way down south, hoping to get flagged down by a trooper so that he could pull over and blow his brains out all over the sedan. After two hours of guiding himself and his car down 395, he came upon one of the meccas where he so faithfully made his hajjes season after season.

How can I win? I've set the game against myself now. Only a loser doesn't know when to fold. I'm tired. I've been at the table too long and I've got a dud of a hand. I think it's time for me to cash out...for good.

He parked his car in the massive lot and was shuttled over to the casino entrance. Over the years, Herman had forgotten the grandiosity of the edifice that stood towering over him as he approached.

Foxwoods opened the same year Herman sired Michael and like Herman's son, it grew and grew into something substantive in the early 90's. In the years between, both had learned to speak to Herman and he tried to answer back but he never found the right words.

Up in his suite, he replayed the splattering of Chantal's blood over and over in his head, and then the acid attack well before, how her cherubic voice turned into the hellish cry of a scorned banshee. In an attempt to forget all this, Herman knocked back the nips in the minibar. But, all the manifestations of all the monstrosities he wrought came roaring back tenfold.

Finally, the alcohol settled into his gut and he felt the warmth in his innards. He adjusted the brim of his cap and bore the freakish memories of Chantal's ruin all the way to the roulette wheel. He watched it spin and placed bets when he was in the mood and only on numbers that had some personal significance.

Hypnotized by the dizzying spin of the wheel, the mechanical pull of the slots and all of that golden grit scurrying around like rats in a labyrinth, Herman had managed to forget himself and that scar-ridden face that began haunting him once more. As he won, like he never had before, not at a casino at least, he tossed chips of various denominations indiscriminately and became quite popular with passersby.

The night pretty much went that way all through the witching hour. Four in the morning hit him like a ton of bricks. His head pounded from the excessive alcohol consumption and excitement. He needed to lie down and so he did. The headache was too much for him to pass into sleep, so he just lay in his suite supine with his eyes closed as the room spun around him. Great dread wrapped itself like a snake around his aging heart when he glanced over at the clock; he vowed to off himself before sunrise and the appointed hour was approaching. There had to be something left to do, some task left to be finished. How could the whole of a mighty struggle culminate into this, a lonely suicide in a hotel suite? Wasn't there some wrong he could have righted?

I could try to go back for Wallace, make things a little easier for my son, so he can return. Herman quickly dismissed that thought as foolish. He knew that he was lucky to get this far, to simultaneously grant mercy to Chantal and take something precious from Richard Wallace at the same time. He went out to the balcony and looked up in the sky and couldn't see a goddamn star because of the wretched light pollution.

'Is it too much to ask to see a star on high before I finally rid myself of...of myself?" The trees beyond stretched out interminably until darkness overcame them in her bosom. Forlorn and gazing in the distance with bloodshot eyes, Herman hoped that he could go somewhere like that, somewhere cool and dark, where one could see the stars pierce a winter sky.

Herman Gilbey placed the snub nose to his head and made his final wager,

What are the odds on God? On an afterlife? What are the chances a paradise is available? Even if, what chance does someone like me have? Should I shoot for purgatory? Suicides, murderers and gamblers don't go to purgatory. That was the only thing that that crusty cunt, Sister Agnes taught me. Nothingness is my only horse now. All my chips are on her. There ain't enough grace in heaven for a wretch like me. Wait! One final act before dying.

⤛✛ ✛⤜

With The Focus packed with ammonium nitrate and a heart that was full up like a landfill, Herman had pursued his destiny as it had been pursuing him; he was tired of running. So, with little brown envelopes full of cash and poker chips he cared not to cash, Herman went on his way back to Boston. His ego screamed to let him out, to run, to survive for one more day, but he overcame the impulse and there he was on Walcott Road with explosives lining his car.

It didn't take long for Herman's beat up sedan to get noticed in this plush neighborhood. In another exercise demonstrating the power of pure will, Herman called Richard Wallace and taunted him.

"I killed her, your little princess. You came after me and mine, so yours gets it. Too bad she wanted it, the little slut. Never saw a dick in her life, so she was eager to ride the old stallion. That girl had a hidden talent. She didn't deserve what I did to her but I finished what I started. I'm in the car outside, so just shake my hand and we'll call it even and I'll be on my way."

Wallace hung up the phone and breathed deep. He rested his arms on those of the chair. He fixed his fedora. It was just like the one that Wallace wore, only it was hound's-tooth instead of fallow. He walked over to the window to witness Herman's audacity. Quivering with anger were those thin purple lips of his.

"That asshole is practically parked in my driveway!" he called. "What are you goons waiting for?" Wallace's clowns scurried about gathering their iron and emptied out of the house like bees from a hive. With their ski masks on, they surrounded the sedan. They were like patrons staring through an aquarium looking glass and Herman was the fish that they dragged out of water.

"Our boss is going to enjoy this" one of the goons said. Another ordered him to keep his mouth shut and get to it before the neighbors saw something.

"Jesus Christ, you boys are slow" the impatient Wallace said with irritation. "I'm surprised you didn't parade him the fucking street. Alright, just put him in the basement. We have to see if five-o shows up." The goons did as they were instructed.

The ever-stoic Goran Perisic stroked the stubble on his chin and drank Vodka from the bottle. He listened intently to his boss.

"So, he's just tied up there in the basement?" Goran asked with a sinister smile on his face. His accent seemed to grow in proportion to his menace. Wallace could hardly sit still.

"I'm going to skin the fucker alive. We just have to wait and make sure the police ain't following suit, so I'm just going to bide my time and keep him here overnight. In the morning, we'll move him to the warehouse."

"His car's still out there."

"I know. The longer we let it sit out there, the more suspicious things get. I was hoping you could move it."

"You think your neighbors are going to report seeing a suspicious vehicle?"

"Well, they call the police every time they see a Negro, so I imagine they might say something. I'm still meditating on that. The people here know who I am and they're helpless against it, so here are the keys. You and some of the boys want to take the old piece of rust for a joyride to the junkyard."

"My pleasure," Goran said

"Strange isn't it? He won all that money and he was on the verge of the kind of hellish malice we are about to bring to him and he still drove that recognizable shit box. I thought for sure he would recycle it. Sentimental, I suppose."

Goran looked at the key as the goons followed behind like sheep. *No electric starter. Been awhile since I've seen this.* He unlocked the door easily enough but soon found that the other doors had to be opened manually from the inside.

"God, this is a piece of shit" he said to the goon squeezing into the passenger seat. "Let's get this shit over with."

"It smells like Phillip Morris in here" one of the goons said. The other goon laughed but Goran did not understand the joke, so it needed to be explained to him so that he could nod in approval.

Turning the engine over took some work as the occupants genuinely worried about getting this thing started. One of the goons suggested turning the wheel but Goran insisted that this was not the problem. In recognition of the struggle, Wallace walked to the edge of his lawn as he had hitherto been standing on the steps, which could only be comprehended by gazing upon his silhouette conceived from the light shining out of the porch window.

Goran got the engine to turn over and for just a second, the engine was idle. A goon exhaled to signal the end of the collective frustration. Wallace waved goodbye to Goran while conceiving fresh tortures for Herman. It was in that moment that his world got turned on its head.

The sedan burst into flames. A deafening thud is the only way to describe the sound that accompanied the explosion as an oppressive cloud of smoke and dust covered the flames. Goran and the two goons were vaporized immediately.

Wallace choked on the dust and of course, he was not unscathed. A large portion of his body was burnt, including part of his face. Bits of steel were embedded in his flesh. Car alarms were blaring and the cars themselves were still reverberating from the tremendous report. It wasn't long before the sirens came wailing towards the fury.

Examining his calloused manacled hands, Herman Gilbey felt his existence to be a very surreal thing in this moment. He was supposed to be in a warehouse at this moment getting his penis skinned off. Instead, he was detained by men of a more refined persuasion.

An agent near the end of his tenure with a fading widow's peak sat so upright he looked like a part of the furniture. Next to him sat an equally intense agent with a handsomer visage. His hair was close-cropped and the lines of his face betrayed his high fitness level.

"Guilty" Herman said. How own visage was pallid.

"We'll get to all that very shortly" the older agent said after attempting to suppress his surprise at the easy confession. "First, are you alright Mr. Gilbey? You look rather sick. We found you tied up in the basement." Herman heard the beginning and the words just tapered off like the sounds on the shore for one going out to sea. The young agent said something but it was all gibberish to Herman who only waited for the murmurs to die down before he spoke these words:

"Thallium is spread over my skin and is coursing through my veins. I will be dead soon so tell me, did I get them? Richard Wallace, is he dead? Goran Perisic too? Speak clearly. I cannot hear too well." The agents rushed out of the room to Herm's disappointment. He needed them to stay, to deliver a final message to his aching soul but they would not avail him.

Emergency medical personnel rushed in covered in protective clothing and masks. They stretchered him out and as he convulsed and his hair started falling out, he called out for his fedora.

"Can't I just die with my fedora? Can't I die as I want to be remembered? Wallace perishes but the Gilbey name lives on!"

Herman was rushed to the ER and became a high priority patient. The staff worked tirelessly and tried every antidote but there was no cure for this. The proclamations of his enduring name withered into low mutters and mumbles about his body being on fire until Herman Gilbey passed from this world at 3:02 PM. His final hand was played.

Richard Wallace woke up in a hospital bed, hooked up to all kinds of machines. The two goons sitting at his bedside urged him to stay lying until the nurse could be consulted. He flipped the pair of them off and penetrated them with a stare.

"Where the fuck is Herman Gilbey?!" he shouted, muted a bit by the gauze covering his face. The goons tried to hush him again but the agents and cops outside Wallace's door took notice of the resurrected Wallace and came strolling in with renewed interest. The nurses lapped the cops and began to tend to the crime boss.

"I demand to be released immediately" he insisted. The physician's assistant explained that he had burns on over sixty percent of his body and that with the metal fragments lodged in his flesh, he wasn't going anywhere. He tried to rise out of bed in spite of the cute nurse's orders but he found it impossible. She hadn't explained that his left leg had been amputated. There was no shock or pity, just the disappointment that the tide of revenge had been slowed. He lay back down and looked up at the colorless tiles. Revenge would have to wait.

It wasn't much longer that Wallace learned Herman Gilbey had committed suicide via Thallium poisoning. It was like watching a child first learn that Santa Claus is not real. When he heard that the son was still alive, Wallace licked his lips and silently promised to exact on the son the heavy punishment that was meant for the father.

When the trial started, Wallace did his best to look like an invalid. He had the burns on his face and was confined to a wheelchair. He made sure to prop up his prosthetic leg as his attorney instructed.

This was Freddie McKenzie's chance to make the headlines. He had been appointed special prosecutor in this case for the work he had done putting some hardcore Cambodians away up on the North Shore. There were no controversies in that trial and McKenzie had made his name as someone who couldn't be gotten to. However, this go round he was working on a federal team with high profile attorneys. Most of them were salty pitbulls like him who would sink their teeth into Wallace and follow the protocol better than the highest of the Pharisees. However, there was once cause for concern, one Dennis Barbour. Farrah Brunson, a member of the prosecution who resembled Angela Merkel, referred to Barbour as being "young, dumb and full of cum" in a meeting wherein all but Barbour were present. Superiors were petitioned to have Barbour removed until it was learned that Barbour's uncle was Senator Adam Thurman O'Neal. To their dismay, the team learned that not only would they have to put up with having a playboy come and go, he was to feature prominently in the trial.

"I guess then it's our responsibility to get O'Neal's boy as seaworthy as possible" Attorney Sandler commented. Sitting round the table, the rest of the team merely breathed a collective sigh and began the work they had set out for themselves.

CHAPTER 11
PERFECT JOY

"Now, somewhere between the sacred silence,
sacred silence and sleep
Somewhere between the sacred silence and sleep
Disorder, disorder, disorder"

- ("Toxicity") System of a Down

With the council of elders seated round the board room table, Barbour rocked up, wearing a sharp grey suit of the finest quality. He spiked up his hair with an excessive amount of gel and carried a swagger that filled the room. Indignant, Counselor Brunson raised herself to her feet and protested the presence of this garish character who batted not an eyelash at the tirade. Sandler, who remained seated, put a gentle arm to the elbow of the infuriated Brunson in order to calm her down. It was almost as if he were reminding her of the futility of their situation. She sat down but her countenance betrayed a seething disposition by virtuc of the rouge hue that animated it.

"It's okay" Barbour assured her. "I studied law at NYU." As he spoke these words, he grabbed the lapels of his pricy suit. This did little to calm counselor Brunson.

"Do we really have to parade Nero's horse around the courtroom?" she asked. Sandler tried to calm her further.

"Listen lady, just because no one has touched your cooch in fifteen years doesn't mean you gotta get all righteous on everybody. You don't even know me." McKenzie let the boy carry on until he issued his own decree stating that the boy was "out of order." Barbour was then instructed to sit down.

"I assume your girlfriend tells you that you're the best and biggest she ever has" McKenzie continued. "Do you ever wonder if maybe it's not enough?"

"Excuse me! Do not make me shame you and whip it out in front of everybody?"

"This is what we worry about" McKenzie said coolly. "If you say this shit to us, how can we be assured that you're not going to have a youthful outburst in the courtroom?"

"This crusty lady just lost her own temper. Why don't you scold her?"

"There's a difference: Anger has its place in the courtroom. Threats of indecent exposure do not. You're here to advance your career, are you not?"

"I want to bring in a shark like Richard Wallace, my very own John Gotti."

"So, it *is* ego driven after all?" Barbour had to think.

"No, it's about justice for all the people that Richard Wallace hurt over the years."

"And you can bring it to them?"

"Yes. I was in the top of my class at NYU and scored magnificently high on the bar. The highest suits at Malone, Brady and Barry say I'm primed for an illustrious career."

"We don't doubt your potential but how many rookies do you see starting game seven of the World Series? This isn't some training exercise. Lives are at stake here. If you underperform or worse yet, fuck up, then Wallace goes back on the street to terrorize more people. Organized crime is finally dying in this city and we have a chance to see it through to its end. Now, to me and everybody else here, you're just some starry-eyed kid from suburban Ohio, whose uncle called in a favor to the District Attorney but I'm not going to hold that against you.

"If you weren't so busy glorifying yourself and waving your dick, you might have done yourself a favor and looked around the room. We have some of the best lawyers in the state and the country at this table. They too want to see justice but just like you, we are all interested in advancing our careers, perhaps more so than you, because we are far deeper in this game.

"This lady that stood up and castigated you like an aunt scorned, that's Farrah Brunson. Do you have any idea the heights that she's climbed and the adversity that she's overcome? Do you have any idea how long she's been waiting for an opportunity like this to take her to the next hypothetical rank."

"I can understand that sir and I won't let you down."

"You're right, you won't because you're going to sit in the background like a good little boy while Farrah gets her name up in the lights and don't even think about bitching to Senator O'Neal or we'll be sure to make sure that this special case of nepotism makes the news. You've got another full generation to make a career like these folks have built and I'm sure that the prophecy that your freshman professor ascribed to you will ring true but for now, you have to learn, as we all do, so here's your seat. Get ready to take some notes."

Attorney Brunson was basically glowing at this point and the rest of the sitting elders were entertained but their staid visages refused to bear joy. Barbour did as he was told.

⊨⊩ ⊪⊨

The trial proceeded as high profile trials generally go, with media credentials packing the courthouse. The attorneys made their opening statements, witnesses were called, evidence was presented and altogether this venture took an entire year.

In this window of time, Eckhart had snuck off to Beijing to disappear in the smog and Gilbey agreed to stay behind on the Tauler homestead that was bequeathed unto Eckhart in Stephanie Tauler's will.

⊨⊩ ⊪⊨

Gilbey set a cord of wood to the fireplace and though he had a healthy fear of fire, which he felt was the result of something traumatic that happened to one of his ancestors, he lit the wood and stoked the fire. He rubbed his hands together, creating as much friction as possible so as to warm himself and he sat before the fire ruminating over Korea. The notion that Seraj was stuck in a cramped cell because of him pleased him but he regretted losing Eckhart to bitterness and what of Bo-kyung? He imagined her forlorn in her cell, a fading beauty, ironing over again and again in her mind the wrinkle that undid her, the miscalculation that wrecked everything.

With his own soft hands, Gilbey had taken a stone to bludgeon Jacob Jung to death. Then, he threw him from the mountain with

Seraj, Eckhart and Bo-kyung standing about. He wondered how such delicate hands could execute such violence.

Was it worth it? Even if I had kept the stains of iniquity from my cassock, I would still be here, before this crackling fire, a hunted man.

Like a maddened king, Gilbey just sat before the fire and watched the snow fall outside. The wind outside was biting and howled like the woman of the barrows. It was amidst that song of winter that Gilbey heard trucks come up the long winding drive. He had an oil delivery not two weeks ago, who could it be?

⊷+ +⊶

Weary from the day's work, Farrah Brunson got into her black Range Rover and headed home to her ocean-view property but not before first stopping in at Wendy's. It was a good night for chili, a baked potato and one of those generic sitcoms she loved so much. She was going to nail Richard Wallace's dick to a wall come trial time but for the rest of the night, she wasn't going to worry a lick about any of that. It was "me" time.

When Brunson entered her empty home, she was greeted by her dog, Birdie, a beagle with sad eyes. She kicked off her heels as if they were the last two weights she would ever know. The animal, eager for its late supper, accosted her owner by sniffing her like a madman.

"Soon Birdie. Man, you have no idea how badly I wish you could do foot massages. I guess Neil never did those anyway." The sound of a squeaky wheel turning and turning. *There must be something wrong with the heating system. I'll have to call the James guy tomorrow.* The sound of the squeaking wheel came nearer. *What the...*

Richard Wallace came rolling in the room accompanied by a trio of goons. Brunson tensed up like a cornered fox.

"There's my jackal" Wallace said. There was a despondency in his voice that he never expressed when he had his leg.

"Do you have you any idea what would happen if any witness saw you here?"

"It would be my life" Wallace said calmly. "However, it would be your life too and with all of your retirement plans that you've put in the layaway, it would be a tragedy to have your face look like the chili you brought here to eat and shit out." Wallace pointed to the gun in one of the waistbands of his goons.

"If you think I'm going to throw this trial, you mine as well shoot me now."

"God, even loveless cunts such as yourself have to be so dramatic." Wallace paused. "I start to understand your kind in my old age. What was it? Your daddy told you it was wrong to steal from the fruit stand when you were fifteen and you did as you were told. Now you think you're some special arbiter of justice. Was everyone you put behind bars guilty?"

"You're different. You're an absolute animal."

"But a rational one. Look, I know that if I threaten your life, you're just going to continue to be the same cunt as before but with added police protection. I can promise you that I'll kill you but that might not be enough. The only thing I can say to really chill you is that members of your family will be mutilated and disposed of as I see fit if a guilty verdict is rendered. That is all." Wallace's last act in the house was to take Brunson's potato and consume it slowly, applying butter and using the plastic fork that was placed in the paper bag. "Next time get sour cream you fucking cunt."

As the trial proceeded, McKenzie noted that Brunson appeared like she was operating with "frayed nerves." She disclosed that this trial was taking a toll on her like none other before. Bearing sleepless nights and endless review sessions were nothing new to her but she was haunted by the specter of Wallace sitting there in her living room with no light in his eyes. This caused her to tremble greatly with self-doubt. Wallace would come after her family with

110

every last fiber of his battered being. This she could not disclose because she foresaw no reasonable way that law enforcement agencies could protect all of her children, grandchildren, nieces and nephews. They numbered in the dozens.

"It makes me wonder about Wonder Boy" Brunson said to McKenzie. He appeared pensive, watching through windows, cars speed over the youth-ridden thoroughfares of Allston. "Perhaps his youth would have served him well. Thirty years ago I could get there in my mind and with my body but now it feels like an aging machine."

"One thing I can assure you of is that you've been putting in a hell of a shift so far. We've got Wallace dead to rights. We can't control whether or not these jurors have been bought but we can control the strength and integrity of our case and you've done a bang up job of that so far. I know you don't want to hand this off and I sure as hell wouldn't like to see Wonder Boy beaming ear to ear. And, you really don't want this blemish on your otherwise spotless career. You want to bow out with a Tour de Force. You were chosen not just because we didn't want Barbour to pull his dick out in court; I (and the others) wanted someone who could carry the load." After this praise, Brunson wasn't glowing. She just thanked him and swallowed the air in her throat. "Is anything else the matter?"

"No, this trial is my life now. I will see it through to the end."

Brunson worked her way through the trial heroically with her primary goal being to conceal her fear of Wallace. Even God Himself and all of his angels might doubt that Wallace ever rolled into her living room with one leg and threatened to wipe her seed from the earth. In that sense, Brunson succeeded.

In the midst of delivering a sermonic closing statement that roused the jurors and would have George Whitefield applaud, Brunson gave to the world that last bit of fire in her bones. Had she ended there, she might have been beatified on the spot by his Holiness himself. However, the livelihood of her family weighed heavier on her than anything that might be plopped onto the scales of justice. Like a Tibetan monk vandalizing his own sand mandala, Brunson in an instant desecrated all that she built during the case – nay, everything she built for the last forty years after she set her teenage heart on becoming a hotshot trial lawyer. Here was her big case. Finally, she had stood within that moment that was to be her most triumphant, one that she had been anticipating since she received an acceptance letter from Georgetown Law.

Citing the wisdom of one Larry Mann, Farrah rationalized her decision to do what could not be undone by telling herself that "one has to chew one's own leg off to survive." The prosecution rested only after Farrah snickered and said, "But, I think we all know the real reason Mr. Wallace refused to testify."

Attorney McKenzie, who had been seated at the prosecution table with his teeth clenched like a boxing fan waiting for a knock-out, suddenly found his mouth agape. She had committed one of the cardinal sins of trial law; she violated the constitutional rights of Richard Wallace. Any first year law student knows that there can be no incrimination based on the exercise of the Fifth Amendment. In boxing terms, Farrah Brunson had just thrown an uppercut from the outside and so there lying on the canvas amidst the flashing bulbs was the case and her career.

Before the verdict was to be read and rendered, McKenzie found Bronson and unleashed a tirade unlike any other he had uttered during the course of his entire career. His bald head neatly waxed, bobbed up and down like a buoy when he spoke:

"How much did they pay you?! How could you do this to us?! You're going to burn Farrah!" It must be said that in the surreality of the moment, Brunson felt nothing, no scorn or hatred. She was in shock and her body and mind were acting accordingly. An eyelash was hardly batted. They both knew the game was up, so eventually McKenzie relented, but only with one final piece of advice.

"I hope it was an honest mistake but I know that someone as talented as you wouldn't fuck up like this even if you hadn't slept in a week. I know that you have too much integrity to trade a verdict for money. At least I'd like to think so. Therefore, I believe that you traded your life for a verdict. I know you won't acknowledge it either way but just as a professional courtesy, I'd like for you to know that Wallace won't let you keep that life for very long. Wallace's secrets die with Wallace and no one else, regardless of what you do with him or how this trial turns out, so not only did you not save the day, you didn't save your own life." Brunson just nodded, barely acknowledging her colleague. "See to it that this is the last case you ever try or I will."

Down in his chambers, Judge Simon appeared grim but remained somewhat reserved. He rubbed the little nick he got from a poor shave job earlier in the morning. McKenzie, Sandler and Barbour sat around Simon's desk eager to hear what the judge had to say, hoping against hope as they never had that he would somehow overlook Brunson's gross error. Judge Simon sighed:

"I'm sure you gentleman are all aware of why I called you in here." They nodded. "Ms. Brunson, Where is she?" McKenzie informed him that she wasn't feeling well.

"I wouldn't be either if I just shit the bed like that. Anyhow, our brilliant prosecutor has tainted the trial but I cannot declare a mistrial because it was a litigator who made the vital error. The jury is going to reach its verdict but if Wallace loses, his people are going to appeal and all legal precedent, as you know, would suggest that a guilty verdict will be overturned." It was the moment they feared.

Outside Barbour raised his palms to the heavens:

"This is why you should have given the game ball to moi. I never would have caved like your cuntly friend. Are you happy now?" he pointed his finger to the chest of McKenzie. "Did that little dog and pony show you did at least get your old dick into the lingerie she bought from Lady Grace?"

"If you tried the case, Cheese Dick" McKenzie said "we'd never have gotten to the closing arguments."

"Would've spared us all the pain." Barbour stormed off and McKenzie went with Sandler to grab some gut-stick food.

When everyone returned to the full court room to hear the verdict, Wallace had a shit-eating grin but the eyes remained coolly fixed ahead at nothing in particular. The verdict was read. Wallace was found "Not Guilty" on all charges. Farrah Brunson had just received her second shock of the day. At once, she was both vindicated and defeated, the former because her intentional mishap had not freed Wallace and the latter because she had not won the trial after a total performance.

Wallace examined his fingertips as if they were strange objects and laughed loud enough to be heard but softly enough to avoid shouts for contempt. He shook the hand of his slick defense attorney and nodded with approval. McKenzie & Co. were stupefied. When Wallace shook the joy from his feet, he would cover his hands with the blood of his enemies and most immediate among them were the kin of the deceased Herman Gilbey.

CHAPTER 12
DARK NIGHT OF THE SOUL

**"One day I'm going to grow wings
A chemical reaction
Hysterical and useless."**

- ("Let Down") Radiohead

As the June Bugs scurried past the picnic table, Wallace wished he could crush them. *I'm a goddamned cripple.* Once revered for the tenacity that emboldened his wiry frame, Wallace was helpless to be an instrument of destruction in and of himself. He had to rely on his goons to exact the violence that was in his head. Yes, it felt good to see someone torn to shreds like some medieval exhibition but to watch and only watch felt voyeuristic and incomplete. Out of the silence, Wallace spoke:

"Bear trap." One of the goons smiled at this. The other remained stoic.

"It's all useless unless we can find the little menace" Wallace's new Lieutenant, Zepp, said. "He's not near Boston because even a moth is too smart for that and none have seen him. He's got family in Florida, Canada and Louisiana. That's a good place to start."

"Five years ago, I would have agreed with you," Wallace said, "but we're under heavy surveillance now if you haven't noticed. I can't have the FBI wondering why I'm making trips to Florida, Canada or anywhere else. Hansel and Gretel can't leave that many bread crumbs on a trail for a hungry witch. We've got to get this right. No murders until we find the only begotten son of Herman Gilbey. And then if we can't, we draw him out, by picking the mongrels off one by one

By the crackling fire and surrounded by hidden stashes of money, Michael Gilbey passed the winter. He sat by the window eating junk food and watching squalls, hoping that when he closed his eyes, they would never open again. Pathetically, this is what he schemed and survived for, to cowardly hunker down amidst a brutal winter and hope for death. He was driven to partial madness from which he hoped he could recover and the sleep he got was troubled by the ever-shifting phantasms of Richard Wallace as they appeared to him.

It was in that benighted state that Michael Gilbey sought out Father Barry (his family name), an aging priest who was in the process of being succeeded by two real healthy looking fellows. He still had his wits about him and was glad to make his way to Florida while still ailment free. Gilbey sought him out one day while he was in the middle of his crossword puzzle, subconsciously counting the days when he would be in sunny Florida with his white knee socks and orthopedic shoes.

Gilbey stepped into his office without appointment:

"What can I do you for?" Father Barry asked with a smile partially shadowed by his moustache. Gilbey wore a hat to conceal his enormous cowlick but the priest could still see the shiny purple creases beneath his eyes. He looked the boy (was a man really) over to make sure he wasn't carrying weapon, wasn't high and wasn't physically injured and then offered him a seat when he was able to confirm this.

"So?" the priest asked after a long pause. Sickly Gilbey introduced himself by extending his hand, which was trembling from alcohol withdrawal.

To get through the harsh winter, Gilbey inhaled on average a single liter of Canadian Rye. He raided the Tauler liquor cabinet before he had to start making sixteen mile round trips to the nearest package store. Coming off of it cold turkey was a hell of a kick to the system. Father Barry pretended not to notice and didn't neglect the notion that the boy could have been suffering from some neurological condition that causes tremors, which only meant that he certainly had his cross to bear.

Had Gilbey been bolder, he would have outright told the priest what he really wanted, a ticket to the seminary, but he couldn't say that. There were too many gaps for the priest to exploit, so Gilbey took a path of lesser resistance and asked if he could take part in the ministry. Even with it mattering little to Father Barry because of the limited time left as an active priest, he did not want to see shaking hands passing out the consecrated host. He already wrote him off for any roles in which the man child would be on display for the esteemed congregation. And, he just wasn't going to ask about the baking of bread because he didn't trust the man child to refrain from defilement. He had an alright voice for a lector, but once again, Father Barry didn't want to see the trembler up on the altar, though he wouldn't be the first weirdo to get up there and read a Pauline epistle. One of Father Barry's greatest regrets is that Susan Winston, the eternal bag lady, would continue her role as a lector after he had gone down to Boca Raton. Even worse, the lady would probably still be reading the responsorial psalms with her wispy voice long after

Father Barry had been interred but I suppose he had an easy time living with it knowing that he would soon be out on the lanai sipping margaritas and joking with the neighbors about their various ailments. Of course, he wasn't going to give the boy any sort of real stewardship, so he decided in his head that he would allow him to be in hospitality and bring the donuts out whenever there was a post-mass bash. *Let him prove himself to the new blood.*

Father Barry had processed all of this in a matter of moments and nodded with pleasure as though he were excited to hear that the boy wanted to take part in the ministry. Now, for the test.

"What parish are you from?" the priest asked. Gilbey paused to formulate his answer:

"I just came back from Korea, Daejeon to be exact."

"Never heard of it" Father Barry said, though he was impressed.

"The church was rather humble and went by no other name than Daewha-Dong church; it was named after the neighborhood it was in."

"I see. Do you remember the name of the priest?"

"It was an immigrant church. There were a lot of Filipino priests who required my help in English. Father Matt was one." As it might be inferred, Gilbey wasn't exactly a regular devotee, but he was going to sell this priest on his piety at any cost.

"Father Barry and Father Matthew will most likely need help setting up before and after certain events. I can put you in touch with them." He was handed the white business cards of the future of Our Lady of the Black Hills. It never dawned on Gilbey that men of the cloth could carry business cards or would have any desire to do so. "Sorry, I forgot to explain. I've got one foot out the door. That's right, come summer I'm free. I'll be road-tripping it with a couple of other former soldiers of the cross and then once November hits, I'll be down in southeast Florida." Father Barry almost added that once there, he would work on his tan and golf swing but chose to remain professional. "I'm retiring.

"What do you for work, Michael?"

"I was a teacher."

"Is that what you were doing in Daejeon?"

"Yes, si...father."

"I see. What brings you out here? Are you from here? You have a northeast accent."

That's right. I'm originally from Connecticut...Oh, what brings me out here? I'm living with a friend I met in Korea."

"I hope you enjoy our beautiful state. Alright, call Father Matt or John Paul. They are very nice guys, young lads; you'll like them."

"I will. Thank you."

"Is there anything I can help you with?" Gilbey rubbed his sore eyelids and informed him that that would be all.

Michael Gilbey did call Father Matt as the first order of business the next morning. The priest did not sound thrilled but he wasn't discouraging either. He wanted to say that they had all the help they needed but didn't want to keep a lost sheep at bay through his own hastiness. "Why don't you come in sometime? And we'll get you set up with Marianne who is kind of our unofficial head of hospitality."

Father Matt, as always, was in a good mood, smiling with his dimples. That smooth-shaven of his face betrayed not a single dark night of the soul. For that reason, he was primed for the episcopacy. When Gilbey sat down to speak with him in person, he was expecting a much meeker man. *Why isn't he married? Why would he choose this life? He must be exceptional at hiding his brokenness from the rest of the world.* Immediately, Gilbey felt that he was making a mistake instead of a friend, but he was there, so he went through with it. Just as Father Barry remained unimpressed with Gilbey, so was Father Matt, but as Father Matt counseled him, he let the man child bring out the donuts on occasion.

While becoming a regular at all church functions, Gilbey found the large families and curious old ladies difficult to navigate as he handed out the punch and pound cake. At first, he didn't know how to talk to these people, most of whom had no interest in Gilbey. What was a bachelor man child on the wrong side of thirty doing hanging around a Catholic Church with no collar? For those who did want to know Gilbey, they wanted him to be a certain kind of person, a cherub who sang his praises lucidly, not the kind of man who harbored dark thoughts. It took him awhile to understand that morbid thoughts of great heft weren't perched in the hearts of other men, so for once in his life he adapted.

He learned Latin and went to the Tridentine Mass in Rapid City to get along with the hardliners, who were few in number, compared to the majority, who were drive-thru Catholics eager to swallow their sanctified bread, shake the priest's hand and get on with it. Gilbey knew that if he could find allies among the hardliners, then the drive-throughs and pleasant elderly ladies would fall like dominoes. For Gilbey, it was nothing more than a political exercise and he passed with flying colors.

A year and a half passed this way and Gilbey's only failure lay in his status as an unemployed single man. For the most part, he had conquered the parish, including Father Matt and John Paul and he was ready to set-up shop again, but somewhere entirely different, a place whose people he understood.

Standing in the front hall and looking out on the plain that would soon receive the snow for Gilbey's third Sioux winter, the man child saw a gleaming ginger-ale colored pickup come up the serpentine driveway. Cars or trucks never came up this way, so Gilbey grabbed the Tauler family Springfield Bolt-Action and readied himself. Who was he kidding? He had no idea how to operate a gun but he would much rather misfire with this than the family buckshot. Panicking, Gilbey realized that he needed a quick strategy for suicide if indeed Wallace and the goons were coming for him. He would never make it to the nearest body of water to drown himself, nor was there any great height on the house from which he could throw himself and be assured of death on impact. Then, Gilbey remembered the eight dollar investment he made in a bottle of Tylenol PM. Surely, there were enough capsules in that bottle to kill him. He quickly dismissed the notion of waving an old hunting rifle in front of menaces bent on torture, so he went to the medicine cabinet to retrieve his pills.

For a moment, he lamented the Gilbey legacy of suicide as an impossible thing: First, Uncle John than his own father more infamously. Were they all just built to spill? Would death bring the end to the Gilbey curse or would Wallace seek to draw more blood?

And then joy. Emptying out of the rental truck was no Richard Wallace but James Eckhart and a fair blonde woman. Gilbey forced the handful of death back into the bottle and waited to greet his longtime friend and what must be his new love.

Gilbey opened the door and extended his arms as one waiting to receive. Nora, the female, was hesitant and Eckhart was downright contemptuous tossing a bag to the floor and ordering Gilbey to get the rest of their luggage. He caught a nudge on the arm from his love for this curtness.

"You don't know him like I know him" Eckhart said. "He deserves this."

"It's no problem" Gilbey said. "Really, it's the very least I can do. This man, as uncouth as he can be, gave me a place to say while I crawled back to my Lord on the cross."

"Oh, I didn't know you were religious" Nora said.

"He's not" Eckhart said. "It's an act. Now, go g…Why the fuck is there a rifle cocked by the windowsill?"

"Oh, wow, well it's really silly. I thought you were…"

"You didn't get my e-mail?"

"I canceled the internet and phone. I haven't been online for months."

"I let this fucker live here for free and he can't follow basic instructions. Are there any other surprises I should be expecting?" Eckhart walked over to the window to make sure the gun wasn't cocked as he originally suspected. "Thank God. At least this imbecile is too dumb to load and cock a fucking gun." He looked down at the ground, found a few of the capsules Gilbey didn't manage to stuff back into the bottle and examined them. "Why are there pills on the floor? Were you planning some kind of murder-suicide? Explain yourself." Nora stood silent, amazed at the character and the bizarre props he had brought down to the window.

"Well, not murder-suicide. Murder or suicide. Have you told your girlfriend?" Silence. "You see I'm a wanted man. No, not wanted by the police. I am wanted by a vicious gang boss. That's why Eckhart extended his hand to me. He hoped that by letting me live here alone, while he scampered off to the bowels of China, he would find out whether he was safe because, sorry, I didn't get your name."

"Nora."

"Nora, great. So, he scampered off to China and left me here as kind of bait, to see if this gangster could find me. A couple years later, he's had enough of breathing in the smoke of where was it? Beijing."

"That's correct" Nora said.

"So he comes back to see that I'm alive if not well."

"Yeah, you look like you haven't slept for a year" Nora said.

"Not sure that I have. Haven't gotten much sunlight either. It's fucking with my memory but the things in my mind are the kinds of things you can never forget.

"I think that this is it for me if the rightful heir to the Tauler kingdom would allow me to pass one more night under his roof."

"That's fine" Eckhart said, "But tomorrow, you take this rental and you bring it back to the airport and you go back to whatever hole you crawled out of."

Gilbey was more than glad to pass the night on the couch and relinquish the bed to the love birds.

"God, this room smells like a gymnasium" Nora said, walking towards the bathroom in search of some kind of air freshener.

"You're going to start to understand why I have no patience with this dude."

"I still don't get why you have to be so cruel. Where are the towels?"

"Good luck getting anything, Nora. Gilbey was the caretaker of the household for the last couple of years, so if you want something, you're going to have to find it in your suitcase."

Downstairs, Gilbey told himself that what was in his hand would be the last half liter of whiskey he would ever drink. He needed it to pass the night. Watching through his favorite window, the man child took a mental photograph of those twinkling stars that he took for granted as they accompanied him through insomniac nights. He would miss this place, just as he would come to miss the bright lights of Korea with all the misery that they brought him. However, all this nostalgia meant nothing without a future and somewhere out there, past the prairie, a gangster with the scars to prove it sought to snuff out any possible future that Gilbey might dream of.

CHAPTER 13

VI AHIN SOLL ICH GEHN

"What hast thou done? The voice of thy brother's blood crieth unto me from the ground."

-Genesis 4:10, KJV

Once again, the sights, smells and sounds of motel rooms joined Michael Gilbey's world. The orificial sheets, old school TVs, smoky room and whiskey stained carpets had to be tolerated once more. Gilbey studied the bottle of pills. *Lightning in a bottle.* Was his father's way the only means out of this mess? He thought about telling the authorities he was alive but what purpose did he serve after the overturned decision? Would the authorities dangle him like a worm before Wallace? Could Gilbey accept this scenario? There were relatives in Florida and Canada but they weren't eager to see the shape of this bearer of bad omens outside their doors. He had the Mark of Cain upon him, and so what was he to do? He was tired of wandering, tired of running, tired of late nights at dirty love motels with buzzing vending machines right outside his window, tired of life really.

Closing his eyes, he fixed his mind's eye on the women he claimed that he loved and would have had if not for those myriad missteps. Moving along, past the memories of the piercing eyes of woman he never really knew, Gilbey fixed his longing soul on his teenage home in Swampscott. If he could just get back there, not through desperate dreams but utterly escape back to those hallowed times, he could redeem the endless nights with their infinite tears and empty bottles. But, with waltzing phantasms occupying his wretched mind, there was no way back to anything resembling peace. Yet, still forward, through the torment ahead, there was work that awaited him and his reasons for continuing lay in them. And so it was that halfway through a bottle of Popov that Gilbey hatched his plan. It was violent and reckless but sudden enough that all parties connected to Michael Gilbey could move on soon, once he was done pressing for the end.

In actuality, Gilbey came up with this plan right in Eckhart's backyard as he never really left the Dakotas. The motel where he thought up his final scheme was not thirty minutes from the Tauler homestead, so Gilbey passed a few nights at the motel against the orders of his only friend. One way or another, it would all be over soon. No more running, no more roaches under lampshades and no more tears. All things would be into position as everything would converge upon the Tauler homestead: beauty and savagery, light and darkness, feeling and sociopathy. A sudden excitement leapt into bones like a wildfire. *Finally, the good kind of insomnia.*

⇌ ⇌

On a rainy morning, Gilbey came up the Tauler drive in the same vehicle that he left in about 48 hours prior. Eckhart and Nora were cuddling away the heavy raindrops and clenched each other harder when the thunder rolled. The bell rang. Eckhart was pulled out of ecstasy. He dressed and answered the bell. It should come as no surprise that when he saw who knocked, his face shriveled up in disgust.

"Did you forget something?" he asked, rubbing his tired seed-filled eyes.

"No."

"Then, why the fuck are you here?" Gilbey had a depraved look about him now.

"Because I invited Richard Wallace over for a drink."

"You're joking, right?"

"'Fraid not. It ends tonight."

"What time did you call him? Why are you doing this to me?" Without invitation, Gilbey stepped inside.

"Last night, as I tossed and turned, I got to thinking; I've asked for a hell of a lot from you. First, the impossible silence over such a weighty matter and the immense stain that you must forever wear upon your soul. How could I ask more from a man who has already given the full measure of devotion? Then, it came to me so miraculously like an angel throng bewinged, bedight in veils and drowned in tears. Why should you be afforded the little slice of peace you have carved out for yourself? Did you earn it by suffering? Or by your unfortunate association with the ever-wretched Michael Gilbey?

"Do you remember the rooftop, James? The fourteenth floor of High Plus? There you were, hoping for lightning to strike you or for some God to catch you. Well, answer me."

"Answer what, Fuckface?"

"Did God catch you from that great height? Did He show his infinite love? Are you now in His bosom? I think I fell off the roof that night but there was no God to catch me. How cruel. Anyway, I shall divulge my revelation." Eckhart puffed out his cheeks and rolled his eyes. "Nature is not some finely balanced machine that moves on a fixed point. It is a hideous thing that churns out beauty on occasion but that's why men kill for beauty, lie for beauty and work themselves into madness over beauty because it's rare. Who would want to seize a thing that is abounding in the world? That's why you have your little Scandinavian princess waiting for you upstairs? That's why you joined the good ol' boys in Korea for – what did you call it, pussy hunting? Most men think that seizing beauty and sucking what marrow out of it we can will sever the anchor of existence. We are trapped in the belly of this horrible machine and it is bleeding to death."

"You really have gone mad. Is there a point to this sad story? Is this all going to end with you saying we should all die together here? If you were worth anything, Gilbey, you would have died along with that degenerate father of yours. You're the perfect candidate for suicide because no one would miss you. No one would shed a tear for you. No one would come to your funeral, not even me. You could put an end to the Gilbey curse once and for all." There was little consideration of Eckhart's words. Instead, Gilbey narrowed his vision on the serene pasture visible through his favorite pane of glass.

"I've decided that if I survive this coming hell, I will not let the Gilbey name die. The curse will live on because of the revelation I had. Creation itself is an imbalance. Peace begets nothing. Violence begets everything. The death of Christ up on that lonely cross, that was the final brush stroke that opened up the heavens. Did Buddha achieve Nirvana? It doesn't matter because what kind of monster achieves peace only for himself and then locks the door to heaven? Peace couldn't open the heavens; only the turbulence of a God being slaughtered can do that.

"Tonight, under this hallowed prairie, the violence that will pass between us and Wallace will beget something beautiful, out of this herky-jerky machine, out of nothing really"

"God, this is what I feared about coming back here. You sound like one of my relatives who claimed to find God in the Black Hills. I can tell you how that all ended for each and every one of them. It ended with a bullet to the brain or from the end of a rope. Wish you had done it sooner."

"Nothing new to the Gilbeys either. Ain't no shame in dying by your own hand. When I have my son, I'll leave it to him to escape the madness. For you and I, there is no way back. That's what my revelation was: a message telling me that those who receive peace like Buddha are not the blessed ones. We are holier than that. We are begetters. We are the vessel that will carry the risen Christ to the Buddhas of the next age, but first the slaughter which will sanctify.

"You may say that I'm crazy but tonight an end will come to either Richard Wallace or my misery and that in itself is a resurrection." Eckhart stormed up the stairs to notify the police of his trespasser.

At the behest of his sheriff, an officer came up Tauler drive. He got some vague instructions about a disturbed individual and prepared himself to usher whoever it was to jail or to Custer Regional to get some sort of evaluation.

Officer Aaron Doten hated the fact that he had to bottle up his piss and vinegar at this job. Unable to get the war out of his head, he was longing to get back to whizzing bullets and whistling mortars, but when you have kids, a wife and a mortgage, you settle for breaking up bar fights but not all of the calls were so basic. The rush just wasn't the same, and so Doten often felt the urge to drive around till he got dizzy, all while the whole town was sleeping.

"So, you're the Tauler heir, eh?" he asked, rolling his tongue around his right cheek.

"That's right."

"Big name in this town."

"It's dying out. I'm a Tauler on my mother's side. The name's Eckhart."

"So tell me, Eckhart: what the heck am I doing all the way out here? I heard something about someone not being mentally well. Is everyone alright?"

"Why don't you come inside?"

"Anything to drink?" Nora asked, standing in the kitchen to play hostess. Doten clasped his belt and politely declined from the side of his mouth.

On the couch with his hands clasped like a ruler, Gilbey sized up the detective.

"Is this the guy?" Doten asked. Gilbey tapped his longish fingernails against the arm of the chair, then took a swig of the gin that bore his namesake. The man child had no words.

"You alright, buddy?" Doten asked. Eckhart confirmed that this was in fact the man in question. With his mouth intoxicated with spirits, the content man child uttered no response. "What's wrong with him?" Doten asked.

"I don't know where to begin" Eckhart said

"Well, did he threaten himself or anyone else?" Doten asked.

"Himself." Doten began to take notes.

"And how did he do this?"

"Told me he was going to follow in his father's footsteps."

"This is all a load of hokum." Doten and Eckhart attempted to ignore Gilbey's drunken ravings but he kept on. "Now, if the two of you want to play Doctor Phil together, that's all well and good. I'm happy to remove myself and go wherever but I must warn you, one of the worse devils you will ever know is going to come up that road and he's not going to care whether or not you have a badge." The long jagged nail at the end of Gilbey's index finger pointed to that wafer of a moon over the hills.

"Alright, buddy" Doten said. "We're taking you to regional to get you examined." Doten then made a half turn towards Eckhart. By the way, does this guy live here?" Eckhart paused.

"He's not associated with the family."

"What I want to know is does he have any legal right to be here that you know of?"

"Well, he's been the caretaker of the house for the last two years or so."

"Ok, well they're probably going to release this dude pretty soon because it's a hospital, in which case he's going to probably come back here, just letting you know. It sounds like as the caretaker, he has some grounds to stay. You got the deed to the house in your name?"

"Yeah."

"Well, that will go a long way in shortening whatever legal battle may arise. Anyhow, he'll be off your hands for the next couple of hours or so." At this point, Gilbey was still sitting meditatively in his chair, looking at the plump moon hang over the vast pasture. "Come on, buddy. You're strolling to the car or I'm dragging you."

"So, you're just going to leave James and his woman to die here? Don't you know they're going to burn?"

"My patience is wearing very thin" Doten said. Gilbey blinked his eyelids slowly and purposefully.

"Very well then" Gilbey said. He blinked his scorched eyes once more and when he opened them peered over at Eckhart and shook his head. Eckhart hesitated but ultimately said nothing. "Look into his eyes, officer; he knows it." Gilbey got up. The officer did sense something amiss in Eckhart's frantic eye.

"Is there something I should know, sir?" Doten asked. Eckhart thought hard. "Is this man telling the truth?"

"Of course I am. I've drunk way too much to resort to lies. There is just the bare truth with me now."

"No" Eckhart said, reaching a resolution, apparently. The officer looked hard at the Tauler heir and pleaded once more with mad Michael Gilbey to come with him. By this time, the man child was standing, but still maintained his view of the moon.

"Look at the moon right now," Gilbey said. "It's as pale as death." He followed officer Doten but looked back at Eckhart like Lot's wife. "I hope you know what you're doing because I sure as hell don't." Gilbey and the truth went marching on.

Outside, Doten hadn't yet cuffed Michael Gilbey yet. He had to ask a few more questions first.

"So, what's your deal? You really insane or are you just one of these eccentric types?" Gilbey kept his eyes on the yellow orb of a moon that hovered over everything like an overgrown onion.

"Who do you say that I am?"

"Well you definitely talk funny but I haven't decided yet. What were you saying in there about him being in danger? Were you just blowing smoke up his ass?"

"Time will tell."

"I'm tired of you acting like a holy man and speaking in riddles. Either way you gotta get your ass in the car to get checked out." Gilbey did as he was told, acting like a man helpless against the fates. He ducked his head as Doten put him in the back of the squad car.

"Don't mind the smell, holy man" Doten joked. He always contended that maintaining a sense of humor was a necessary aspect of the job.

And then something shattered the serenity underneath the glowing orb that scattered its light between the quaking aspens. Headlights came up the road.

"Anyone else live here?"

"It's what I prophesied. Here come the four horsemen of the apocalypse." Doten almost hesitated but quickly got out of the car, grabbed Gilbey in the passenger and walked him up the steps. He banged loudly on the door. Nora answered and he all but bowled her over with Gilbey as the bowling ball.

"What's going on here, officer?" Eckhart asked. He marched over to the door defiantly, demanding answers.

"Does anyone else live here?"

"No, just…"

"Then, why is there a cavalcade coming up the road?" Eckhart shivered and then answered:

"Oh God, they're going to kill us all!" Doten then did something he had never done before as a Custer County officer; he drew his service weapon.

"We're going to need a whole lot more than that puny pistol" Gilbey joked. Eckhart ran to the basement to get the Springfield Gilbey fumbled with earlier. Doten called for backup but the way the hills work with great distances lying between nearly every point, help was a long way out.

At the end of the drive, the cavalcade arrived. In pairs, the headlights vanished.

"I hope you've all made your peace with God, though I confess I haven't" Gilbey admitted.

"Would you please be quiet?" Doten requested. "We need to think a way out of this predicament."

"I warn you," Gilbey replied, "that often the schemes of men fail and that only faith will see us through. What's the point? Why not avail me? One final drink before death." Gilbey knew Doten's response without looking. "You boorish military types are all the same, all raging against the dying of the light."

"I've got kids man" Doten said. Gilbey did not respond. Eckhart came running back with the rifle cocked, but with no real plan to speak of. A single solitary bullet whistled through the wind and shattered panes of glass. Everyone dropped quickly to the floor, except Gilbey, who descended deliberately.

"We need to barricade the doors and windows!" Doten called. At once, everyone followed. Eckhart pushed the couch in front of the door and Nora and Doten moved the fridge in front of the window. Even Gilbey volunteered himself for the task of scattering chairs around potential apertures for the goons to get through. With impressive speed, Eckhart went down to the basement along with Gilbey, whose speed was not as noteworthy. They grabbed two by fours, nails and hammers and began to board up the windows. The most surprising thing was that no rounds had been fired since that early warning shot, but none inside questioned it, not even Gilbey. They just worked steadfastly until the invasion came and then they waited and waited further in the darkness with nothing about them but their own breath and body heat.

The muffled sound of a cacophonic loudspeaker squeaked through. A few words could be discerned: Gilbey's name and "deliver."

"Are they saying that we get to live if we hand Michael over?" Eckhart asked.

"Don't listen to them" Gilbey insisted. "They're like Trojans bearing gifts. Once you open a door, they'll come storming in, guns proper like the original Don Dada." Gilbey could feel the eyes in the room darting around attempting to find one another. The only thing audible was the wind warbling through the glass-less window.

Finally, Gilbey heard it, what Eckhart had been talking about, darkness within darkness, the sound that Eckhart's ancestors heard before their damnation or redemption. It was calling him forth but interrupting his march to the prairie with a handful of pills was the rattle that all had been waiting for. Lead pierced glass, brick and wood from all sides and surely terror beset them. It was as though that gentle tiny eye of the storm had passed over-head and the eyewall was coming down with great fury upon them.

Doten thought of his only begotten son, Eckhart of the future fe-
licity that was being pried away and Gilbey the distance between
him and his deceased father. Like undead things, Wallace's goons
started coming through the small holes that their blasts had created; they were nimble burglars. As Eckhart and Doten fired away
at the bodies coming through holes, Gilbey marveled at the cease-
less loyalty these drones had for their master. How could they value
their lives so little that they would just burst through walls and
take open fire? They were not serving a flag or a country but some
maleficent crime boss who urged them forward and like lemmings
they followed.

When the number of bodies was so great that the Tauler homestead risked being overrun with ease, Doten & Co. fled upstairs.
The logic was that they had the high ground, which came with a
very narrow but sound vantage point. With their limited ammo,
they would be able to pick off Wallace's goons as they came rush-
ing up the stairs. Nora hid in the bathroom and in the midst of the
panic laughed that she always picked the wrong men.

Another lull fell upon them, but the gun smoke still clouded
the house and the light fell in like javelins through the bullet holes
in the window boards. Doten wondered where his backup was. In
all the confusion, he almost forgot that he had a radio but now
that the lull had settled in the house, he switched his radio back
on and was grateful to learn that help was only ten miles out and
coming up the highway at extraordinary speeds. It was a matter
of mere minutes; they just needed to endure through the silence.
Maybe the gangsters had somehow caught wind of the police arrival and were scurrying out the drive. Hope, anxiety and exhaustion were the emotions that characterized the hiding.

Abruptly, the sound of steel teeth buzzing through wood could
be heard, albeit faintly by rocked eardrums. The goons were using
a chainsaw to cut through a breach that had been created through
persistent gun blasts. Would they all pour in like water through

cracked glass? Doten wasn't willing to wait. He abandoned his perch to investigate and hopefully seal up the chasm. When he got to the bottom of the stairs, the window boards fell. The radio was abuzz with news that the police had exited the highway and were just a mile or two from the Tauler homestead. As Doten fired into the cavity in the wall, he thought how quickly his companions would swallow up the dirt road and gravel in pursuit of this besieged house.

He felt a sting and then another. They were coming upon his torso like bee stings and when he looked down, he say that he had been affected by a spray of rapid fire. One got him in the rib cage, another in the collar bone and one got him flush in the lilac crest of the pelvis. He dropped to the floor. Now the goons could get in with ease and they did. Without hesitation, they shot Officer Doten to death; he didn't even get a chance to beg for his life and tell them how he wanted to live for his son.

Working quickly now, the goons scoured the downstairs, not realizing that Eckhart was camping on the 2nd floor with one full five-round cartridge left to spend. The goons moved the objects used for fortification and opened the bullet riddled door. Where was the light coming from? Surely, it took more than just moonlight to illuminate so boldly the frame of the open door. The vehicles were again shining their high beams at the house.

Squeaky wheels rumbled to the front door as though they belonged to an ancient chariot. It was Richard Wallace bound to his chair, just hanging in the threshold with no concept of time and possessing no fear of police arrival.

"Border this thing back up" Wallace ordered as he was finally pushed over the hump of the threshold. "They're probably hiding in the basement." Eckhart had a shot at Wallace but the shot was compromised by the fact that Eckhart had to conceal himself with the bannister post at the top of the stairs and letting one fly amounted to giving up his location. Gilbey sat on the edge of

Eckhart's bed trying to regain the aberrant ataraxia that provided him with the will to call Richard Wallace and bring everything to a head. Reality became his curse and he had lost that strange cultivated refuge in his mind, so now he was powerless to escape it. He left his drink downstairs and so he didn't even have his only consoler and so Gilbey began to pray under his breath, "The Lord's Prayer" and "Hail Mary." Gilbey knew he didn't deserve mercy but he argued before God that none really did. *Die if I must but please Jesus, don't let that devil torture me.*

The door was bordered up and the basement was cleared out by several goons.

"There's no one in here, sir" one of the goons said. Wallace cast his devious bloodshot eyes towards the stair and he had moved about enough that Eckhart no longer could put the mobster in his sights. Wallace ordered the goons to bring alive all whom were found upstairs. Eckhart's hands were sweating profusely now. He tried to control his breathing as his renegade father once taught him to do; he massaged the trigger and as the goon squad came up the stairs, he let a shot rip, guiding the lead bullet to collide with an unarmed musclehead's fibula. The goon rolled down the stairs head over heels trapping the leg of another under him, which broke that leg and sent that goon rolling down to the bottom of the stairs as well.

Eckhart opened and closed the breech with the bolt and took aim at the Taser-wielding goon who nearly made it to the top of the stairs. Because Eckhart had to shift the bolt with each round, the goon was able to fire a fraction of a second before Eckhart was. The electrodes stunned Eckhart as they landed in his back but like a pro, he did get his shot off, sending his bullet through the goon's thigh, narrowly missing the femur. Dropping to his good knee, the goon writhed in pain.

Wallace watched with disinterest as though he could not be harmed. The last of Wallace's two goons came charging up the stairs and seized the rifle from Eckhart's stunned hand. From the master bedroom, Gilbey could hear the police speaking over a megaphone. Rather than feel relief, Gilbey soon determined that the police weren't going to risk more of their own by going in with guns blazing. Frantically, Gilbey hurried over to the window to wave at whoever was out there but the goons came after him and hauled him away from the window. The next person to nab up was Nora, who shrieked at the sound of the bathroom door being kicked in. The goons took joy in hauling her down to the basement.

CHAPTER 14

YELL DEAD CELL

"Never. Oh, never. Nothing will die. The stream flows, the wind blows, the cloud fleets, the heart beats. Nothing will die."

-Merrick's Mother in *The Elephant Man*

"This is my final work of art" Wallace said, examining the three captives (Nora, Eckhart and Gilbey) as one empty canvas upon which he could splatter his paint. He didn't bother about having the goons gag the prey for he knew that if the police outside hadn't laid siege to the house to get their own, they would certainly take their time moving in. Eckhart scanned the basement and felt that he and his party made a grave miscalculation by taking the high ground. The basement would have been an easier keep to defend. He looked into Nora's eyes and saw the tears carry the mascara down her face. She was another casualty of Gilbey's calculated recklessness. When Eckhart turned the other way to get a good long look at the sloppy ruiner of lives, he saw the boy trembling in his chair. He almost felt mercy for the poor boy.

"Nora, I love you" Eckhart said. Gilbey shook his head at the absurdity of the comment and the moment. Wallace smiled widely because the deeper the love, the greater his torture would prove to be.

"Where are the police?!" she screamed. Wallace chuckled.

"Some people go their whole lives without feeling this kind of desperation" he said. "I once let a man pray for twenty minutes before I killed him. I told him that's all I was giving him and his God to enact a miracle. Needless to say the clocked ticked on and no lightning came from the sky to smite me. I think me and that guy lost our last shred of belief in God in the same hour, me with smoke coming out of my gun and him with his brains splattered all over his living room for his wife and kids to find. I was freed then. My hypothesis was correct. This universe is bound together by nothing, but humans ceaselessly try to hold it together. Being in this world is like trying to repair Mansell's femur with Elmer's glue. I would be remiss if I didn't compliment you on your good shot, Mr. Eckhart"

"You can let Nora and I go, or you can let just Nora go" Eckhart pleaded. "She's innocent in all of this."

"The words 'innocent' and 'guilty' mean nothing to me. I am not a court of law. I am not here to distribute any kind of justice but the personal kind. I'm not attempting to establish order to the universe. Don't you understand that there is no order? That was already explained to you in the story about the guy whom I let pray. Have you been listening to anything I've been saying? Of course not, you've all (even the so-called innocent one) been looking for avenues for escape, but if you decide to open up your fucking ears, let the last lesson you learn be that your petty lives are all up to the fates now. You're just puppets, my little puppets hanging from shredding strings." Gilbey pissed himself and Nora continued to scream while Eckhart churned the gears of his mind, trying to find a way out of this hell.

"Alright, I've had enough of this" Wallace continued. "O'Riley, bring sweet tits over here." O'Riley untied Nora from the chair and wrestled with her for a bit, though it was no match really. "No matter how crippled I become, there is always one part of my body that continues to work. Slap her around, O'Riley, so that she's ready for a good seeing to." The goon faithfully performed this task, switching from forehand to backhand, until the girl was kneeled. "She's got a fat ass. That's okay I can handle it."

"Nora!" Eckhart screamed. From his chair, Wallace dragged the girl by the arm so that she was only on her knees and not on all fours.

"I want you to unzip it slowly" Wallace said.

"You really think this affects me" Gilbey said, interrupting Wallace's moment.

"I don't care about your feelings. You'll get your turn and it will be far worse than the sexual acts I am about to receive.

"It would be hard to get it hard, I would imagine, if one were to meditate on your daughter's decomposed face." Wallace grabbed Nora by the hair and resented being denied his blow job. Eckhart didn't know what to make of things. He was afraid Gilbey might incense the mobster further but was also happy to see that the mobster was reconsidering his plans to violate his girl.

"Place her head on the floor" Wallace said. Eckhart screamed and convulsed in his chair. O'Riley did as he was told and with a smile on his face, Wallace rolled over her head and crushed her neck. She screamed in agony. If Eckhart hadn't had his hands tied down, he would have reached out and touched her to console her. "Beat this cunt to death." O'Riley scowled at Eckhart and Gilbey, took a breath and then bludgeoned Nora to death with a hammer. She struggled but it only took a couple of whacks before she lost consciousness. Just before the third strike, Wallace held up his hand for O'Riley to stop.

"What did I teach you, Mr. O'Riley?"

"Death is mercy."

"That's right. We don't want to let this woman off easy. We want her to be a survivor. We want her to go on Oprah and live with the memory of my ghost. I want her to be as my daughter was." O'Riley took out a small bottle of nitric acid, of which there were many, from the bag hanging from the back of Wallace's wheelchair. He flipped Nora on her back and poured the nitric acid on her face.

"Will you still love her now that she is a monster? I still cared for my daughter after her face was gone. When she wakes up, she's going to be very mad that much of the living tissue in her face has been destroyed." Eckhart sobbed. "Come on, be a man. Do you want my last memory of you to be you crying in the chair like a little bitch?"

"She was innocent" Eckhart cried.

"Here we go again" Wallace derided. "Honestly, Gilbey, I wish I had more that I could take from you, but your life is so pathetic, and you are so alone that all I can really take from you is this whiny friend of yours and your worthless little life. I want to cut Gilbey's dick off now, in case the police man up and actually do something."

Nothing could prepare the man child for this moment. He finally got to begging Wallace and tried to explain that our father's sins were not our own. The mobster rubbed his weary eyes:

"The worst of it is that as I craft this masterpiece, you fail to understand; it's not about you. It's a goddamn waltz; you must glide with me if we are to do it right." O'Riley held up the straight razor. "That razor used to belong to Doyle 'The Mohel,' so it's somewhat of a sacred artifact in my world and now it shall be used for one final uncovering."

Gilbey started kicking about like a fish out of water but a hammer to the patella steadied him so that his legs could be tied down. O'Riley used the straight razor to cut open Gilbey's khakis and boxers. Between his thumb and his forefinger, O'Riley held Gilbey's penis. He had a laugh about it with Wallace.

"Not much to cut" O'Riley joked.

"We made a crucial mistake" said Wallace. "We forgot to bring tweezers." Mirth rose again from the mouths of the insidious. Gilbey leaned forward to bite O'Riley and got a chunk out of his neck, which he chewed defiantly. O'Riley retreated back a step in surprise and held the part of his neck from which the flesh was taken. Blood ran through his fingers.

"You little shit" O'Riley said. He stepped forward again and made a backhand slice with a straight razor cutting the inframmary crease wide open. Gilbey tried to head-butt O'Riley but the two men were too far apart. With a rougher grip, O'Riley held Gilbey's penis in his hands again. "Say goodbye to your little friend" O'Riley said.

Boom! Just before the harrowing severance could be made, the basement door got kicked in and a stun grenade landed at Wallace's feet. True to his character, Wallace gritted his teeth and winked at Gilbey as if to say he would back again to hunt and torture Gilbey and all that he loved. The grenade exploded leaving those gathered in the basement senseless. Only Wallace remained unmoved. Finally, the siege was upon them.

⇥ ⇤

Looking for his reflection in the cup of coffee and rubbing the fresh scar on his chest, Gilbey listened to the detective.

"You got quite a fright there. You were about ten seconds from getting your dick cut off."

"Tell me about it" Gilbey said, surprised by his own hoarseness.

"Well, we've been learning quite a bit about this Wallace dude as we've been briefed in the last couple of hours or so. This dude's a major player and he killed your father and then he came for you."

"Unlucky circumstances, I guess."

"One thing we can't figure out, and maybe the FBI can help us out when they get here, is why your personal cell phone number is on Wallace's call log. You actually called *him,* so what we need to learn is the nature of these phone calls." Gilbey sighed, took a gulp of his coffee and swirled it around a bit, studying his warped reflection. "You look tired."

"Nerves must be shot. I think I'm going to need a lawyer."

"These questions are going to be a lot harder when federal agents are standing around." You mine as well answer shit while the going is good."

"They're going to hound me regardless of what you ask and discover here. I can only make things worse for myself."

Still in shock, Eckhart listened to Detective Pizzolatto ask him about Gilbey.

"Bane of my existence really. I met him in Korea."

"North or south?" Eckhart curled his lip and shook his head.

"It wouldn't be the only strange thing in this narrative."

"We both taught in South Korea at the same time or I should say that our contracts overlapped."

"He lived with you for a time?"

"Not exactly. I left him to squat in my house."

"If this guy is the bane of your existence, why let him live in your house for free while you're away in…?"

"Beijing."

"You must like the Asian girls."

"They like me; that's for sure. I probably have a couple of Ji-seung Eckharts running around Seoul looking for their father. Sorry. Sometimes you just need humor, especially with what I've seen. I promise I used a condom every time, not that that assures us of anything. Eh, what was the question?"

"I think I was asking about your travels to Asia."

"What specifically?"

"What attracted you to the orient?"

"Plain and simple, they gave me a job when America either couldn't or wouldn't."

"Did you ever think about joining the military? That other survivor told me how good you were with that hunting rifle."

"If I had a faster gun, a modern weapon, I could have saved Nora. Any word on her? I hope she doesn't have to live through..."

"She's in the hospital and she's expected to live; that's all we can say at the moment."

"But her face, God, what those men did, why?"

"Only those men can answer that. We want to bring them to justice though."

"It's all that bastard's fault."

"Who? Wallace?"

"No, Gilbey. He's cursed. He's won't leave me and the stench of murder follows him like a goddamned dog."

"What are you talking about?"

"Back in Korea, I watched him kill a man with a stone for insurance money he didn't even get. Sometimes, I think he did it just to watch him die." The wide-eyed detective jotted this down.

"Why didn't you stop this?"

"I felt paralyzed. He pinned it on some poor Indian Muslim fuck, Seraj Mukhtari, a friend of mine. Poor fuck is rotting in Cheonan prison."

Detective Pizzolatto took a break to discuss the most recent revelation with his colleagues.

"Forget it Tom [Pizzolatto]. How the fuck are we going to overturn a conviction in Korea based on some rant from a dude going through shock. Let's just wait for the suits to get here." And wait is just what they did.

Agent Owens, the middle aged gentleman who worked the Wallace bombing case, showed up with his capable understudy, Brian Tally. They discussed the preliminary interview and the details of the extensive home invasion with the Custer County Police, who were more than happy to hand off this mess to more competent and well-equipped investigators.

To get an orange bit out, Agent Owens sucked his teeth and then swallowed. He spoke:

"So, Mister James Eckhart, you've had a very eventful 48 hours."

"That's what the last guy said. I just want this to be over."

"I hate to inform you that these things don't pass quickly like giant kidney stones. We're talking years of witness protection program with a long public trial and then you can get on with your life." The prospect of losing another two years to Gilbey's mess drew Eckhart deeper into despair.

"I mean, what choice do I have? This Wallace dude is still alive and as long as that's the case, he will not rest until he can exact some torture upon me."

"And from Mr. Gilbey, the almost castrato, he wants even more."

"I could care less if they skinned his penis off."

"It would be helpful if you could explain why you have this feeling towards Mr. Gilbey. Detective of Pizzolatto, the man who interviewed you before, mentioned something about a possible foul play homicide in Korea."

"It's complicated."

"Facebook relationship statuses are complicated. This is something else entirely."

"No, I suppose I just blame him for everything that went on there and beyond."

"Well, that definitely stands to reason. He made the call that brought Richard Wallace to your house."

"Then, why don't you charge him with something?"

"With what? I mean, we'll try to rack our brains to think of something, but all we have is a record of a phone call. Creating a case around a call log is not something we can do."

"Damn it. This fucker gets away unscathed every time. We need a certifiable crime."

"We'll do our best to relocate you as far away from your nemesis as possible."

"You look pretty well for a dude that almost had to pee out of his asshole for the rest of his natural born life." Owens toasted Gilbey with his own Styrofoam cup and jotted some notes down. "We would like your help in taking Wallace down."

"Sure thing. I just wish you shot the fucker during that raid. I lost ten years of hearing during that whole affair and I'm none the better for it."

"What say you to the Witness Protection Program?"

"I'm all for it. Get to move to a new town with a new name and the government pays for it."

"You're a strange one, Mr. Gilbey."

CHAPTER 16

WE'LL MEET AGAIN

"In a book in a box high upon a shelf
In a locked and guarded vault
Are the things I keep only for myself
It's your fate but it's not your fault"

- ("For You") Barenaked Ladies

At the still waters of Saint Croix, Gilbey had a thorough view of Saint Stephen, Canada. Gulping his swill from his brown bag, he felt grateful for his survival. With no job, no children and no love on the horizon, the dark days of autumn merely blended into one another. Where was Eckhart now? Was he also hidden away in some cesspool where the fangs of winter would also be upon him? Couldn't get much worse than Custer, but then again, Calais, Maine was no great improvement.

Such brilliant hues were resplendent in the foliage but they did little to raise up the spirits of the still-faced Gilbey, who was finding it increasingly difficult to become enraptured by the wonders of the world.

What will become of me when this trial is over? Shall I flee again? But to where? I'm out of running moves. The FBI hasn't seized all of it; I've got plenty saved. Am I to live like this forever, hiding myself wherever I go?

For the first time in a long time, Michael Gilbey was out of quickly conceived calculations that would fix his disjointed life, so he recited the prayers he had been taught but he lost utter belief in them. When he opened his eyes, he was not hit with any kind of spiritual sweetness, just the agony of an existence that was seemingly squandered calculating the value of and observing intently the lives of others.

In the back pew at the hour of penance, Gilbey meditated on the anguished Christ birthing the soul of heaven in his final mortal hours. He didn't believe in all that and probably never would but if a healing balm resided in embracing the unlikely mystery then let the lie live, for it was in a bitter hour in a darkened church kept open for adoration that Gilbey once felt the chorus of angels piercing him with joyous hymns. But, the ecstasy that carried him away flew on and he was dropped back into the rut that tried to wrap and pull him under ever since it was born.

He drove his wobbly Sebring back to the secluded dump that Witness Protection secured for him through Craigslist. The paint and the shingles were coming off. He didn't give a fuck though. It was shelter enough to let him through his drunken stupors and the television with its old-fashioned antenna allowed him to see some sports emerge amidst the static lines.

On the stairs, Gilbey picked up a half-devoured bottle of vodka and took a few gulps to erase a little further the endless questions jostling around his brain like cumbersome stones. His memory became short while his power of concentration and overall cognitive ability fell to all-time lows. He often found himself looking for booze in the dryer or forgetting that he needed soap, only to find a case of Dial in the trunk of his car on his next trip.

Just another hour or so before this blinding sun drops away. Then he could doze away the evening with the static hiss of the television serving as his lullaby.

What kind of plan is this? All these brilliantly calculated moves and I can still feel the checkmate coming upon me. I survived and I laughed and danced and stamped with madness but for what? Jacob Jung will forever be considered a victim, the loser in all of this, but he's the only one of all the men I've encountered who knows mercy as his struggle has ended. I wish that I too had been dashed with a stone. Lord knows that there are plenty of men who would be more than willing to give me a hand. What now? I live on to see Wallace put in chains and an orange jumpsuit. Can I at least call that a victory? But, what do I head back to? Even this fucking decrepit decaying white mausoleum will be snatched away from me? I have nowhere to go and nowhere I want to go.

As he felt himself doze off, not to sleep, but to lessen the sting and breadth of his consciousness, Gilbey heard his doorbell rang. His right eye shot open and the left one twitched. For a moment, he thought that Wallace had found him and that he had come to pick up where he left off, so Gilbey brought his Vodka and his newly acquired heater to the door.

"Who goes there?!" Gilbey asked through the door.

"Agent Owens." Gilbey scurried around to find a place for the gun. He placed it under the couch and opened the door to see the tall middle aged man standing in the doorway looking intensely at Gilbey, examining him from the outset. "Jesus, you really let yourself go."

"What the fuck else am I going to do in Calais, Maine?"

"I don't know; set off fireworks."

"In the winter? I'm not asking for a tropical resort but did you have to put me here? I feel like I'm being punished."

"Have you run into anyone suspicious since you've been here?"

"I've run into more moose than actual people. Is this some kind of checkup?"

"How well did you know Ryan Chase?"

"I think that's one of my cousins down in Florida, round Miami way. I haven't seen that kid since I was in elementary school. Probably grown now."

"He was a data systems analyst."

"*Was?* What happened? Did someone ice him?"

"That's exactly right. He was murdered by a biker at a stoplight."

"Veronica Guerin mode."

"Who?"

"The Irish journalist who was shot by a drug gang. I saw the movie a couple of years ago."

"You don't sound very sympathetic. Anyhow, we have reason to believe that Richard Wallace hired someone to do the deed. I'm sorry, Michael, you look bored. Don't you care? Your cousin died. I expected to see a little more pathos."

"Second cousin and I hardly knew the dude. You could tell me that my third grade chemistry teacher died; it would be the same."

"Sounds like the booze has gotten to you." Gilbey rolled his eyes and retorted sarcastically,

"My grief is so great, whatever shall I do?" He sang the chorus of Leann Rimes', "How do I live?" like his father would.

"Well, it's just a start. The trial proper will not commence for another couple of months. In the meantime, I have the feeling that Wallace is going to use that time pick off your family."

"Don't you gentleman have heat on him or something? I thought all you geniuses were supposed to be better than folks like me with my failing brain."

"We can't protect your whole extended family. Some are north of this dump and some are as far south as Louisiana. We just can't put that much manpower on this. We're talking about dozens and dozens of people."

"So, what the fuck do you want me to do? Just be aware of the impending doom of my entire bloodline. That's great; now, I can sulk further and drink more grade B liquor."

"We just thought you should know."

"Well, I'd much rather be blissfully ignorant. Now, I can't even soak in my misery in peace." Owens offered government protection, but Gilbey seemed to imply that he only wanted peace.

"So, you don't care if Wallace's crew kicks in the door, straps you to a chair, and tries to go after you with a straight razor again?"

"As long as Richard Wallace remains in custody without bail, he's going to want to keep me alive. Knowing that I was tortured and killed will do nothing for Richard Wallace. That psycho needs to see me bleed in the flesh. Otherwise, his sacrament yields no grace; nothing is uncovered."

"I see. Well, I'm afraid that's all the news we have, not a lot of positives."

"That's fine, but for future reference, can you not roll up here in that 40,000$ car. I don't need people asking questions; you assholes will move me somewhere worse than Calais, Maine. I don't know where the fuck that is but you assholes will find it."

"Valid point."

Gilbey loathed having his usual evening nap interrupted by that slick visitor. *What the hell was the point of it anyway? Why can't they just let me be? Oh God, can I let them do it? Can I let Richard Wallace order the slaughter of my family through a prison cell?*

For hours, he lay draped over the couch, rubbing his tired eyes that would net let him sleep. The thought of all the aunts, uncles, cousins, nephews and nieces killed in cold blood haunted his psyche. With his clouded mind, Gilbey tried to conjure a plan as if by magic.

They all looked down on me when measuring themselves against me at weddings and such and now they must trust their lives to this decrepit thing of misery. How the stone that the builder refused has become the head corner-stone? There's nothing I can do for them and what would I be saving them for? A bullet in the head from a renegade biker sounds like a good end...would certainly put an end to these pernicious thoughts that swirl around my head. To sleep and never wake again, how this would be heaven.

A week passed. Gilbey whittled his days away wandering the woods out back. Wandering had become a metaphor for his life. Even as a fifteen year old, he would walk to Star of the Sea cemetery and read of the desperation of the confessional poets. The same doubt of surviving in the world was already manifest then; it just persisted with greater intensity in his twenties.

A white-tailed doe galloped gracefully a hundred yards ahead. Gilbey thought of what it might be like to dash so carelessly with no thoughts to chain him. He wished he couldn't recall so vividly his childhood expectations of his adult self. Where was the beautiful woman he had promised himself or the house she would occupy? Where were the kids she would pop out and the prestigious job that would clothe and feed them? Where was the rich social life that would come with it? They were all vain pursuits but vanity seemed a lot better than enduring opening mental wounds.

He looked down the barrel of the glock and considered how easy it would be to silence the demons once and for all. There'd be no more sorrow, but the dishonor of it all. He didn't want his Episcopalian relatives to shake their fingers at him at his funeral. He had to make it look like an accident. He could drown himself but if the body were found, then it would get back to the Gilbeys and the Chases, that his death was no accident. There was no way he could die with the closest judges of his character determining that he was going to burn for all of eternity.

Life is a curse, especially for the Gilbeys. I vow here and now to end this curse. I can impose it no more. For now, though, I must wander on with my head held low. My clan is condemned to die. May God have mercy on their souls.

It became a habit for Gilbey to take a Monday ride down to the Calais Free Library to use the internet to see if any other kin had been slaughtered. He was mostly concerned about the New England Gilbeys, specifically those inside of Massachusetts. Why had Wallace bothered to kill some insignificant second cousin that Gilbey had seen all but once in the last fifteen years? Was he saving the best for last?

Within two weeks of learning of Ryan Chase, Agent Owens informed Gilbey of his great aunt and her dog getting waxed in Naples, Florida. Gilbey laughed at the thought of the little labradoodle catching a slug. *The little bitch probably yapped its tail off until the glock burst.* He even told Agent Owens that they were the two most merciful bullets he had ever heard of.

Then he got the call that hit him like a stone. A body washed ashore in Winthrop. It belonged to a little girl, Sarah Yorke, whose mother was a Gilbey. The last great champion of the Gilbey name was beside himself. It was one thing to put Aunt Chase out of her misery, but an innocent little girl, that was beyond malice. Could Gilbey prove it with Cartesian certitude? Was there a chance that this was an accident?

When Agent Owens came to bring the news he already knew, this time in a vehicle far more modest, Gilbey was gone. Owens waited on the steps in the blistering cold, drove around a bit and finally broke in when he had had enough of waiting.

"Gilbey!" he called. *God, this place is a fucking sty.* Owens combed through the filth to obtain something of value. It was mostly old clothes and discarded bottles of liquor, but in the rubble as it were, he found a picture of little Sarah Yorke playing amidst the sand dunes. The photograph was cut out of a periodical. Owens nodded to the silences, respectfully acknowledging that Gilbey finally had a fire lit under his ass.

⊶ ⊷

Down on Hooper Street in Chelsea, Nick Waits rolled a blunt with satisfaction. He was happy to be done with work for the day and happy that his nagging sickly mother had been cremated two weeks ago. The house had been bequeathed to him. He was now the king of the peeling paint, tacky furniture and smoke stained garments.

The news was on, so the TV blasted dramatic music to accompany its frightful yet brief graphics. Waits inhaled and scoffed at the vignette about a girl who got stuck in a tall tree. A can of Coors occupied the other hand once he got to smoking.

The doorbell rang. Waits pretended not to be home, but the rings were persistent. *Jesus Christ, can I get a moment of peace?* With a doobie still between his teeth, Waits strode to the door ready to unleash a lecture on whichever Jehovah's Witness or Girl Scout dared interrupt him. His belly was popping out of his grease-laden shirt and his blue janitorial uniform was swaying around as he swaggered about.

He looked through the long thin window by the door and had to do a double take when he saw Michael Gilbey standing there in a blue polo and green khakis. Waits forced the door open and looked behind Gilbey to see if anyone was following him. Nobody was in plain sight, so the janitor used his impressive forearms to grab Gilbey by the collar and force him into the house.

"What the fuck do you think you're doing here, boy?" In a matter of moments, Gilbey was lying supine with Waits' Wolverine boot on his chest and neck. "You want to end up like your father."

"No" Gilbey pleaded. "I only want justice for Sarah."

"Why the fuck did you come here then? Wallace is in jail."

"So you know he did it?"

"I don't know but a man can put two and two together. What? Did you think you could just come here and I'd feel so much sympathy for your loss that I'd offer to band together for the sake of justice? I'd much rather sell out to Richard Wallace. That way I could move out of this shithole that my mother gave me."

"Wallace wants me alive though."

"Bullshit. That dude wants to drive a rusty screwdriver through your skull."

"Of course, but he has to wait until he gets out of jail, which may be never if this trial goes right. Eventually, he may cut his losses and try to off me before the trial but there's at least one other witness. As far as jury tampering goes, that's a distinct possibility...."

"You talk a lot for a man with a foot on his throat."

"You're not the first."

"What the fuck do you want from me anyway?"

"You're the one who gave my father the acid and the thallium?"

"By whose account."

"It's pretty obvious. My father told me that he procured the acid from a janitor and I know only of one such colleague."

"I'm not a goddamn apothecary."

"You did it before and it remained a secret all these years. Why can't you do it again?" Waits let his foot off of Gilbey's chest.

"What the fuck do you want? Rickie Wallace is in prison."

"Let's give him a hot shot."

"Hot shot? Does he even do drugs? And, how the hell are you going to get to him? I'm a janitor. I have access to chemicals. I'm not a player in the drug game, not a major one anyway. I have no idea what gets smuggled in and what Richard Wallace takes if anything, but you're barking up the wrong tree. You need to get someone on the inside. Now get the fuck out of here."

Gilbey spent each Monday at Dedham Superior Court looking for a specific once and future convict, one who could get close to Wallace and one who was daring enough to deliver a death blow. A lot of scum passed through the court. All the small timers were arraigned in their local courts: the public drunkards, the delinquent payers of child support, etc. The alleged rapists, murderers and pedophiles were all arraigned in Dedham. For Gilbey, the challenge became not only finding someone, but finding them outside of court and offering them a devil's deal. Negotiating with a reasonable man over the cost of a car at a dealership is one thing but asking a bona fide animal who has shrugged off any notion of a social contract to kill is a whole different ballgame altogether.

Jimmy Nguyen stood with a bowed head as his young public defender entered the "not guilty" plea for Nguyen for the charge of first degree murder. In the back of the courtroom, Gilbey looked up after being mesmerized by the fingernail he forgot to cut. *Oh, this is my dude right here. He has "life without the possibility" written all over him.*

It was just that simple: Gilbey looked up Jimmy Nguyen online. Knowing the address didn't matter. Of course such a charge would warrant that Jimmy Nguyen be held without bail. Gilbey could only get to him through his homeboys but he really had no strategy save for rocking up to Essex Street in Lynn and asking for the Deuce Boyz or their leader.

Checking in and out every couple of days. Gilbey had become a veteran of the North Shore motel circuit. Gilbey daily visited Kennedy Fried Chicken and Chef's House on Acorn Street in his effort to learn about Lynn and the gang to which Jimmy Nguyen belonged. When he wasn't devouring a fried chicken cutlet or some pesto, he was cruising around the streets learning about the drug trade.

After two months, Gilbey learned which gangs held which turf, where the disputed territory was and even who sold which package. Every couple of days, Gilbey would roll up to Trinity Avenue and buy the black tops from a house that was the color of the Caribbean Sea. If Gilbey waited long enough in the Sebring, a dealer would come outside, usually some Cambodian just a tick over five feet who was known to his peers as "Borey Mode." The stocky kid always walked with long low strides as though he were pretending to masque an injury. His oversized white-tee was generally the garment of choice. He could have seen Gilbey one million times but he still would have played the act of a stranger.

"Whatchu want, Whitey?" Borey asked.

"You got black tops? I got twenty." Borey reached into his jeans pocket and grabbed three vials. It was foolish to pretend not to know Gilbey because the exchange of drugs and money had become flawless at this point, like Stockton to Malone. Tired of waiting, Gilbey made his play:

"You know Jimmy Nguyen?" Borey Mode was more than a little perturbed.

"Who's asking?" Gilbey thought about slipping another twenty but he didn't want to be mistaken for a narc.

"I need a favor from him."

"Nigga's in jail so sounds like you shit out of favors. Is there anything else 'cause it's cold as shit and I need to get back inside?"

"Wait. I know he's in jail. I was hoping one of your leaders could assist me."

"Man, I don't think you want to fuck with gangsters. You've got your blast; now get on your way."

"But I need this" Gilbey said as he drove away. He felt nauseous and needed another drink. He went to the package store in defeat, racking his brain to figure out a way to get a meeting with a street general. Gilbey grabbed his date for the night, a bumpy bottle of Seagram's Classic, and paid for it at the counter. The Cambodian clerk held no gaze or judgment. She just smiled.

Walking to his car, Gilbey noticed the purpureus sky smeared with streaks of pink. The sun had almost set beyond the rows of decayed dwellings. It was another unfolding mystery he could not quite feel in his bones. He manually unlocked the door and soon found a heater pressed against his back. Shutting his eyes, he prayed for a swift merciful death and for God to have mercy on his soul.

"Borey Mode said you was looking for Deuce Boyz and Jimmy Nguyen. What business you got? You police?"

"I need a murder done in Souza-Baranowski."

"Nigga, we drug dealers. You think we just knock off niggaz like they roaches. You get life for that shit. Not only that, they put you in the hole."

"So, you've been to jail then?"

"Did six years on a drug charge, ain't never goin' back."

"So you know the inside?"

"Alright, get in the car. We mad obvious out here." Under the instructions of the jive-talking Asian gangster, Gilbey drove off towards Barry Park.

"'Know the inside,' nigga. Now you talking like Prison Break. Why some white bread dude like you want someone dead in jail?"

"Can you do it for me?" Gilbey looked at the gangster in the passenger with conviction.

"It's gonna cost ya forty thou" the gun-wielding gangster called.

"That's fine but I need to work out the particulars with one of your leaders. You said it yourself; you're just drug dealers."

CHAPTER 17
THE TRUTH THE DEAD KNOW

"I don't know just where I'm going
But I'm gonna try for the kingdom if I can."

("Heroin") The Velvet Underground

White Mantis had just come out of jail on a drug trafficking and money laundering bit and nearly half of his life had been spent in confinement. In that time, the only toxins his body knew were nicotine from the Joes he smoked and alcohol from the hooch he drank, but now, on the outside, he had come to know heroin again.

Sao Mellow waited for the sweetness to abide in Mantis' veins before unceremoniously ushering Gilbey in to plead his case. The bespectacled face of the ginger belonged more to film director and less to the leader of a violent gang of ruthless Asian thugs.

"You don't have to call me Mantis." Gilbey looked into his revolving eyes with some surprise.

"What should I call you then?" Gilbey asked.

"Joe" said Mantis in a thick Boston accent.

"If you don't mind me saying, you sound rather peaceable."

"I do fucking mind and if you say that shit again, I'll put you through this fucking wall. Prison took a lot out of me; that's why I seem mellow. Don't get it twisted though: Any one of those thorough dudes you just got grilled by would be happy to beat you to a pulp at the snap of my fingers, so tread fucking carefully. Anyhow, let's get down to business: Who's the target?"

"Richard Wallace." Mantis laughed.

"Get the fuck out of here. We don't have a rod to catch fish that big. He's in PC, monitored constantly by the COs. He gets one hour of rec time and isn't dumb enough to mingle with the other prisoners."

"How do you know so much?"

"Do you know what taking out a target of this magnitude would do for the man who made that kill? Charlie Manson survived thirty years in San Quentin, why? Because he's in a protected hole where no one can get to him. Wallace is more of a man than that psycho pussy –I actually admire his work – but the problem remains: he can't be gotten to. Please see yourself out. If you want some product, Manny at the door's got you."

"Wait, what about Jimmy Nguyen?"

"How you know about Jimmy?"

"I saw him arraigned in Dedham Superior Court."

"You some kind of attorney? What sick game you playing?"

"I've been going to court to look for a person on the inside."

"You wasted your time. That's a common theme with you. He wears our colors on his skin; he ain't going to be anywhere near Wallace...Might end up in another correctional institution. No matter what, he'll live and die in gen pop."

"Might go free." Mantis laughed at the notion that a knight of the criminal world might be judged innocent.

"Seen stranger things. I forgot, before you go, I got a man in PC at SB. He's not affiliated. In fact, any boy with the Deuce Colors sees him and he's going to bleed like a stuck pig but we can turn him. He can do this favor for me and I'll let him live, since you'll pay his debt of 32 grand, plus the cost of waxing him, which brings the grand total to 64 g's, 32 up front."

"You want 32 thousand dollars up front. That's a yearly salary for some people."

"I'm not *some* people. You asking for a lot, brother. I hope you ain't coming around with a thin wallet to ask for some heavy shit. Come back here with 32 g's or don't come back at all."

"Sounds like a deal." Gilbey spoke with little confidence. He got up awkwardly.

"Oh, you didn't know."

"Know what?"

"Before you leave, you gotta shoot up."

"Man, I don't…"

"I heard you buy product from us all the time. The only kind of person who buys dope and doesn't use is a narc; you a narc?"

"Do I look like I can hold down a job?"

"It's hard to make you out in the dark. You need help finding a vein?" Gilbey did. Mantis turned on the light, wrapped a leather belt around Gilbey's and sought the vein out with ease.

"This vein is like a green valley, untapped beauty." Mantis put the spike into Gilbey's vein and waited for the visitor to reach the paradise that is one's first high. The peace Gilbey had sought for almost a decade now flowed through his veins. His eyes rolled back into his head and he surrendered to all the hurt leaving him.

Sunlight penetrated the tiny slit of a window in Father LeBlanc's' cell, and as it did, he chanted the Latin version of the Apostle's Creed while clutching his rosary. The sheets on the bottom bunk rustled. Inmate Ryan poked his head out of the sheets and told his cellmate to give it a rest.

Indignantly, LeBlanc turned his wrinkled face with its promi-
nent pointy upturned nose to the complainer. The grey hairs on
his head never quite remained kempt, though ever the bachelor,
he rarely tried. With the tops of his ears jutting outwardly, LeBlanc
resembled a gargoyle, especially now that he was scowling at Ryan.

"You're going to burn for what you've done" Ryan said. "Ain't
no use praying. There's a special place in hell for you and all the
fairy bishops who protected you."

"They're all going to burn for what they've done to me, not the
other way around."

"I read what you did. You destroyed almost 200 lives."

"I'm worth more than 300" Leblanc retorted defiantly. By now,
inmate Ryan was sitting up, shaking his head.

"You praise your glorious church. Well, those fuckers with their
tall hats and long dresses probably wish they castrated you when
they had a chance."

"I'm worth ten million more."

"So you're worth 300 lives and twenty million dollars. Well, I'll
be damned; I thought only ballplayers were worth that many dollars and that many lives."

The guard rattled the door with his nightstick for morning reveille, putting an end to the conversation. It was time to play nice.
The cells were opened and after a quick inspection, the inmates
were allowed to enter the modest common area where they could
confabulate and play cards.

Richard Wallace sat there dignified, trying to not look perturbed that he could not capture the "spy two" in a hotly contested
game of Casino. He nodded to Ryan who took a seat at the long
cafeteria table to stare at the small mounted TV screen. LeBlanc
got a little less respect but was still acknowledged.

Taking the quietest spot possible in the farthest corner of the
room, LeBlanc continued to pray the rosary in Latin right where
he left off. Whenever he did this, a few inmates wanted to knock

his block off, but he wasn't the only freak in PC; some sought him for counsel and even believed that his absolutions could confer grace. Those in PC that were not sexual delinquents referred to LeBlanc's spot as freaks corner.

"Gloria Patria…" he mumbled with his frail purple lips quivering. He looked over towards Wallace just before the act and paused his prayer out of reverence.

With half of a can lid, Ryan had gone straight for the neck of Wallace, but he knew this wasn't enough to slay the beast, so he took his toothbrush, the end of which had been filed into a shank and proceeded to stab at Wallace. The sexual misfits gawked, frozen to their respective spots, except for LeBlanc, who looked sullenly at the scene, almost with glazed eyes.

It never occurred to him that human flesh being punctured sounded so vociferous; how could he know? This was the first time he had ever seen something so violent. I mean, he fondled boys and forced them to perform sexual acts but there was a finality to this that revolted him like Himmler when he inspected the ditches of the einsatzgruppen.

To the bitter end, Wallace fought, using the end of his glasses to poke at Ryan, throwing the attacker off at times. At no moment, did Wallace's eyes betray despair, even as Ryan got his hands to the throat of Wallace. Inmate Ryan wanted his penetrating eyes to haunt Wallace in the next world but the crime boss never flinched; he would not relinquish his wicked soul. He even managed to crack a smile while he fought to remain in the world.

As blood spouted and oozed from every orifice, guards rushed to the aid of Wallace, clubbing the assailant, who was enjoying the fruits of his labor. Gracefully, LeBlanc walked over to the scene like something grotesque ready to spread its wings and fly off its perch and performed the act of extreme unction. With the prisoners commanded to lie prone on the ground, the guards gave LeBlanc a little space, but when they realized how long it would take, they brushed him aside and moved Wallace to the infirmary, where he did not stay very long as the staff and equipment were not sufficient enough to deal with the problem at hand. Wallace was rushed to Nashoba Valley Medical Center but died along the way.

The news of Wallace's death did not move Gilbey to celebrate nor did he feel any real sense of relief. His attitude approached incredulity and doubt. In order for Gilbey to really believe in the death of Wallace, he would have to see his inanimate body resting in the casket with his dry mouth sealed on his waxen face and that may not be enough; perhaps, he would have to witness the interment of that pernicious figure in that very casket.

In some ways, Wallace could not die, for he would always haunt scores of families who had lost their fine sons to Wallace's unyielding violence. When Gilbey shut his eyes, and passed into sleep, Wallace, even in death, became an ever-advancing figure and the faster Gilbey ran in these nightmares, the closer Wallace got. Every mirror held behind its exact silver gaze a potentially cruel revelation of Wallace's obdurate visage.

It wasn't long after Wallace's demise that Gilbey went to see White Mantis to pay the remainder of what was owed. Michael loathed the idea of walking into gangland with a bag full of money but knew that there was no other way to pay. He could get robbed en route or even worse, he worried that he knew too much.

Once I hand them the money, they'll have everything they need from me. I'm a loose end for them. Why keep me around? But, I'm tired of running. I gotta learn the lesson of my father: gangsters don't take IOUs.

Staring at Trinity Avenue through his rearview, Gilbey lamented the other sight in his mirror, his pale wan turned that way by the sweet poison the Deuce Boys had given him.

I have got to get off dope before this shit kills me.

Tremulously, Gilbey grabbed the bag and headed to that hideous green house with the hoods watching him. The Deuce Boyz knew him by now, a few even nodded to the fiend.

"Mantis is waiting for you" a Cambodian hopper announced. He was chilling on the steps, smoking a blunt contentedly.

"Do I just go in?" Gilbey asked. The hopper dapped him up and nodded coolly for him to get inside. With vigilance, the hoods were still watching. Once inside, some lieutenants inspected the bag and patted down the visitor, then told him to proceed.

"Have a seat, fiend." Mantis was chilling in the spot he occupied in Gilbey's last visit, still adumbrated in his rotting kingdom of junkies and crooks. Fruit flies were buzzing around the place.

"As you know, it is done."

"Thank you. Excellent job."

"You were notified about the price amendment."

"Yes, it's fine. A little bonus is in order for a job well done."

"I trust we'll see you around the way, but as for hits, this is it. We landed you a shark."

"No, I pray to God on high that this is the end of all the violence in my life. I have a feeling that peace is coming my way but no, I don't plan on being 'around the way' as you call it."

"Don't lie now boy or else I'll know. You a fiend if I've ever seen one and I know our product is bomb 'cause you always come here for your highs. And, violence, what violence? You ain't even squashed a bug before. You know why they call me White Mantis?"

"I assume it's because you're white and predatory."

"When a Mantis stalks its prey, it sways its head side to side to gain depth. I used to do that in fights."

"Shit, how did you know that?"

"I copied the technique from boring science videos that my middle school science teacher used to show me. Yeah, we're not all dropouts."

"You seem kind of smart and articulate for this world."

"You talk too freely, boy. Any person that survives and becomes anything in this game is smart. The smartest people I know I met in prison, geniuses of cruelty and efficiency really. In the end, there is a place for everyone. Aidan Ryan was a nobody in general society, but put him in a prison and he becomes a fable, an imbalanced offender who schemed his way into protective custody to make a hit for the Deuce Boyz...so, now he has his place.

But, you fiend, I can't quite put my finger on you. This mantis can't quite gauge our distance. It took me a long time to decide whether I was going to let you walk out of here. I'm still not quite sure. I like innocence; it belongs in the world. However, I hate when people get a free pass from violence. It's like they've opted out of being human. Violence is our nature. Look at the animal kingdom; it is full of it."

"And yet it is against our nature. Isn't peace preferred to violence?"

"Only to those minds who ignore the primal calling to shed blood. I see what this Wallace business was all about. I did my research on it. At first, I thought it was all revenge because I learned that he killed your old man and your mom and her boyfriend too. Then I thought: damn, this dude is going after your whole tree, trying to wipe your seed from the earth. It really tripped me up, thinking about how both you and Wallace were both like these...I don't know what word to use, 'pivots.' His death would free you but your death also would have been his final step on the road to vengeance. Then again, for men like that, the path of vengeance has no end; the road he walks is paved with the corpses of his enemies, just like me.

"I knew there could be only one and in the beginning, I chose to give life to Wallace but he would not accept my terms. He needed to be there for your death or your final passing would have been null and void like when you use the coin to scratch the forbidden part of a scratch ticket. Nobody wanted you alive more than

Wallace. Your final torture and death were going to be that dude's masterpiece, that is if he ever got out of prison.

"I thought he might never get out of prison and when he did, he was never going to employ our help, so I just went through with the hit. Some might say that it's against the code to do an OG like Wallace the way we did. He deserves a fair fight but if there is one thing the gangster world taught me, it's that we don't get what we deserve. The mind looks for fitting ends: the glutton chokes on food, the slut chokes on a dick and so on and so forth. In reality though, it's all just kind of random. I wish there were a way to collect and store the final thoughts of people. It would range from everything to, 'I need to pick up the dry-cleaning' to 'I can't wait to show off my beach bod' to the more common 'oh shit' before a car comes and takes that person out.

"So, here you are free, getting more than what you deserve, so how does it feel?"

"Hasn't really hit me yet but I'm looking forward to starting a new life."

"And do what exactly?"

"I don't care what, just far."

"It's all the same. What makes you think anything will change, fiend? Wherever you go, there you are. I gotta be honest, I never wanted to see you free. That's why I put you on the pipe. You're going to have to earn your way back now. I thought about killing you. Then, I thought it mercy to jump you out like we would a gangster. I doubt your drug-battered body could take a beating, so I'm going to show you even greater mercy: I'm going to give you a farewell shot of heron. What's one more shot anyway? That way we'll be on equal footing when you leave." Gilbey wanted to say that he thought that the transaction didn't warrant any more sacrifices from him but the sweet lull of opiates called to him.

Gilbey still had not perfected and probably never would perfect the art of finding fresh vein. Although he felt eyes upon him,

Mantis was dozing off. Foreseeably, he could fake his shot but that would be in bad faith. He wanted one more flight to the angels anyhow, so he removed his belt, tied it around his meek bicep and injected the syringe he had taken from Mantis.

Although there was no time like the first time, Gilbey could feel himself drifting weightlessly, leaving this earth and its heft for a bit. It was never euphoric but it calmed him and let him feel more pleasant about existence. The more he relied on it, the more he needed it just to keep from getting dopesick. This shot would help level him out but the snake would call again a few days later.

Gilbey thanked Mantis, who was still savoring his stupor and then headed off for the motel. The future lay before him but the high he felt palliated that burden.

In the scuzzy room provided, Gilbey sat in an angry chair, trying to hold a candle of thought up to his clouded mind. While his peers were struggling with debt from college loans and mortgages (the lucky ones anyhow), Gilbey still had 87,000$ to his name.

A great mind would know how to turn this money into paradise, even less of a fortune than this. My tragedy is that I have nowhere to take this money. It's in the wrong hands. Men kill for this or for as much but it's worthless with a corrupted mind. All that really matters is health and sanity and I have neither. When was the time that I went wrong? Is it the drugs that are ending me, my improprieties in South Korea? Was I merely born under a bad sign? Is there a way out of this? Is it worth carrying on through this torment? Isn't it the perfect time to die, before spring? I have nothing left invested in the world; what reason do I have really? This fear of living on is making me restless. Seems like the perfect time to drown myself in an icy river, just shoot some dope into my veins one last time and let go like a Buddhist.

What will Eckhart think? Will he shake his head or will he actually have some sympathy for me? What's he doing now? Alas, this is my only reason for carrying on, to see how things play out in the world with the players that I know. It's nothing more than grand curiosity. If I drown myself, not only will I kill this body, I will put an end to all those pernicious thoughts swirling around my head. Everything gets flushed away with one giant tidal wave. Why not commit the final act of violence that will set me free?

Gilbey meditated on these morbid thoughts for a moment. He found no flaw in his pessimistic logic as though it were neatly wrapped in tight syllogisms. Then, a single thought undermined his whole train of thought:

But if I die like this, I lose. Indubitably, I lose. I cannot bear to think that those who survive me will curse my name as if I were some kind of cowardly loser. No, I'm going to smile through these crooked chompers and with this frail drug-ridden body, I'm going to strut. That's right, I'm going to make sure that this world looks at me as though I've got the winning ticket right in my trousers. Ages and ages hence, Eckhart will be sitting on his porch and his memory of me will be nightmarish; I know that. However, something will twist inside him like a screw driven into a socket and he will see things my way for once and he will forgive me. He and God on High will know that suffering led me to all my sins and that I can't be held responsible. If there's a heaven, maybe we can all be there together. Eckhart and I can chill at a convenience store and spit conjecture as to why certain folks didn't make it. Mr. Jung and Seraj won't begrudge us for the good years we robbed them of and off in the distance, my father and Mike Powell will be holding onto their tickets after placing wages on who gets in. For all of that, I must live another day, at the very least.

CHAPTER 18

ANTHEMUSA

"Like the mist of morning, my dream remains
Hanging in the burnt fields of my memory
The flames hiss a chorus of your disdain
Picking up the past I left behind"

-("Women and Wine") Martin Sexton

At Cheonan Prison, Eckhart sat across the table from Seraj, regretting that he had spent thousands of dollars of hard-earned money to gain some sense of closure. Seraj was full of rage, ready to pounce at his counterpart at any notice.

"Y'all bitches did me dirty" Seraj exclaimed. "I got my money saved and I'm putting together an appeal. You and that Dough Boy friend of yours better make sure that you're living in a non-extradition country when I'm done."

"How are you holding up?" Eckhart asked, for he could not conjure a better question.

"Holding up? I'm in a cage like a goddamned animal. I left my apartment half-drunk and when I woke up I was in the legal battle for my life. You and that fat prick killed Jacob, and then pinned the shit on me."

"I don't know what the laws are here so I can't speak to that. What's important is that I'm here to help you."

"How you can help me, you cheery Midwestern fuck? Go back to your father's cheese farm to fuck the cows. Your time is coming."

Eckhart had flown fourteen hours to Incheon International Airport and spent an additional three hours on buses to be in this strange edifice, only to be spurned by Seraj. He didn't expect to be met with open arms, but how could a man so plagued by the loneliness of confinement be so unequivocal in his rejection of an old friend.

"Do you have anything left to say? Because I don't, unless you feel like walking down to the nearest precinct and clearing this thing up...I didn't think so."

"Is there any message you would like to declare to your family in Florida?"

"Yeah, don't trust Eckhart. I may be stuck in this cage like an animal, but I'm going to spend the rest of my existence, getting out of here and getting my justice." Eckhart just continued to sit there and observe his irate counterpart, who looked as though he might explode at any moment. He feared the threat of this forlorn man raging against the absurdity of his condition, but the fear soon dissipated and instead Eckhart saw the contortions in his friend's face and the bulging veins in the neck as theater worthy of savoring, so savor he did.

Eckhart walked on through the mist of morning in a foreign city (Cheonan), whose streets felt awfully familiar. Through a bus window, he envisioned what these desolate misty streets become when day turns night. Deep within the marrow of his soul, the smoky barrooms and the flood of neon beckoned to him in the way that the sirens called to Odysseus to rest his ship on the shores of Anthemusa.

'I could be the king of the roost once more and preside over this neon kingdom. It would be nice to hear those charming voices sweet-talking me back to my room at two AM." As the city faded behind him, he thought of Seraj, and the probability that he would rot in that jail until his youth had gone from him. He imagined Seraj sitting in a dark constrictive space, plotting his revenge. And, he wondered if Seraj, a careless miscreant, wasn't worthy of his cage.

If I stayed any longer, Neon Hell would have claimed me forever. Should I have breathed my last breath there? Maybe I can go back to that endless snowy desert and cleanse myself of these neon demons. Seraj is gonna rot, Gilbey's gonna be an average frustrated chump, the people here are going to work slavishly until every inch of this peninsula is glittering with neon, and onward we march.

PART II

CHAPTER 1
EIGHT YEARS LATER

**"Well now everything dies baby that's a fact
But maybe everything that dies
someday comes back"**

- ("Atlantic City") Bruce Springsteen

Father Gilbey was like a waxen figure staring out the window of the baby blue Sebring he purchased for posterity sake. The enraged faces of Eckhart and Seraj haunted the caverns of his mind. Paranoia struck deep. He had begun to believe that cars were following him on the interstate and even along the byways.

Did the bishop who sent him here know that the drooping cypresses spooked him, especially at night along the long and lonesome freeway that seemed so open and endless? Was this some kind of punishment from on high for wasting his former years in sin and speculation?

Eight years passed since the cell door had been shut on Seraj. His time was soon to be served but he was still using every square inch of that cell as a gym and he was still brooding on the faces belonging to those who put him there. Gilbey hoped that Seraj had found peace in the four walls of freedom but he also knew that there would be no peace in Seraj's soul nor would there be freedom in the walls that confined him.

Eckhart had moved on, which was his method of putting the past away. Of all things, he found a comely Asian girl, born in the states, to love and hold him dearly. They married and had three kids, two older sons and a daughter. The past often visited him in the form of nightmares but he refused to attempt to explain Korea to his wife or children. Although his ethereal night visitors would keep him up and weaken him at times, he merely waited for the darkness to pass and found a balm in his wife and children.

Eckhart was out on the deck with his wife when he got the call. He answered the phone and the nasally tenor on the other end immediately inspired him to remove to a quiet area. His wife smirked, assuming that it was a business call.

"Is this Eckhart?" The nasally voice asked.

"Gilbey, how the hell did you get this number? Why won't you leave me?"

"Listen James, I'm just telling you this for your own good: Seraj has been released from Cheonan prison." Eckhart had no words to rebut, complain or express surprise. "I know. I never thought this day would come either but it's here and while that man has no moral spine, we robbed him of his dreams and the latter years of his youth. A man that broken has only one thing on his mind, vengeance.

We're both stuck on the same wretched peninsula together but it's not China's dick that we're on this time; it's Florida. I'm just giving you a heads up."

"Goddamnit, Mike, I have a family now. I've done everything right for the last decade to build this family and now you're telling me that Seraj is coming out of hell to drag us into it. This can't be happening."

"It is happening. You had better hope that he comes for me first. After all, I deserve it and maybe that way, the authorities can arrest him before he comes to your home. "

⇥ ⇤

At 6 AM in the blueblack cold, Seraj rose to greet the rude prison reveille for the final time. His countenance betrayed nothing of his inner turmoil and he went through the morning of his release as he had done the decade prior. When it came time to be free, he shook the hand of the Filipino thief who had become his cellmate over the last month or so and walked down that narrow corrugated hall to be processed.

When freed, there was no one to greet Seraj. He was simply put on a bus to Seoul and flown back to Apopka, Florida, where his father resided.

Seraj requested that there be no grand homecoming. Upon arriving in Apopka, he would need to sleep and sleep he did to the rhythm of the falling rain. In his sleep, Seraj raged. The horrors of confinement chased him in his nightmare as he dreamt of being entombed in the catacombs of a medieval palazzo. A giant roach entered the room but instead of scurrying across the floor, it stood upright. The roach swallowed the key and then peeled back its own face, revealing another beneath, that of Bo-kyung. Seraj shuddered and woke. The clock read 2:38 AM. Seraj wasn't tired, so he got up and paced the small room as he had done in his cell and whispered shrilly over and over again,

"Gilbey first or Eckhart first?"

⇒ ⇐

Bo-kyung had also done time, but just the nine months. For that time, she played the part of the widowed martyr and victim but the people of Korea, who watched the drama unfold on the nightly news, knew her to be an adulteress and even though they forgave the couple who let their child starve in their basement while they were off at the PC Bang building characters in a Role Playing Game, here they refused to forgive.

To free herself from intense public scrutiny, Bo-kyung had wandered like a Gypsy from city to city, finding work in restaurants and then packing up once the people around her began to get a fix on who she was. There were a few places left to set up camp after years of wandering but a year before Seraj's release or thereabouts, Bo-kyung threw in the proverbial towel and resigned herself to a life of hard agrarian labor in her grandmother's village in Boseong county in southwest Korea. She quickly grew bored. There was nothing there to dazzle her. On the contrary, for the first time in her life, she had been appointed the task of cultivating the soil and raising the cattle. She was not used to stiff fingers, blistered feet and mud drenched hands.

Just before evening fell, her aunt, Na-ra Jang, commanded her to visit the Jee residence a couple of kilometers down the road. Bo-kyung was to collect a couple of jars of tea leaves from Jong Suk Jee, the elder of the family.

After stumbling down the muddy moonlit road to the Jees on blistered and cysted soles, Bo-kyung knocked. A small paper lantern hung over the door to illuminate the threshold and the space just beyond it.

A crude woman answered the door in a conical hat and looked over Bo-kyung with a critical eye. Bo-kyung greeted the wench with the warted face as pleasant as her capacity for such things allowed and explained that she was a distant relative of Na-ra and had come to fetch the leaves.

The ajumma motioned for Bo-kyung to come in with the repeated wave of her right hand as she held the door open. When Bo-kyung stepped inside, she removed her shoes and looked through the modest but well kempt home. Jong Suk Jee was seated at the table drinking tea that was poured for him with the air of dignity and stoicism normally expressed by English nobility centuries ago. He hardly looked up at Bo-kyung, making the girl wonder if he noticed her at all.

While staring at Jong Suk's long sleeves, Bo-kyung was ushered forth to the pantry by the ajumma, who pointed to the two large ceramic jars and left the girl to her own devices by festinating to the low table to serve Jong Suk another small cup of Chrysanthemum tea.

As Bo-kyung took her leave, she looked out the window to where the faint mist was gathering in the light. Boots trudged but she could not see the figure through the window as he approached. She thought nothing of the mystery and opened the door, expecting another country bumpkin covered in grit but the sturdy man she saw walked far more gracefully than the sound the steps betrayed.

When he greeted her with his soft unjudging eyes upon her, it caused her to tremble. She struggled to greet him with the same disinterest and remained fixed on his face, so much so that she nearly reached out her arm to prevent him from moving through the doorway but she held back her heart and hand and walked on through the mist.

With the aching joints and hands of a seasoned ajumma, Bo-kyung ambled softly with her head held towards the January stars, cherishing what she just saw. Each step was precious and took her farther into her fantasy with the mysterious stranger as the full yellow moon guided her way.

The house was dark when she got back; everyone had retired to their rooms. She set the jars of tea down on the counter and walked to the creaky washroom and dreamt more as she cleansed herself of the filth and the labor. The hot water felt good, clearing the caked filth and soothing her aching joints and muscles. As she scrubbed intensely, she thought of the ways she might make the pieces fit so that this mystery when unfolded before her, would be hers to seize.

Sitting on the hard frameless bed and seeing branches out of the window, Bo-kyung gleefully whispered a common nursery rhyme one of her aunts used to sing before she left the farm for big city dreams:

> Mr. Elephant's nose is a hand
> If you give him a cookie, he'll take it with his nose!

⚊⚊ ⚊⚊

Seraj stood motionless at the bath & plumbing section of Home Depot, unsure which way to go. This was not the simple matter of not knowing the correct aisle; it had everything to do with living the last eight years in a confined space with very few choices to make.

"Can I help you?" a girl asked with her pronounced tongue-ring stud bobbing up and down.

"I need a shovel, masking tape and some rope." The girl paused for a moment and then pointed Seraj to the correct aisles.

⊨⊧

"Thanks for coming, James" Gilbey said. They sat by the Bayfront gardens of the Ca D'Zan Palazzo of Sarasota, drinking the beverages Father Gilbey had purchased. The one man musical act was strumming his guitarra with a capo on it, singing "The Weight" by the Band.

"What are we going to do about Seraj?" Eckhart asked. Gilbey stared into the sun.

"I hired a private investigator, Billy Swift. He says the bastard got off the plane two days ago. Followed him into the Home Depot. Said he bought a shovel, duct tape and whatever else you need to buy whenever you're going to kidnap some fucker, put them in a trunk, burn their bodies and bury him in a sinkhole. Also, says he purchased a .22 at the sporting goods store.

"Let me ask you a question" Gilbey said. "You packing?"

⊨⊧

"Who was that girl that came round the way two days ago to collect the tea leaves?" the robust Jin-hee asked his mother (Ji-soo Shim). They were seated at the low table. The patriarch of the household, Jong-suk Jee, had retired to bed just after dusk as was his custom, so this left just the mother and her son.

"I suppose she was pretty" Ji-soo said. "Don't be getting any ideas though. This line and this farm are pendent upon you marrying Se-ra Choi...Maybe she doesn't wave your flag but she's honest and will grow on you in time."

"She's boring."

"Do you think only of yourself? You can give relief to these aching hands." Ji-soo held up her hands so that the light would shine on the callouses and blisters. "I don't know how much picking is left in them. If you need to let loose a little bit, I suppose that's okay but don't do anything permanent." Jin-hee let the words steep like the tea he poured in his mother's cup.

Running out before twilight, Jin-hee hastened to the Kim farm to deliver the final tea that was owed for the last shipment of beef. The Kims had gone to Unjusa Temple to seek favor from the gods that inspired the strange pagodas, but Bo-kyung had stayed behind to await the arrival of the man in whose mystique she wrapped her sorrows.

While milking the cows and tending to the mushrooms, Bo-kyung fixed her mind on the clothes she would use to dazzle the bachelor. What she chose could not be too elaborate, for a large part of the game resided in making the choice of clothes seem undeliberate. She asked herself what would stand nobly amidst the Eulalia and thought of the sun that often appears over the reeds.

Of course, after her release much of her wardrobe had been left behind. She wondered if she still had a yellow dress. When she returned from the field, she rummaged through her wardrobe to find nothing of that color, save for a pair of ankle socks.

When the rest of the family left, she knew she had to rummage through her aunt's closet and happen upon a dress that was no longer a fit for the older woman. It didn't take long for her to find it in the faithful light and she knew not how it remained so well kempt over the years. She shook the dust off the garment, pressed it and let it fall over her flesh. It was a perfect fit. Now, all she needed was a pair of shoes. At the bottom of the closet, a pair of blue leather ballet flats never danced in felt smooth against Bo-kyung's groping hand. When held up against the light, she instantly knew that there would be no other choice. She slid the slippers on and pushed her hair back behind her dress. The delicious reflection in the mirror brought back memories of wild nights gone by in smoky motel rooms and along dusty streets.

She thought she buried the girl who strove for stars in a narrow jail cell but seeing Jin-hee reanimated that part of her that fluttered to the light like a moth before a flame.

And then there was the sin that she authored that took the life out from underneath another, a man whom she had no love for, whom she professed a solemn vow to, bouncing off crags to meet his end at the bottom of a mountain. It was not the life that was lost that she lamented but the way it was lost and what it meant for her reputation. When she first learned to strive heavenward, she believed that even if she could not touch the heavens, cosmic forces had aligned themselves to bring upon her an ordained romance. However, she loved love, or the notion of it, too much and so when more than the time of mourning passed, she grew mad, wondering which miscalculation had thrown the stars out of whack and how she might rectify her life to realign the pieces in the cosmos no longer stuck together.

She wasn't going to wallow and obsess over questions of worth. She was going to win the heart of Jin-hee and by uniting his heart to hers, she would redeem the ghosts she wrought, still dwelling in the rain.

He came up the road in an unimpressive sedan. Ten years ago, the car would have been enough for Bo-kyung to write off Jin-hee, regardless of his stunning looks but now she thought nothing of it. It made him more down to earth and less desirable among the foolish lots of women, a group to which she used to belong, and therefore an easier catch.

She pretended not to notice the headlights coming up the dusty drive. In order to make it appear that she was in the middle of things, she took clean dishes off the shelf and began to sort them on the table. When the knock came, she purposefully clanged the two ceramic cups together in order to make it seem that she was busy about her work. She scurried along the floor with the ballet flats and opened the door, doing her best to look surprised albeit pleasantly.

Jin-hee was wearing a blue wool coat that he had unbuttoned for comfort and dungarees with boots underneath.

She smiled, doing her best to form an impression in Jin-hee's eyes but he was less than mesmerized. He smiled back and it was she that was enraptured. She could not find a single imperfection in his face. All the words she rehearsed she could not find. Instead, she just smiled back in autopilot.

"I remember you" he said. She remained silent. "It's a small town here, so we notice strangers. Jin-hee." He held out his hand and she grasped it as she rocked back. Something surreal fell upon her and she announced her name but she did so faintly.

"Where is the rest of the clan?" he asked.

"Out" she replied. "They went to the temple."

"Just chilling alone, then. The boredom out here can be enough to drive you mad at times."

"What do people do out here for fun?"

"Drink. It's considered a blessed life if you do it in public more than behind closed doors. There's a couple of annual festivals but I can tell you are not country people, not wearing that dress." She had begun to question her wardrobe choice in light of these comments. "You from Seoul?"

"Not originally, but I spent a lot of time there."

"What neighborhood?" he asked.

"Seodaemun Prison."

"Did you live in the prison there?"

"I was obviously joking."

"Right. It's not in use. Have you got something cooking?"

"Yes" she said playfully, forcing a giggle. "I had to prepare something with my aunts gone. I made enough for more than myself."

"I wouldn't dare rob you of leftovers."

"Oh, I wouldn't worry. My aunts will cook generous portions of much better food in the first light of morning."

"Well, when you put it like that." Jin-hee's manner was rough but his healthy boyish smile vindicated his rude way.

Finally, they moved on from the threshold, which they had remained trapped beneath for the whole of their exchange, to the kitchen.

The Lees did not have a low table, just the waist or belly-button high wooden table upon which they ate all of their meals. It was awful big for the two souls but they sat across from each other and picked at the same plate with their chopsticks.

"Not bad" Jin-hee said.

"I try."

With the kitchen window slightly ajar, Bo-kyung and Jin-hee could hear the wind brush by the swaying Eulalias. Bo-kyung wanted to bridge the physical distance between them but feared that if she reached out to touch the flame of love, she might be burnt, so she looked into Jin-hee's eyes and waited. She tried to glean something from them, but only remained mesmerized by their brilliance. When Jin-hee returned the gaze, his face betrayed tranquility.

"When do your parents get back?" Jin-hee asked. This question satisfied Bo-kyung, who bit her lip playfully. Now, she was able to close the distance by leaning across the table for a kiss. Jin-hee accepted the invitation by meeting her halfway and holding her in. Decent folk with time on their hands would have moved the action to the bedroom but they had to make the most of this precious hour and were deliberate yet purposeful in exploring each other.

The blue ballet shoes and yellow dress were off and Jin-hee's denim quickly followed suit. Finally, in the state of Eden, they removed to the bedroom but even in the throes of passion, they managed to maintain enough decency to gather their clothes with them in case the others arrived sooner than expected.

When the real intimacy began with its gentle biting and kissing below, Jin-hee wondered if he was not going to it too soon. Had he waited, perhaps the consummation would have been sweeter but once under the weight of a beautiful woman straddling his nether regions, there was no turning back.

The act was gratifying but there was no time to relish in the afterglow. The whole Kim family would soon arrive back at the farm and neither Bo-kyung nor Jin-hee wanted to have to explain what they had just done, so they quickly assembled their clothes, shared a long parting kiss and Jin Hee went on his way. In the doorway, she watched him leave and sighed deeply, wondering how long she could savor the moment. What would it take to retain Jin-hee?

When the Kims got back, Bo-kyung pretended to be asleep to avoid any questions about her encounter with Jin-hee if any came about. In the mirror, she could still see the imprint of Jin-hee's teeth on her neck and belly. It endeared her to him but it was two things to explain. Would they even care about or notice a hickey?

The next morning, Bo-kyung greeted the new rays of the rising sun gracefully. She opened up the dirty window and gazed over the Eulalias, towards the horizon, out of which the yellow sun rose.

For the first time in a long time, she greeted the morning peacefully, putting on her clothes without consideration of her husband's ghost. She forgot how good she looked. Prison hadn't worn her the way it had some women; she was not weathered. For now, the cloud had been lifted and so she did her best to put her hands to work and put her heart to God.

CHAPTER 2
THE SECOND LAST STAND

"I would be willing, yes glad, to see a battle every day during my life."

-George Armstrong Custer.

"You look like you've seen a ghost" Myra Eckhart said to her husband after he had just returned from his meeting in Sarasota with Gilbey. She was reading on the back patio and put her book down when she saw the sickly visage of her husband coming into view.

"I might just see one soon."

"What are you talking about? Are you okay?"

"You all have to get out of here. Find a motel, I don't care where just far. I can't contact you until this is all over."

"Why won't you tell me what's going on?"

"I'll tell you when this is all over if I'm still living but right now you're in danger and don't even know it."

"Shouldn't we go to the police? Are you some kind of criminal?"

"There's a man, Seraj Mukhtari, who has just gotten out of prison in Korea. If he has his way, he's going to kill all of us but not only us. His father lives twenty miles north of here and he's already come home. To my knowledge, he does not yet know my location but his anger will propel him to find me."

"His anger? Why would he want to kill you, us?"

"Let's just say that everything that dies someday comes back. In my foreign travels, I was no saint and I did my best to bury the sins of the past but oh how they have reached triumphantly up from the grave."

"You're scaring me, James. What haven't you told me?"

"Just tell the kids that you're going on a vacation and that I'll meet you there. I have some business to take care of."

Eckhart left his wife to sort out the mess of packing, pulling the kids out of school and running away. He went to the Sports Authority in Altamonte Springs, the same one where Seraj purchased his own .22. Not realizing how limited the selection was, he ended up with an air rifle, similar to that of Seraj and a Cold Steel Dragonfly Wakazashi sword that was marked down 200$ bringing his total to around 900$. He paid in credit.

"What the fuck is this?" Gilbey asked Eckhart, examining the sword and rifle in Eckhart's garage. "Are we making Custer's last stand? Why didn't you go to a proper gun store and buy something with power and speed?

"We're in fucking Florida, dude. Can buy an AK in this hillbilly haven without so much as a driver's license and you buy the Civil War starter pack."

"It's better than nothing and we'll stock up soon, maybe as early as today" Eckhart replied.

"Maybe there *is* a better way than a showdown at the OK Corral. After all, you've got kids to look after."

"Well, that's part of the reason I don't want to stock up. If we kill this dude by standing our ground or make it look like so, then they are going to search us and if they search us, I don't want them to find a whole arsenal. They'll put some resources into finding out why. In fact, even without the guns, they are going to want to know why some dude just released from a prison 8,000 miles away came after his expat buddies and why they were ready for him."

"Well, we can obviously play it off that he is the same killer who went into Cheonan and that eight years of being in a cage made him even more sinister" Gilbey said. "What are you going to do about this samurai sword?"

"Yeah, I guess it is kind of an impulse buy. I can't really carry this in my trunk. Good point. I'll just gift it to some businessman's son for his Bar Mitzvah."

"It's a strange Bar Mitzvah gift, though it could work in a circumcision if the Mohel is in a pinch." Eckhart squirmed and Gilbey cringed and looked downward upon realizing that he just conjured up images of Doyle the Mohel, which forced Eckhart to replay the incident that happened in his family basement in South Dakota.

Silence fell in but Eckhart persevered to break through it:

"I bet he's coming to your parish first."

"He can burn that superficial edifice to the ground so long as no one is in it."

"Like you care if someone dies. The only person you care about is yourself."

"Do you think I have no shred of human decency? I may not be Mother Theresa but I wouldn't want to deal with hearing that my parishioners were immolated."

"So what do we do until he starts in with his wrath?" Eckhart asked.

"Motel circuit?"

Bo-kyung held her rounded stomach and looked at herself in the mirror. Would today be the day that she told her family that she was carrying Jin-hee's baby? Would they discover it on their own?

As she examined herself in the mirror, she heard a knock at her door and let her overalls hang loosely over.

"You're late to the field" Na-ra called as she stormed into the room. Bo-kyung apologized and proceeded downstairs, trailed by her aunt, who barked the orders for the day.

"And one more thing" her aunt said. "You will need something to wear for the wedding."

"What wedding?" Bo-kyung asked, misty-eyed, her head held forward

"The one with that gorgeous man the family down the road are keeping you from. I think you know who I mean." She did. "You need to find a man like that, someone who can strengthen this family."

"What if I told you that I already have?"

"How is that possible? What that crooked toothed, pot-bellied Gyun boy over the hill? Well, I suppose any man has his claim"

"Not quite."

"That city bound Gong-yoo? What can that twig do for our family?"

"No, Jin-hee, the man that is set to be married."

"Whatever do you mean? Talk plainly girl. Have you been fooling around with some wildflower?"

"I've been carrying his baby inside me for the last two months." Bo-kyung felt a firm slap from her aunt.

"Why haven't you told me? We could have leveraged this. The cows and mushrooms can wait. We must go to the Jee's at once." Excitement stirred in Bo-kyung but also an element of fear. Revelations softly spoken to her in late quiet hours were to be trumpeted to the unsuspecting on this sunny morn. She readied herself for the vitriol of the Jees, who surely would not welcome the wrench from her stomach to be tossed into their well-oiled machine. Bo-kyung and her aunt marched down the road like soldiers in the rain but the sky was clear.

The Jee homestead stood there awaiting them. At its center was the house Bo-kyung had longed to return to. The lights were on inside so the niece and her aunt waltzed gracefully past the interminable fields and grazing animals to that house but 1,000 paces from the door, Aunt Na-ra stopped her niece. She winced from the power of the sun and with one open eye, she rubbed her niece's belly to make sure she was pregnant. Feeling the baby bump pleased her. With her pointer finger waving in her niece's face, Aunt Na-ra promised that if her niece was lying or if the nephew belonged to someone else, Bo-kyung would be on the first bus back to the city. Without looking for a response, Na-ra cast her eyes downward at her upward facing palms to look once more at a pair of hands ravaged by time and painstaking labor. For the last thousand steps, Aunt Na-ra practically danced to the entrance, thinking that this could be the end of that labor and the beginning of a prosperous retirement.

A little boy with no bottoms on answered the door and proceeded to run around the house, so for a few moments, Bo-kyung and her aunt waited in the threshold. Desperately, Bo-kyung wished to turn back and wait for a time when she would be greater prepared for such an intrusion but her aunt's hand placed gently at her back trapped her like a vice within the doorway.

The shouting of an adult female could be heard and soon the speaker came into view. Ji-soo Shim was surprised to see the two women in her doorway and politely asked them to state their business.

Aunt Na-ra laughed loudly:

"I come bearing profound news. Gather your family round."

"Your whole clan is strange" responded the woman. "Come out with it and I will be the one to determine whether it is worth the time of my ailing father, whose remaining hours on this earth are precious."

"Well, you can wake him to tell him of his future great grand-child" Aunt Na-ra Jang said.

Ji-soo clenched her hands into fists.

"Get out of here at once!" she exclaimed. Her irate protest brought the presence of Jin-hee, some brothers and sisters and her dear old dad, who squinted at the members of an ignobler clan standing in the doorway.

"What's the meaning of this?" he asked. His daughter assured him that there was nothing newsworthy and that this was just the usual antics of the disgraced Lee's. Aunt Na-ra was hearing none of it and gesticulated with great pathos, pointing to the very center of Bo-kyung's stomach. The father demanded silence, which he got.

"This matter requires careful consideration." Jin-hee tried to shrink from the scene but felt the eyes upon him increase in number and grow ever larger. "Jin-hee" his grandfather asked. "Did you sleep with this woman?" Jin-hee looked at Bo-kyung and even in her farm clothes, a great sense of beauty and elegance emanated from her. Ji-soo shook her fists violently and screamed something in gibberish to the heavens. Once more, the ahjussi demanded silence. Still squinting, he asked Bo-kyung if there were any other men. If he were a man of lesser esteem, Aunt Na-ra Jang wouldn't have bitten her tongue; she would have had a fit of righteous indignation.

"No" Bo-kyung assured him.

"Play actor!" Ji-soo accused. "Enough" the grandfather said and summoned the Lee women in for some tea.

⇒⊹ ⊹⇒

Gathered tightly around in a circle, the Jees and the two Lee women listened to the elder Jee speak.

"I must be honest to the Lee family in admitting that some of the hysterics expressed by my daughters is in my own heart, though expressed far more placidly I hope. We were all hoping that Jin-hee would marry the fortune-covered Se-ra Choi, for it would change the fortunes of this family, which has feared a decline for a decade now."

"Decline?" a bewildered Aunt Na-ra asked.

"There is always one rung to ascend and a million others to descend. This alliance would have meant climbing several rungs for pretty much all of my descendants that sit with you, so you can see why they have such a vested interest in this matter, but let us not dwell on what might have been. Let us meditate on how we can proceed with the situation that lies before us.

"First things first, there will be no June wedding with Se-ra Choi." Jin Hee's mother gasped and tears rolled down her face. She wanted to slap her son. "But, we must proceed with such matters prudently. The Lees will not be happy with us but we must conceal the truth, to save face and in case something happens with this child, God forbid. But, I'm not going to sugarcoat things for you. If a miscarriage occurs or if it turns out that the baby is not Jin-hee's, then we will seek once more to grant a union between Jin-hee and Se-ra. Surely, you must understand.

"For the Lees, the temptation surely will be to inform Se-ra of Jin-hee's indiscretion to remove any possible competition but I assure you that this is not in your best interest for I assure you that

193

I will use what remains in my aching bones to avenge whatever dishonor and hardship you bring upon this roof."

Both members of the Lee clan nodded that they understood. When Bo-kyung got home, she lay on the couch and was treated to the fattest cuts of Kalbi

"Rest up" Aunt Na-ra said. "We need to make sure you have a healthy baby." *This is our ticket.* Uncle Lee walked in with a look of wonder.

"Who died and made her a princess?!" he asked indignantly.

"It's not who died but who is going to be born that has made her a princess." Uncle Lee remained puzzled. "She's carrying Jin-hee's baby, fool. Now, go get us some gochujang sauce for this beef." Uncle Lee sprang joyously to the kitchen as though he were a deer in flight.

"I knew agreeing to housing her would bode well for us. We put the cosmos on our side."

"You held no such pretensions" Aunt Na-ra said. "Get us some Kimchi while you're up."

In-Sung Jo rolled up to the Jee farm in his Mercedes. Dust swirled around the car as it braked on the gravel road. Out stepped In-Sung.

He was tall for a Korean lad, a couple of inches over six feet, which meant that whenever he walked into a room, he was generally the tallest person in it. He also had the extraordinary fortune of being quite a handsome fellow. His life was of a charmed nature really and he owed much of the enchantment to his stature and the success it propelled him towards. Jo was not an introspective man and who would blame him? There was little to lament because little went wrong. His only goal was to keep the essence of the talisman that blessed him flowing, so he became a lawyer and not even a good one, but with his good looks and thespian presence, the folks at PL Group's agricultural division were sure to make him a visible figure albeit a powerless one. That was fine with In-Sung Jo. His work was limited to distributing papers and visiting farms. At best, he was a glorified bean counter, but PL Group gave him enough money to live the lavish life of a hedonistic bachelor.

With confident steps, he approached the Jee home and knocked. While he waited, he held his briefcase in his left hand and examined his spotless gray woolen suit in the other. One aunt answered and welcomed him with open arms. She remarked that he grew taller and more handsome every time she saw him. He returned her complement with the grin that had won him over so many unsuspecting lovers. She ushered him to the table where he waited for the rest of the family to arrive.

The Jee family rushed down to greet the sitting In-Seong Jo, who already devoured his first cup of green tea.

"You need to savor it" one uncle joked.

"This is too good" Jo responded. "I could drink this until I die."

"Marry one of our daughters and you can" an aunt rebutted humorously. Her collegiate aged daughter blushed.

"So, what is the urgent matter you wish to discuss?"

"This is sensitive and I wish to only inform Ji-soo, Elder Jee and Jin Hee. It will be up to them to inform you at their own discretion." Jo gave a polite smile to all the disappointed faces, but they complied and Jin-hee, his mother, and the elder Jong-suk removed to the elder's private quarters to discuss matters.

Jo sat in a wooden chair and opened the briefcase. The elder sat on his bed and his two descendants seated themselves on the wooden floor.

"It appears that the girl who is allegedly carrying your baby is the infamous White Oleander. Did that famous case make it all the way to the countryside?"

"We don't read the papers much here or watch the news but the name is familiar… It can't be! The horror of it! She's the one who conspired to have her husband killed for insurance money?"

"That's right" Jo answered. "And, she may be running a similar scheme here. How certain are you that this woman is carrying your child?!"

"Let's just say that it is highly plausible" Jin-hee answered.

"Stupid country boys don't know how to use condoms" his mother gibed.

"Her getting pregnant for the sake of her own gain is the least of your worries" Jo said. "It's like a virus, once it gets in, it spreads."

"What can we do?" Ji-soo asked.

"Besides pray for her downfall?" Jo asked. "There's not a whole lot of options if that baby is one half Jee. Basically, you better hope that the antibodies naturally fight this virus."

"Speak plainly" the elder demanded. "I can't understand you. We can't go to the court and use her criminal history as a reason to dissolve any responsibility?"

"I'll get back to my people but if you go that route, chances are that you will have to pay hefty child support in lieu of a wedding."

"This is madness" the elder said.

"The best we can do for now is hire someone to uncover more" Jo answered. "You know it's hard to surveil a place with you impenetrable country types. Only family members get to come in, but I think I have the man for you."

Detective Hye-jeong frantically put her papers in order. She always presented the air of working to live but there was a quiet confidence in her way as well. She wore her bangs in the exact same way for the last ten years. Some of her pantsuits were new but you would never know that she ever refreshed her wardrobe.

With her papers in order, it was now time to sort through the mail. Most of it was the same old interdepartmental crap: memos, official reports, etc., but there was one envelope that caught her eye because it was so out of place. It was from PL Group (Agricultural Division) and the address was handwritten.

Hye-jeong used her monogrammed letter opener to unseal the missive. There was a typed letter with an ornate signature at the bottom. The letter read:

Dear Detective Lieutenant Hye-jeong,

I hope this letter finds you well.

I am writing to update you on the whereabouts of one of Korea's most infamous criminals, Bo-kyung Lee. She has gone to her family's farm in Boseong.

While it may appear to the untrained eye that this is an exercise in the rehabilitation of a prisoner, Bo-kyung has reverted to her nefarious ways. She has found the life of another man to destroy, that of Jin-hee Jee, whose family cultivates green tea leaves. Using her devilish guile, she has found a way to trick this man into impregnating her. I am sure that if this fetus is born and develops, it will be used by Bo-kyung Lee to gain an economic advantage.

Jin-hee Jee could become the next Jacob Jung. I am requesting your assistance in the matter. Any resources you can divert would be most appreciated.
Sincerely,
In-Seong Jo

For a good six minutes, Hye-jeong rested her chin on her closed fist and visited the past in her mind's eye. The characters of that arduous case were like caricatured phantoms dancing through the rain: the motel clerk, the three foreigners and the widow with that outlandish bombazine veil that she wore everywhere.

I can't wait to show Woo-jin this letter.

CHAPTER 3

I STILL CAN'T SAY GOODBYE

I've grown up here now
All of my life
But I dreamed
Someday I'd go
Where blue eyed girls
And red guitars and
Naked rivers flow

- ("Whistle Down the Wind) Tom Waits

As Hye-jeong approached Woo-jin's cubicle, she could hear the pool ball rolling around his workspace. Having very little ambition, Woo-jin was happy to be reassigned to the Evidence Unit, where he whistled down the days with computer solitaire and novels. In fact, he was working on a book of his own, and was almost 60,000 words into it. The book, he decided, would be called *Plucking the Oleander*; it was a piece of nonfiction chronicling his involvement in the 2010 investigation into the murder of Jacob Jung

"Busy, are we?" Hye-jeong asked, catching Woo-jin off guard.

"Even when I kick my feet up, I'm working."

"How's the novel coming?"

"It's not a novel, stupid. It's nonfiction. I'm already in touch with an agent. She said she's going to make me rich, which means my ex-wife is going to be rich.

"By the way, I should have trusted my instincts about getting married. It was a bad idea. Without In-Hye Oh, I would be able to retire to Jeju Island after this."

"How is your personal life by the way?"

"In shambles. When I do get to see my daughter, she doesn't want to see me. Maybe everything will change once *Plucking the Oleander* hits the shelves. Anyways, are you?"

"Good, Seong-Won and I are going to Thailand in a few months. Until then, it's nose to the grindstone but things have been in order for a while."

"With you, things have always been in order."

"I'm an organizer, I confess, sometimes way more than a policeman."

"It's not only that, Hye-jeong; you know how to move forward." Both cast their eyes on the red resin carom ball. "No matter how joyous or painful the past, I can't let go. Maybe when this book is all over." Hye-jeong didn't dare suggest that finishing his book might make matters worse.

"Just make sure you run a copy by the Captain when you finish."

"I'm going to run out the door when I finish...So, you just stopping by one your way to gather evidence?"

"No, of course not."

"It's okay. I know I'm not the highlight of your day. Can you believe it's been about a decade since?"

"The glory days, right?"

"When I mattered."

"This is what you wanted, right? You asked the Captain for something easy after the big case and we all thought you just needed some time to gain your equilibrium but you never hungered for more action or a promotion."

"I just had too much in my life. If I just stayed away from that woman and the altar, I would be all good now. I would have had the kind of life, where I could really go for it. I would be more than a lieutenant and with all that I won, I could have found a real woman, a beauty with real devotion and an irresistible feminine charm and I wouldn't hit the bottle hard, so I'd have a daughter who wasn't ashamed. On the contrary, she would be proud of her father. But, none of those dreams matter, because I never recovered. "

"You don't blame me for…"

"God…no, not directly, anyhow."

"What do you mean 'not directly?'"

"I mean you kept pushing and pushing the idea of love and marriage on me and I thought it was what I wanted."

"I tried to prevent you from losing your faith in the world and becoming a recluse. I didn't tell you to marry her. I only told you not to abandon tradition."

"Because no woman wants to see a man free. You all think it's cute when one of your friends has her man trained. If he leaves the toilet seat up or one of his socks on the floor, then it calls for a riot. You really will make a great captain with all those memos. Every man under you will have his balls in a vice."

"Woo."

"Sorry, I'm just looking for… I've driven away everyone else who could possibly be held accountable. In the end, it's all on me. I built this life and I must rise with it or go down with it."

"Have you seen a psychologist recently?"

"To be put on lithium. That shit killed my good friend."

"To talk to someone other than the wall or Captain Q. Who said anything about psychotropic drugs? You really have lost it. You didn't even ask why I came here."

"I'm sorry; I've lost all manners."

"I'll just say it to avoid any more awkward exchanges. I got a letter from PL Group (Agricultural Division)"

"So, you're going to switch jobs and become a farmer."

"No, can you just listen? Jesus. The letter was from some lawyer or businessman and in it, it said that Bo-kyung Lee was back on her family farm in Boseong."

"But you gotta give her credit for trying to make it in the city." Woo-jin jotted down some notes and then continued speaking. "To think of her humble origins and how she almost got away with it all and how she would have had that tower to herself like Rapunzel."

"Do you remember how badly you wanted her?"

"Well, she was gorgeous and had all that money. I wanted to believe that somehow she was innocent and that she wanted lowly ol' me."

"Turns out neither of those were true." Woo-jin raised his mug to cheer her quip and they shared a moment of laughter. "Inside she was rotten, like a cancer. You were better off poor, then be rich with her."

"It's hard to imagine that this life could be worse."

"Stop being so melodramatic; you've still got life. If only you would live it. Sorry, I..."

"Ugh." Woo-jin rolled his eyes. "Anyhow, what did the rest of the letter say?"

"The writer of it urged me to divert resources to Boseong to keep an eye on the White Oleander. Even if it were within my power, which is certainly is not, it's foolish. Oh yeah, apparently, she is pregnant with the baby of some farm family that makes green tea."

"I don't see how it's foolish. You should notify the Boseong police and tell them that they have a dangerous killer in their midst."

"The only dangerous thing about that girl is that she is drop dead gorgeous. If you men could look beyond looks that girl would have no power."

"If you women could only see the power your looks have over men, then you would not make such statements.

"I would very much like to go to Boseong to write an afterword for my book. Do you think she's sincere? Do you think she's rebuilding her life down on the farm?"

"She probably needs a man like you to keep her warm when the nights get lonely."

"I would like to say 'in my younger days' but I never had a chance."

"Seraj had a chance, then so did you. You realize that you're lamenting the fact that you weren't able to get with a woman who had her husband murdered in cold blood"

"Allegedly. I know I just – Well, I have a vacation coming up and I think that some respite in Boseong is just what the doctor ordered.

"If I run into her, do you think she'll recognize me?"

"You're a riot, Woo. You have no desire to do any work when you are on the clock and then when it comes time for vacation, you want to investigate a closed case."

"Like I said, I can't bury the past and the past is in Boseong. Maybe if I can confront these old ghosts, I can get on with..."

"Maybe" Hye-Jin answered. "Anyhow, I've got to get back to things; just thought you should know about the latest developments."

"Most appreciated."

"See you soon" Hye-jeong shouted cheerfully.

"See you soon." Woo-jin peered into the carom ball as though it were a seeing stone.

⇥ ⇤

Eckhart and Gilbey booked two queen beds at the West Tampa Bay Travelodge.

"We're all going to die soon" Eckhart said. "We mine as well get our own rooms. I can't decide whether you're too much of a monk or too much of an old man or both. Hey, think of it as the bonding time you always wanted."

"Ha! We're like John Candy and Steve Martin in *Planes, Trains and Automobiles.*"

"Yes! You saw that movie as a kid too? I know which one you are."

"Hey, I'm not obese."

"Yes, but you are the more comical of the two."

"True. I have the blood of a jester but I traded my motley for a cassock."

"This room is only 76 bucks but we're going to spend another 100 at the mini-bar" Eckhart said.

"Yeah, you can afford it."

"Oh I know, and I thought I'd be teaching those fucking devils for the rest of my life. They were good kids though."

"They really were. I wonder what Cass is doing now."

"I bet she's all grown up and has kids now," Eckhart said.

"Little Casses running all over the place, it's hard to imagine. I hope she picked a good man. You know, someone who offered her something. She had a sweet soul so I imagine she found someone worthy."

"You *have* become a bit of a priest. You never used to talk like that."

"I suppose that I've been inculcated. This religion with all of its candles and carnival lights has made me a better man somehow. I know for some people I'm hell bound no matter what I do but maybe I can aim for a higher circle of it. Am I really such a bad guy after all?"

Gilbey's phone began to buzz.

"This thing is a cancer I tell ya" Gilbey said. "Fifty percent of the time I'm getting calls from the parish to administer the act of extreme unction to some geezer."

"So you just don't answer it?"

"I do. Sometimes, I wait for a voicemail because I need to mentally ready for myself. One cannot be a priest all of the time. I have to get into character. Shit, I chose this gig because I thought that it would be little work. You get to hideaway from the world for seven years – wasn't a fan of the supplication but it is what it is – and then you've got to spend all your hours pretending to be saintly. It's exhausting relating every answer to every question to some Jew who lived two millennia ago.

"Don't even get me started on confession. I thought I'd get to hear about raunchy orgies and double murders but it's all old ladies afraid to die and fifteen year old boys coerced by their parents, trembling because they beat their dick to the image of some cheerleader in their physics class.

"Did I ever tell you I had a priest ask me how often I beat my dick? That was the last time I truly confessed. I even stopped confessing to lust because they always asked follow up questions about masturbation. Do you know what I find? The priests who were pure of heart, the gentle souls that I really looked up to, would just shrug it off and move onto the next sin but the real jerks, the wise guys with a chip on their shoulder liked to dangle you (metaphorically of course) by the very dick that caused you to sin over the pit of hell. I tell kids to shrug it off because I for one let off more rockets than Hezbollah when I was in the seminary. Of course, I can't go around telling kids that it's okay to beat their dicks because then they can go tell their parents that Father Michael Gilbey gave them a pass. I know they're inclined to keep that sort of thing private but you never know. One thing I've gotten better at over the years is covering my own…"

"Jesus Christ, you've got a lot going on up there. Ever think about going to see a shrink."

"We have psychologists. I think they're mostly looking for pedophiles but once again, how confidential is confidential? If I tell a rival priest, even in the confessional, that I let them fly like Brett Favre in his prime, then someone might start looking at me."

"This right here is why you never got laid. You are the most paranoid and neurotic man I have ever met. Some Swedish supermodel could be hinting that she wants to take you back to her flat and you'd be in the CVS lamenting how expensive condoms are and how it should be a woman's responsibility but me, I'd just buy a pack of Trojans and be on my way."

"Trojans, yeah right, more like Slim Fits."

"Coming from a man who never gets laid, that means a whole lot. I was a legend back in Korea and my wife ain't too bad. I do well in that department, my friend."

"I mine as well check that voicemail."

Gilbey punched in the code to access the voicemail. It was a message from the bishop:

"Father Gilbey, oh dear, it seems there has been an accident at Saint Florian. I was surprised you weren't at the rectory, as these are your office hours, but I am more concerned about you being alright. Please get back to me as soon as possible so that I know you are okay."

"Wow!" Gilbey said.

"What is it?"

"Seraj just tried to burn my parish down.

"Wait, what the fuck? Holy Shit! Was he actually identified? Our crusade could be over if he has to do another bit, this time for arson."

"I wouldn't get your hopes up. This old rickety bishop sounds clueless and they haven't even investigated the fire yet. I'm sure that they will discover that it's arson. I think we need to find a clever way to drop a dime on Seraj.

"Well, I must be traveling on. I'll listen to some Gregorian chant in the car to get me in the mood for talking with Bishop Glynn. Here's forty dollars; I hope that covers my half. Priest's salary, you understand."

"It's worth something. Ten years ago, you probably would have tried to sneak out the door."

"I'm a Gilbey; it's in my nature to be shifty. There's no use in fighting it."

"That's a sorry excuse for sins."

"God made me this way. Go take up your complaint with Him. I have a performance at what remains of Saint Florian parish."

"Yeah, break a leg; I really mean it."

Gilbey parked his car at "Just Gents Inc.," an upscale barbershop across from his parish. He took his sweaty palms off the steering wheel and took a deep breath to access Father Gilbey and shake off the sin-plagued Michael. The Aquitanian repertory had taken him almost all the way there. It took that extra deep breath to shut the door.

Hurrying to that uninspiring building in the style of Spanish Colonial Revivalism, Gilbey held the countenance of mock concern. From Just Gents, there was no direct view but he could see the trails of smoke over the roof of the barbershop.

Gilbey choked on the smoke that was thick in the air as the sirens wailed on. Finally, he stepped around Boca Bargoons Sarasota, a rug store, to get a full view of the extinguished conflagration and the damage it caused. People gathered in rows along 2nd and Acadia Ave to watch the whimpering end of the show. Little did they know that they would get an encore when a panicked Gilbey came to join the crowd.

Individuals in the crowd patted Gilbey on the back, offered their condolences and inquired whether anyone was inside as though he would know.

The spectacle to be witnessed though was not the fireman nobly putting a cessation to this conflagration. It was what Gilbey had stepped into, what was just across the way from Saint Florian. The real rector of the Parish, Father Benedict Matthews, was kneeling on the sidewalk with a couple of old ladies and a few college students and they were fervently reciting the rosary.

"Hail Holy Queen…"

Great, now I've got to do this shit.

For a moment, Gilbey just sat there and watched but he could feel the eyes of strangers on him and those eyes seemed to ask him whether would join in, so he braced himself as one would for a tremendous kidney shot from Mickey Ward, and approached the circle of prayer. He attempted to make eye contact with Father Matthews but the pious man was so lost in rapture that he couldn't get so much as an acknowledgement.

After letting out the faintest of sighs, Gilbey joined in with his back arched forward and his eyes to the curb.

What an embarrassment, to be on display like this. What the fuck did I spend seven years in the seminary for? To be some kind of carnival freak that they roll out when a church burns down? I should have stayed a lay man. I might be dead or even worse but I'd have a shred of my dignity. Perhaps, I should have become a monk or a brother; that way my religious expression could be kept in private.

When Seraj gets taken care of, this will all turn sane again. I'll go back to my regular duties, but I don't even like these regular duties. They want me to be a chipper and I have to strain not to be my morose self. This was a poor investment. Eckhart had the right idea: Don't be a play actor. Go put your nose to the grindstone, get into a business, make some money and live away from things. I thought being a priest would allow me to live away from things. You get your room, your board and there isn't much to worry about but darn it, if I'm not spending every waking hour pretending to be someone that isn't me. This is supposed to be different from the workaday world but it's really the daily grind on crack. Can I really do this for another two decades or more? Will there come a time when Michael Gilbey and Father Gilbey become one person? Is that something I want? To lose the parts of myself, as flawed and broken as they are, that make me who I am? Lord, give me a sign.

CHAPTER 4
KHUSARA

"And to which of the saints wilt thou turn?"

- Job 5:2 KJV

Once again, Gilbey found himself across from a detective eager to know answers. On this occasion, Gilbey was seated in a parish office at the Diocese of Venice, instead of that cold dwelling so familiar to him, the interrogation room.

"Do you know anyone who wanted to hurt you or Father Matthews or wanted to do harm to the church? Any suspicious characters in the pews as of late?" Detective King asked. Gilbey scowled at the southern drawl. It made King sound stupid.

"There is a gentleman I met while I was in South Korea named Seraj Mukhtari. Ah, so this is a complicated story. Back in 2010, Seraj was sentenced by a South Korean judge to life imprisonment without the possibility of parole for killing the son of a wealthy tech magnate."

"I don't follow."

"I and another man named James Eckhart testified against Seraj in that trial."

"And?"

"He was very recently exonerated."

"By forensic testing?"

"Not sure. It's possible. I know that he did it. I heard him brag about it. They uncovered a rock in his room with a blood all over it."

"You seem to know a lot about the law for a clergyman."

"How do you figure? Given that I was a witness in this case, I paid close attention to the facts for the long thereafter. If you put a guy behind bars, wouldn't you want to know about his release and everything about his case?"

"I do put men behind bars and I do look into what happens after the fact; you're right. Can you tell me about this incident in South Dakota?"

"More garbage luck. If the Gilbey family ain't cursed, I don't know who is. My father, God rest his soul, was involved in some nefarious affairs with some of the more notorious local criminals in Boston. As retribution for what my father did, bad men sought me out. It all culminated there. I already told Detective Pizzolatto all this back in Custer. I was cleared of any wrongdoing."

"Thanks. I'll inquire about the file. No need to be on edge though. You are not under suspicion of anything yet, though I must say your case is a curious one. Trouble seems to follow you wherever you go."

"I was born into trouble as sparks fly upward."

"What?"

"It's from The Bible."

"Right. Where were you when the fire started?"

"Tampa Bay, visiting an old friend."

"Ok, because Bishop Glynn and his little mascot Father Matthews were in a tizzy that you were not around at the time of the fire and you notified absolutely no one that you would be out of town."

"Sometimes, you gotta get away. I know I'm a priest and I live under different rules and stipulations than other folks, but I'm human and I get tired of living like a fourteen year old girl always having to tell some superior where I'm going."

"That's how it is in the military."

"But when they return home from basic or active duty, they get to be free, not me."

"I suppose. Are you new to this whole priest thing?"

"I haven't been out of the seminary for very long if that's what you mean."

"Yeah, maybe that's why you don't strike me as a priest."

"What do you mean? There are priests with all kinds of temperaments who come from all walks of life."

"But, Father Michael, when I look into your eyes, I see the shadow of skepticism. I don't see that in other priests, not in Bishop Glynn and certainly not in Father Matthews. Only Star Trek fans make me more uncomfortable than that dude. He told me that I should investigate abortions because that's the real crime of the world. I don't think you would do something like that in a million. Am I right?"

"Yes, but does that make me less priestly or just less Vatican-friendly?"

"Sorry, we're getting off track. If you have any more information or you can think of something that slipped your mind during this interview, don't hesitate to give me a call."

"Will do."

Detective King rolled up to Seraj's father's house in his 2016 Chevy Caprice. His partner, Detective Shore, an African-American male of equal heft and age, sat beside him.

"This case is already the strangest thing I've ever had the mispleasure of dealing with" Shore said. "This fire that took down a church is now linked with crimes that happened in South Korea and South Dakota."

"Think of it this way" King said. "This might be our chance to be on *Forensic Files* talking about fibers and refraction."

"What does Mr. Mukhtari do for a living?"

"He works at Alibaba in Longwood. Judging by the looks of things, he probably just washes dishes."

"Any record?"

"Yeah, a couple of small drug offenses, could have been a small-time dealer, nothing over 25 pounds. He did a couple of very small stints but I would expect that from someone living in this dump. This home was purchased for 49 grand."

"You ready?"

"Ready as I'll ever be."

The two detectives approached the house.

"Well, I'll be" Shore said, "This roof is crooked." King laughed. "You know he's no major player in the drug game with a roof like that.

A dark Pakistani male opened the door. He was as thin as the day he left for the United States.

"What you want?" the man asked with indignation. "My son innocent. Find real criminal." Detective Shore wanted to snap Mukhtari's spine in half because of the open disdain he showed and because he looked like Sideshow Bob from the Simpsons with his curly hair dangling below his shoulders. He possessed what the Germans would call a "backpfeifengesicht" because of that elongated nose that stood dead central in that rodent-like face that generally expressed disbelief or contempt.

"We're not claiming that your son is a criminal" King said, "and he's not yet been charged with a crime. We just want to ask him some questions."

"When they put my son behind bars for almost a decade, they say 'we just want to ask questions.' He's not here. Leave us alone."

"Do you know where he is?" Shore asked.

"He works at restaurant. My son is good person. He not criminal."

"At Ali Baba?

"Yes, he washes dishes there. You can find him there but he is no criminal."

"Damn, this is in the same place as a Korean restaurant" Detective Shore said to his partner. "I bet they have some good dishes there. Lebanese is straight but it depends on when you go. It's one of those hit or miss things."

"Shore, we're looking for a suspect, not a good place for Dim Sum."

"Good food helps me during hard cases. I suggested that wood composite test in the Newman case after the most sublime pecan pie of my life. I refuse to have another slice until I hit another dead end in an important case.

"What happened was I went to the John to read the sports section, but I ended up bringing in an article about some Bradentucky prison warden who was stealing farm equipment and property from the state. I don't remember the facts of that case so clearly but I do remember that Ackles, who was making more than six figures at that time, had the prison farm firewood loaded onto his truck. The synapses in my mind were firing and I started to think about wood and how Newman's body was burned with lighter fluid in a burn pit. We couldn't find the lighter fluid in the Newman home but we were able to find logs that had the precise same chemical composition as those found...well, you know the fucking story. I was a hero for that. I celebrated with a Soft Shell Crab BLT at

Owen's Fish Camp with Sharmell after the verdict. I got drunk off my ass that night."

King sighed deeply and dismissively but started to understand that there was some real connection between food and Shore's ability to solve cases.

"The way this case is shaping up, I think you're due for some 25 cent wing nights at Gatorz."

"I love me some wings, King, but you're missing the point. That cheap grub does me no good mentally. You have to be like Catherine Medici."

"Who? Is that one of your exes?"

"Man, Catherine Medici was a Renaissance bitch. She was a patron of the arts. She paid money to artists so that they could live and craft beautiful works of art but she couldn't just give them sustenance. Michelangelo doesn't paint no Sistine Chapel on 25 cent wing night. Michelangelo needs a Filet Mignon to have the energy to aim Adam's fingertips towards the Father, to reach out and touch faith. 25 cent wing Michelangelo slaps some Hooters waitress on the ass and burps his beer, then draws a fucking paint by number."

"I'll keep that in mind. By the way, Slade and Wysocki from the Apopka Police Department won't be joining us today but they do want a report no matter what happens, and if we do end up charging Seraj, they are willing to assist."

"Cool. All this discussion of food has made me hungry. I feel like Jiro, but instead of dreaming of sushi, I'm dreaming of a good old southern fish fry and this foodie has his pick of hot sauce."

"Discussion? Sounded a lot more like a monologue. I'm sure this place has Kebob."

"Yeah, I'm hoping for some Sujuk. I haven't had that shit in forever. I'm hoping they have that Lebanese soft drink I had back in a place in Tampa so many summers ago."

The two detectives stepped inside.

"I heard they had a Hookah Bar in here" Shore said. King shrugged his shoulders. "Yeah, I'm just saying that moving it away from the regular dining area was a considerably wise decision. The last thing I want at 2:30 in the afternoon is Hashish in my face."

"Hashish is illegal, Shore."

"I mean Hookah; you get the point. I'm just commending them.

"They also have shows at this place, dancing girls. They don't take their clothes off but they do that belly dancing. That shit is erotic. That's how I lost Sharmell. I took her to Acropolis Taverna. See Sharmell is originally from Burbank, California and unless you from the south, 'specially Atlanta, you're not down for no exotic dancing girls while you're with your man.

"So, I was cool until this song that sounded like 'Big Pimpin' by Jay-Z starts coming through the speaker and this angel named Hafsia comes out in some angel winged costume and gets into it. You know when you watch them adult films and most of the time, you can tell that even though the dude is bringing it, the girl is less than interested. It makes sense; getting slammed by something that hard in various body cavities is probably equal parts pain and pleasure and with dudes standing around with that long ass mop looking mic and HD cameras, it makes even more sense but every now and then, you can really see it, especially with the chicks new to the game, you know, the ones who haven't been stretched out like pizza dough if you know what I mean. They get really into it. They lose theyself in the moment just like that Eminem song says.

"That's what this Hafsia chick was doing, only she wasn't nekked [naked] and there was no dick under her but when she got to gyrating and vibrating, Sharmell could see me licking my lips."

"Well, yeah dude. Women get jealous. I've treated my woman like a lady for fifteen years and I don't watch porno or would dream of exploring your nuanced theories regarding it. My woman would never walk out on me."

"That's great. I'm so proud of you and Jesus is proud of you too but let's be real, Sharmell was jealous that what this woman did for money had an effect on me that she couldn't produce in a million heartfelt Stripteases. She stormed out. I paid the bill and for the night; I had my angel. You better believe I asked her if she had a man. She did. If she hadn't, I would have spent my bottom dollar trying to hit that."

"And that's what separates you from me."

"Settling down ain't for me, man. I need to explore the world around me. Wanting to know the world around me is what makes me investigate cases; it's what makes me get to the bottom of the truth.

"The whole department likes to pat Zuley on the back but that crooked cracker plants more guns than he does daffodil bulbs. You see the way he coerces defendants. You know damn well that that Dulli kid didn't commit no triple homicide back in '09 but Zuley mentally and physically tortured that kid for three stinking days and that crooked Judge Grisham wouldn't throw the confession out even though he saw the shiner and cracked ribs."

"Hey, you on the side of the criminals now too?"

"I'm on the side of justice, a rare thing in this world and let's be honest, a rare thing in this profession. That's what I'm trying to tell you. I'm not some amoral Christian Bale *American Psycho* character running around with an axe. Other detectives and police look for convictions, I look for the truth, so don't go around slandering me like some lowlife.

"Yeah, I'm not married and I don't have much of an anchor in my life and I've watched pornographic films and drank alcohol and pigged out to deal with the accidental fucking characteristics of my existence."

"Sorry Shore. I know we don't always see eye to eye. You have to understand that as a man with two daughters, I have a hard time dealing with sexually aggressive men."

"Sexually aggressive? That's a reach. I haven't had more sex than the next guy. Most of my sexual experiences involve some serious wrist action if you know what I mean. I told you I wanted to nail some hot belly dancer; it doesn't mean I'm going to rape some woman in an alleyway."

"You should strive to be a good man."

"Man, I could never be no square. The only way I can help the world is by solving cases and I can only do that by being this man. As soon as I become a family man and I have a mortgage, a wife, and a dog and some kids to play with, I can't go back to interviewing sex offenders about their whereabouts. This world is too dark and gritty to bring back to all of that. It might be different for you, Bob, but I'm limited to one of the two worlds and I have chosen the one with delinquents and strippers. I wish I could compartmentalize, which you are far more gifted in but I can't and knowing that I can't is wisdom if Saint Francis is right:

"'Accept the things you cannot change.'"

"What's wrong with wanting to cultivate a good world that my daughters can breathe in and feel safe in?"

"I hate to throw some splatter on your living Norman Rockwell painting but that world will never be. The best your daughters can hope for is that they have enough money to keep themselves locked away from the monsters we try to capture.

At the end of the day, what difference do we make? The killings and blastings continue. Mothers cry and if we're lucky we find the dude who did it so that he can't do it again but prisons are filled with innocent men, or good men who don't deserve to be there, men put there by men like us."

"Why do you do this, Shore, if you don't feel like you're making a dent? Can't be for the money. The sleep this job deprives you of, there would have to be a better way."

"You do what you're good at and I'm good at this gig. I don't know how to succeed in any other game."

"I think you could have been a sous chef but let's just agree to disagree and get Seraj."

"There's something we can agree on."

Although Shore was more desirous to try the fare offered by Korea House, he settled for the Salmon Kabob at Alibaba, which was better than he thought it would be.

"King, this is the kind of grub that is going to get me to solve this case." King rolled his eyes. He got the Gormeh Sabzi, which was satisfactory, but his contentment was overshadowed by the sound of Shore licking his lips and groaning in pleasure. "You have to admit for the middle of the day when these kinds of places phone it in because the chef is some amateur and the kitchen short-staffed, this is pretty impressive. Time for some coffee and baklava and then we'll ask that kid some questions about the fire at Saint Florian."

While debating when, if ever, it is appropriate to use the women's room, King and Shore enjoyed their dessert and coffee in silence and when they finished paying their bill and when King finished thanking the old Lebanese waiter for his service, they showed their badges and asked about Seraj Mukhtari. His shift had ended twenty minutes prior when the owner, Hamad Alanazi, sent him out the backdoor.

In actuality, the restaurant's owner, Hamad Alanazi sent Seraj away after he got a call from Seraj's father regarding the police visit.

Seraj drove his clunker, a 1999 Bordeaux Red Pearl Buick Le Sabre. Every time he switched gears, the exhaust would boom after a short delay. He was surprised that the beater hadn't died out every trip and he knew that if this thing kept running, he would grow attached. The radio was as clear as a bell, so he moved the dial past the stations of thumping honky tonk music and holy speak and settled on Mix 105.1, a top 40 station that preferred dance hits to all others.

He slowed his car down on Dog Track Road and promised himself that as soon as he found a cheap motel, he would go back there and spend some of his dishwashing money and a portion of the restitution granted to him in Korea on the dog track. The least the world could give him is some vulgar pleasures after being denied every sort of comfort for the last eight years and what pleasure is more vulgar than watching abused animals chase a fake rabbit around the track in the hopes of winning greater glory?

There was a room available at the Suburban Extended Stay Motel for 40$/night so he booked it, and got back in his car. He was filled with rage.

Do they know about the fire? Can Eckhart and Gilbey see me through their rearview? First things first.

Seraj drove a couple of blocks to the nearest strip mall. He was glad to find that there was a Boost Mobile between Bright Light Books. Inside the Boost Mobile, Seraj purchased a burner and put 60 minutes on it. The first call he made was to this father.

"What trouble are you in, Seraj?" his father asked.

"Dad, I ain't got time for this shit. What did the police ask you about me?"

"They looking for you, only this. Maybe talk to them and they go away; I don't know."

"That's what the Korean police said. Did the detective leave a name and number?" Seraj's father gave his son the personal information on Detective King's card.

"Son, when you comin' home."

"When I got all of this sorted out. I'm going to call him. I'm going to be home soon. It may not be tonight but I'm coming home."

When Seraj got off the phone, he took two slow minutes to gather himself and then he called Detective Shore.

"This Detective Shore speaking. How may I help you?"

"I ain't going the fuck back to jail so you better tell me what the fuck it is you pigs want from me." Shore was caught off guard.

"Ah...Is this Seraj?" Shore pulled over to the shoulder over the road and put the phone on speaker so that King could hear. His partner perked up.

"Let's just say that I am. I want to know which little piggies are looking for the big bad wolf and why?"

"Where are you? We'd love to pick you up and have a chat."

"Shut up!!! Everyone keeps saying that. Nobody wants to have a chat. That's what I used to say to chicks to get laid. I'm not spending another decade behind bars for a crime I didn't commit."

"Seraj, we know all about you. We know that you were wronged and we want to set things right. We know about your troubles with the two men who falsely testified against you and we know that they live not too far from you and we just want to make sure you're safe and we definitely want to get your side of the story."

"Sorry, I want to believe you but what I suffered the last eight years, I'm not dealing with the police."

"You're a free man now. Enjoy that freedom. Don't do anything stupid that's going to jeopardize that liberty. Just tell us where you are."

"In your bedroom screwing your wife, cocksucker." Seraj hung up the phone and stared contemptuously at the whitehaired throngs pushing carts in on out of ABDI, the grocery store next to Boost Mobile. He knew that this slow easing into death through decay would probably have been his fate too had a horrendous crime not been pinned on him.

Am I that unlucky? At least, I won't become that. My world will end with a bang, not some whimper. I need to stock up.

In Florida, you're never far from the nearest gun store. He didn't even have to ask about. He merely looked for the first redneck, semi-redneck or wannabe redneck he could find but they would be in short supply in ABDI and less than abundant in the boost mobile, but lucky for Seraj, there was a Northern Tool & Equipment and it didn't take long for him to find a bearded man in a camouflage patterned tank top to point him the way albeit with skepticism.

At Southern Guns LLC, Seraj purchased a .38 to go along with what he bought at the sporting goods store a week before, but it failed to assure Seraj. He needed something with rapid fire capacity and with the 80 million Won (roughly 67,000$) in restitution granted to him by the Supreme Court of Korea, it was a small price to pay for someone who had no plans to live beyond the next month.

I'm not going back to jail and I'm going to buy this 900$ M4 to make sure of that.

The gun store cashier and clerk, a thin old white man, had no reservations about selling to a brown-skinned man. Of course, Adolph Hitler, Saddam Hussein, Mao Zedong and Lyndon Johnson would all fall under the category of "just another customer."

After purchasing the guns, Seraj carried the two boxes in which they came out to the LeSabre.

4:17 PM

It's time to roll up to Kissimmee and pay Mr. Eckhart a visit. With that church fire, he and/or the police may be onto me. I need to phone a friend to drive by the Eckhart residence before I drive this obvious loud fucking shitbox down that road and get myself into a situation that I can't get out of. I don't mind a shootout with the police but not until those two shitbirds are lying six feet deep, not until they suffer what I have suffered. It is wrong for them to see any more of the light.

The first phone call Seraj made was to Matthew Sanders, an African American acquaintance of his. Unfortunately, he was currently serving the end of a one year sentence for selling an ounce to a cop, so he had to rely on Esteban Agreda, a "Solutions Engineer" for a cloud secure web gateway platform.

"Seraj, Jesus Christ! I thought you were in some foreign prison in Korea for killing some dude. Your picture was plastered all over the news."

"Yeah dude, it was fucked up but I was exonerated. I was framed by two imbeciles."

"You still living in Clermont?"

"Yeah dude, living the life. How are you? You back in central Florida?"

"Yeah man, fresh off the boat. It's hard to adjust after sitting inside a cell for eight years but I'm loving the sunshine and I'm loving the freedom. I went to the beach for the first time in ages the other day."

"Nice dude. I wish I could get out there but there are no beaches in Orlando, just swamps and I am tied to my wife and job. Fun is a remnant of the past.

"But, ah, what's up? You want to chill some time? I can't get out much with the wife and kids but you can stop by sometime; I just have to clear it with the old lady."

"Ha, you got the old noose around your neck."

"I confess."

Yeah man, sounds good. We'll put some steaks on the grill have a couple of beers and talk about old times."

"I can't wait. I don't have many friends around here. I just have the wife and kid. It really would be nice to catch up."

By the way, I have a favor to ask of you."

"Yeah, shoot. I don't know what I can do for you because in terms of time and money, my hands are pretty tied. I finally paid off my fucking student loans and now I'm starting on my daughter's college fund. I'm telling you, she's is doing two years of community college and then a state school. A private education is far too expensive and you don't get shit out of it. These kids, they leave school with...Anyhow, what was it you were seeking?"

"Ah, I need you to stop by somewhere for me?"

"Where at bro and why?"

"Somewhere in Hiawassee."

"What the fuck is in Hiawassee besides nothing?"

"A girl, dude."

"Ah Seraj, my dude, back to your old ways."

"I've been in the slammer for years with no conjugal visits. The only thing I've been making love to is the memory of hot chicks that I used to know. This chick Amber Dawn, future or current stripper, knows nothing about my prison history. Hell, if she did, she might be more attracted to me and encourage me to get some more tattoos to make me look a little more hardcore."

"I gotta ask, Raj, what does this have to do with me?"

"Nothing, I promise. I'm going to head over there soon. I just want to make sure that the old man isn't home. Can you make sure that the he isn't home? He drives a 1999 Ford Taurus like a 93 year old lady. Can you just drive by and make sure that no Ford Taurus is in the driveway?"

"I don't have a problem with it but why don't you just call her to find out? Wouldn't that be simpler?"

"I know, right? She actually left her phone at the cafeteria at her school."

"Seraj, how old is this girl? Don't be going for that jailbait. You already served enough time."

"I know, I know; she's almost eighteen, but she's worth it and I deserve it. I suffered enough for two or three lifetimes so on her eighteenth birthday, I am going to annihilate that cooch."

"Damn man, take it easy. Let her live. I'm envious even though I'm not at the same time. I haven't looked forward to sex in years."

"Well, I finally have a partner besides my right hand man if you know what I'm sayin.'" Agreda mustered sympathetic laugher.

"You do deserve it; I will admit that. Well, if you really want me to drive by, it's not a problem. Hiawassee is mostly on the way and I'm just driving down a street, right?"

"Right."

"What's the address?"

"7226 Rex Hill Trail road."

"Cool, I'm on 408 now. The exit is coming up shortly. Looks like you got me just in time. Once I get off the highway and get onto the suburbs of Hiawassee, I'm going to have to plug in these coordinates."

Agreda stopped at the Shell along 438 to plug in the coordinates. He filled the tank of his Chevy Cruze since he was stopped, even though the price wasn't right, and continued on his way. The destination wasn't much farther past the Shell station.

When Agreda came down Rex Hill, he observed the empty driveway, phoned Seraj and warned his friend about getting into potential trouble.

"Don't worry" Seraj said. "I will wait. Lord knows I've become a master of doing just that."

"Right on man and definitely one day soon, we'll have to grab some brews or you can come over and meet the wifey and I really want you to meet my daughter. She's ten years old. It's crazy how fast the time passes."

They exchanged goodbyes.

Perhaps Eckhart is not back from work but the Private Investigator told me that he has a family and the wife ain't home either. I'm going to use that bit of intel and see what I can do at the witching hour. I should get back to the motel and get some rest.

Seraj made a couple more purchases before going back to the extended stay motel: a bottle of Jack from the liquor store and over the counter sleeping tablets from CVS. He watched the Florida Panthers get thrashed and gleeked the whiskey onto the covers.

I don't even like sports.

He changed the channels but nothing could hold his interest. He was too numb to get amusement from the sitcoms and so-called thrillers, so he popped two tablets as the instructions indicated and took a big swig from the bottle.

It wouldn't be so bad to die in my sleep but I want my fucking revenge. I'd hate to see chemicals put a stop to that.

Even with the antihistamine and depressant in his body, it took Seraj some time to fall asleep, till darkness set in, which was sometime after six. When he woke, he had one hell of a headache.

I can't fucking think right now. What time is it? 1:37.

He tried to fall asleep but there was too much rage in him.

The police, they could find this shit car I drive so easily and be on their way here. I could get raided and lose my chance that way. If they drag me out in the middle of the night without my guns and they find the evidence of the fire, I might be going back to the slammer for another couple of decades. I'll get out when I'm sixty. By then, Eckhart will have lived a full life. What revenge can I get?

He got up and dressed and give himself a quick look in the mirror. He wasn't quite used to seeing his own reflection. In prison, there weren't too many mirrors. A colleague once remarked that Seraj looked like "Ramses II, or some other Egyptian Pharaoh" and he could hear those words ring as he focused in on the trace of the scar that Gilbey left with a broken bottle.

I'm going to take my time with this one.

CHAPTER 5
NO NEED TO BE A MARTYR

"Stop me Before I Dream Again"

- ("Teenager in Love") Jim Steinman

"We're not killers" Jung-hae Jee said to his spouse, Ji-hyun. "We wouldn't be killing the woman, just the unborn baby inside" she replied.

"And how would we do that without hurting the woman? Even still, it's wrong."

"Do you want to live in this squalor for the rest of our lives? When we got married ten years ago, you promised me that we would get out of this. I'm tired of working my fingers to the bone?"

"So, do you just want me to get a ski mask and punch her in the stomach as hard as I can?"

"Don't be stupid. There are drugs we can mix into her drink. The longer we wait, the greater chance for more complications for the mother, so we'd better hurry."

"You know far too many evil things for a simple country girl. I don't want you to go anywhere near that woman. If I find out that something happened to that baby, you're going to join him."

"So, you're sure it's a boy?"

━╉╀╄━

When Elder Jee walked, he had a distinct limp and crooked his neck as a means to reduce the pain.

Accompanied by his daughter, Ji-soo, he examined the fields of tea leaves and nodded silently, keeping his observations to himself, but to look upon him for more than a moment was too see the sadness of an old man who was becoming aware that the prosperity he imagined for his family would soon be carried away in the yellow dust.

"We must give them a chance." When he spoke these words, he leaned more heavily upon his daughter's propping arm. "She is not my first choice but if we keep them apart, what future does their marriage or this family have?"

"Yes sir, but if she is pulling some kind of ruse…"

"Let's be honest, how many men in this village are worth doing the deed with?"

"Father!?"

"It's the truth. Even as a withered thing, I am far more capable of charming these young girls than these dim-witted youngsters.

"But, your words bear weight. How can we plan for the possibility that she is scamming us? Apparently, it wouldn't be the first time that this girl carried on in this way.

"We have to rely on Jin-hee to make the right decision but this woman is likely holding our future in her womb, so we must not drive a wedge between our house and that of the less blessed clan."

━╉╀╄━

Jin-hee took Bo-kyung out to where you could see Goheung and the spit of blue sea between it and Jeonnam.

"It's not the best place to take a pregnant girl but maybe you're not that far along."

"No, it's wonderful. I don't recall many serene places like this from my childhood, though I feel that if I should stand here long enough, they should come back to me. At some point in my life, I was given the city but looking back, looking forward and looking out on the water, I see that I made the wrong choice."

"Country people are not as simple as you think and even the most serene beauty can grow tiresome. People grow very bored here and do rash things. It's open and beautiful but the older you get, the more this place seems like a prison. You were right to leave and go for it in life."

"So many of my family members left to run restaurants and shops in bigger cities. Some came back but most stayed away even if the jobs were just mediocre. They were probably right.

"Family farms are dying out. They are being bought out by corporations who can do more with the land and turn large profits. My grandfather has turned down Gold Partners on several occasions because he wants a great future for the family, for me and my offspring really.

"Had he known that I would impregnate the first beautiful woman I saw…Sorry, I didn't mean…I mea…"

"It's okay. You shouldn't shy away from the truth, even if it is harsh and hey, you just called me beautiful so that's a plus. I just want to know. How do you feel about the future…with me?"

"The more I spend time with you, the more optimistic I feel about the future. As you know, the family was hoping for a different marriage, one I didn't want, with a prude I've known since grade school. Forty plus years with her would have been a disaster.

"Now the future is wide open again. I don't know how prepared I am to be a father or take this business over, so many people are counting on me and my mom is right; I'm still just a boy.

"This farm life takes its toll on the body. It turns those once nimble fingers into slow arthritic twigs. So, some things I'm looking forward to but with others, I'm looking for a way out.

"I don't know if we shouldn't sell the farm once my aunt and grandfather die. I could care less about the lot of those schemers. I want my grandfather to die thinking that we own our little niche but I want something different from life. I'm just not sure what.

"I want to go to Seoul with the bustling crowds, bright lights and big opportunities."

"You may be in for a rude awakening. Working the land is hard but I've lived in a goshiwon [extremely tiny room] and done regular fourteen hour days. Why do you think I jumped at the first chance to marry a rich man?"

"You know, Bo, that's something we have to talk about, what happened up in that mountain. I just don't understand how someone so lovely could marry a man that she didn't love."

"I had to take care of myself. I am an orphan. If I got sick, there was no one to take care of me. How long could I live in that cell and work those endless hours? I thought I might die there. It's hard to see any kind of a future when you're working at the department store and so when Jacob Jung pulled up in his 100,000$ car and promised to whisk me away, there really was nothing to decline."

"Did you kill him?"

"No, I had a foreign lover who thought he was acting in my best interests. He killed my husband in cold blood so that we could be together and still have the money. I never wanted that. I wouldn't have been able to live with the ghost of that. I wanted to keep the life of luxury and lose Jacob but I never would have done it at the expense of a life."

"Where is your lover now? Why are you apart?"

"He's in jail for the rest of his life for first degree murder."

"Did you visit him? Are you still in love?"

"I'm not a nun, Jin-hee. I'm not going to lie here and be a martyr. I need to move on with my life. Marriage with Jacob would have been a sacrifice and I was willing to make that sacrifice but I shouldn't be barred from happiness, should I? I want what I always wanted, a life."

"How are you getting along with the girl?" Jin Hee's mother asked.

"I think I could love her but I don't think I'll ever be really free with her. I'll always be thinking: what if she orchestrated the death of her husband? What if I'm the next mate to be devoured by the jaws of a praying mantis? Se-ra was vanilla and there would be little she could do to excite me, but she's the kind of girl that could get behind me and with the alliance of our families, I could have taken care of everyone.

"The night I had with Bo-kyung was magical but it was just that, one night and now everything your father and my grandfather worked for is mere dust. I wish I hadn't thought with my loins but she was like an angel fallen to earth."

"Ugh, trust me, we are all wringing our hands and stamping our heels at the fact that you made an irreparable mistake but you have little choice now but to proceed forward, albeit with caution. You might think of this girl as damaged goods but in the eyes of all potential suitresses, you are just as damaged. No young woman of good esteem and health wants to marry a man who has a love child with another woman. You've made your bed; now you must lie in it."

"Thank you for understanding."

"Let's get one thing straight. I'm not telling you what you did is okay. I'm just giving you the maximum support so that you can do what is in your power to rectify the situation."

⊱⊰

The party of the groom proceeded behind Jin-hee, who with two hands held up the paper veil. Country musicians plucked the kaya-geum and blew on the daeguem as he approached the altar and what stood before it. Slow and dutifully he went to it. At what a westerner might call a "side altar" with a folding screen with print-ed images of flowers, Jin-hee placed a wooden duck as an offering to the bride's family.

He then walked up to the side of the central elevated altar that was on display for the gathered family and friends and faced stage left from where his bride arrived in a resplendent wedding hanbok in all of its heft and many folds of blue, red and white. This hanbok concealed Bo-kyung's rotund figure so that she looked mostly as she had before the fertilization of her egg.

Jin-hee washed his hands in a bowl for the sake of symbolic pu-rification. His bride washed her hands on the opposite side of the altar. The bridegroom joined his bride to be at the center of the altar where the low table was with the food for the ritual on it: rice cakes, chestnuts. They bowed to each other and took their seats to become the lone spectacle.

Taking up the wine gourd from the table, Bo-kyung poured it into the two cups that were also on the table instead of drinking directly from the gourd cup. Locking arms, the two lovers drank, embraced in a kiss and the important members of both families joined their family at the table to complete the ceremony.

At the reception, you could tell which people belonged to which family by measuring the degree of joy or resignation on their faces. The Lees were overjoyed and danced as if the whole world were dancing with them. This is about as close as a Korean wedding came to a Chasidic one. The Jees on the other hand had hands on hips. They were content to sit back and survey the scene like a 13 year old ginger with acne and braces at the middle school sock hop.

In fifty years, no woman witnessed such unbridled ecstasy on the face and in the movements of Aunt Na-ra. She introduced herself enthusiastically as the "motherly representative" of the bride and bowed and shook hands with the reluctant Jees.

The newlyweds did the best they could to preserve the luster of what is generally a magical evening but having revealed themselves several times before to that point of ultimate vulnerability, it was less than enchanted. Moreover, Jin-hee found his bride's growing belly and swelling legs to be an obstacle to his arousal but he knew that once he got into the act, all would be fine. This would be the smallest of obstacles to hurdle in the preservation and ascension of the Jee name.

After the act, they lied in the stillness, doing what they could to hold onto this fragmented moment, not quite what it should have been, as it passed. They did what they could to resist sleep, especially Jin-hee, knowing that once they awoke, they would have to start out on their way to blaze the trail for the future.

At 3 AM, Bo-kyung woke and clutched her flank and sides in pain. The frantic movement was enough to wake her husband who watched the outline of her whirl through the dark. When he could hear her faint complaints of the pain, he muttered:

"I knew I punished it but damn."

"It's not funny." When Jin-hee heard the severity of the tone, he perked up as his wife hurried to the bathroom like a cockroach scurrying back under the fridge.

"I'm bleeding! Goddammit Jee, I'm bleeding! What have you done?!"

"Where are you bleeding from?" Jin-hee asked.

"My vagina, stupid!"

"How can you be menstruating? You're halfway through your pregnancy."

"Exactly, you fucking moron! Call a fucking ambulance!"

Exercising prudence, Jin-hee called for an ambulance and refused to contact any familiar member on either side to avoid a drama show in the ER. By the side of his woman, he listened to the phlegmatic physician explain that high levels of Mifepristone and Misoprostol were found in her blood, meaning she either induced her own abortion or someone slipped her the pill without her knowing.

Jin-hee's mind oscillated between pondering who might have done this and whether this was his ticket out of a bad marriage. He teetered on the threshold between revenge and flight. Yes, he loved this woman, but the love was not overwhelming. If he needed, he could have found the strength to carry on and from that strength, he could move onto a higher love and thusly, a better existence.

It was then, with his new bride wailing that he stepped into the hall to call his mom, who promptly answered with sleep still in her voice.

"Are you thinking about me on your honeymoon?" she asked jokingly. "I'm touched but creeped out as well."

"It's Bo-kyung; she's bleeding out the baby."

"What do you mean?" The tone in Ji Soo's voice quickly shifted from jocularity to horror.

"She had some kind of miscarriage; I'm not quite sure, really. She started complaining of cramps and then bled into the toilet but they did a sonogram and the baby is definitely gone.

"How's Bo-kyung holding up?"

"Poorly. She's been crying her eyes out for the last five hours."

"It's important for you to be with her now. I will notify everyone in both families. I'll make the important calls tonight and word will spread.

"I know this is a very hard moment for you and I don't want you to think of me as cold, but you need to think. If you want out of this marriage and a life with Bo-kyung, you should decide soon while you can still get it annulled. The longer this thing goes, the harder it is to undo. Even if you can't get it annulled, you can still get divorced and begin anew."

"It's like you were hoping for this to happen. Did you or someone else in the family plan this?"

"Just think logically. I would never do anything like that and would report any such person to the police immediately. I'm just telling you there is no need to be a martyr."

When Jin-hee hung up the phone, he couldn't ignore the irony that his mother's words mirrored what Bo-kyung had said about her own life in the clearing. If he left her now and had the marriage annulled, he would only be following her way, but who would he be if he turned a blind eye to a grave injustice committed against a woman, albeit a convicted criminal and potential killer? Se-ra, as plain as she was, would be waiting for him but with a dowry like that she wouldn't be waiting for much longer. For a life with someone as stunning as Jin-hee, she could overlook the scandal and the controversy. She didn't need him pure; she'd be willing to receive the bejeweled vessel in its most broken form.

⊨ ⊨

Bo-kyung went back to the hotel the next morning to gather her belongings. She was trapped in a cloud of surreality as she passed the curious eye of the concierges. In the suite, she gathered her belongings and lamented the fact that she couldn't pass just a few more moments of sweetness in that still kind bed. Jin Hee waited outside in the car and stared at the digital clock, doing his best not to think. The temperature was just above freezing and the cool air felt good against his face.

The face of the future had been distorted into something freakish entirely. Jin-hee was now doomed to spend the remainder of his existence fighting the demons of this calamity or running from them.

When Bo-kyung got in the car, they just sat there waiting for the other to speak of the horrors that had just passed or something to cut through the awful silence. "What now" or "what's next?" seemed to be the logical questions to ask but they remained as the mists of morning dissipated.

Sullen Jin-hee drove up 27 from Eojeon-Ri, through the island of Sorokdo, cut across Goheung and continued to the Jee home on the mainland. The same eyes which observed her with disdain at the wedding now darted away in pity. How quickly word spreads.

"I can't live like this!" Jin-hee complained when they returned to the room.

"We're going to put all of this behind us but we have to be strong" he continued. The one thing that great sorrow has in common with joy is that it will pass shortly but what lasts forever is glory. We need to find out who did this and punish them to the fullest measure."

"Revenge...Most people think that my forced miscarriage is a kind of justice for the sins of my past."

"So, you don't want revenge? What do you want?"

"I want to eviscerate whoever did this to us, to my womb. I'm just tired of fighting and this quest for vengeance is going to take a lot out of us. Maybe what's best for your family is that we sweep this under the rug."

"Nonsense. If someone did this, they would risk doing it again. I think someone in the family really doesn't want a marriage with yours and what that entails. Today, we mourn and rest; tomorrow; we fight."

CHAPTER 6
EVERYTHING IN ITS RIGHT PLACE

"What I've felt,
What I've known
Never shined through in what I've shown"

- ("The Unforgiven") Metallica

After five hours of driving from Daejeon to Boseong, Woo-jin needed a drink, or two. He stopped by the nearest restaurant for some beef soup with glass noodles and pounded back a bottle of soju.

The other customers in the restaurant observed Woo-jin intently because not only was he guzzling liquor, he was doing so alone and he looked like somewhat of a wild man with his hair grown long and his facial hair undisturbed for the last several days.

He paid his tab, tried a force a smile to the waitress who was much better at it than he, and then went to the hotel where he had booked a reservation.

Why the fuck did I book a reservation at the bottom of Goheung? All the action is north of this island in Boseong. I need to find a motel there and find what this girl is up to but first, I must relax and take in this beautiful view of the pacific.

Woo-jin greeted an old woman passing by and then was amazed by the sight of one of those ghosts of his past, slightly aged but still beautiful, stumbling through the hotel with her heavy bags, somehow able to keep from falling. Even in this moment, her grace shone through, so much so that Woo-jin wanted to step forward from his obstructed dwelling behind the a column and help her on her way, but he just watched. Before she could step out the door, he noticed her grown belly and swollen ankles and could confirm that she was indeed pregnant.

Why is she in such a hurry? I would follow them but there is only one road out of here and they're going to notice.

With the lights on in his modest room, Woo-jin called Hye-jeong.

"Are you calling to apologize?" she asked in a tone that was slightly playful.

"I was hoping that you would forget my behavior the other day. I hate to make excuses but I've run my life into a nosedive while you've managed it so well." Woo-jin knew that a compliment was the best way out of a full blown act of contrition.

"Aren't you on vacation? You already miss life at the station. What's going on?"

"Don't freak out but guess who I just saw at my hotel?"

"I'm waiting."

"Bo-kyung."

"Did you reacquaint yourself or did you drool at her from afar again?"

"Don't ask questions you already know the answer to."

"This is not an open case and you're not working, right?"

"Just snooping."

"Just as long as you know: if anything happens, you are on your own. Is there anything else?"

"I'll be in touch."

"Please don't be. I can't believe you've gone to Boseong to re-live…Just don't ruin things for yourself. Enjoy your vacation and I'll see you when you get back here."

Woo-jin was disappointed that his former partner had no de-sire or curiosity regarding the familiar ghosts that had wandered away from their manor. This slight meant that Woo-jin would pur-sue relentlessly what was left of the Jacob Jung case.

Well, here is the softest applause to Hye-jeong for being able to move so swiftly forward and never look back. Good for her. Now she gets to walk through the world with light steps and smiles but I'm already battered and broken and I can't be that person that sings and holds my grandson in his arms. I need glory in one form of another, either through this book or through this case because only miraculous glory can vindicate a life so far fallen. When I catch the Oleander in the act of poisoning an otherwise good soul, and I get my name in the paper, they'll all have to agree that I had to live this way and that there was a reason why everything went so wrong when it seemed that it should have gone right. They'll say "Woo-jin was a hero. Even though he was a lousy father and drunk, he saved a life." Redemption, that's what I'm seeking.

He checked into the hotel, lay on the bed and plotted his investigation.

⊷+⊶

At 3AM, the houses of Hiawassee were all sleeping. Seraj stopped at the same shell station that Agreda used earlier to finalize his plan.

If this shit ends up grizzly, the first thing Agreda is going to do when he reads the paper is snitch to the police. Even if I ditch this phone, he'll swear to a jury of my peers on a stack of bibles high enough to stand on and head-butt Yao Ming that I called him to scope out the place and I'm not going to kill this dude and I can't take any loose ends, so how the fuck am I going to approach this?

Let me just drive by and scope out the driveway...should've never made that loose fucking end.

Seraj drove up North Hiawassee, cut left at Clarcona and laughed madly at the quaint suburban homes.

So much work to build high castles, moats and drawbridges but safe from nothing in the end. There is nothing more beautiful than a trebuchet to assail the wall or a wrench forced into a machine. I'm the fucking wrench.

And there it was, the quaint home on Rex Hill Trail.

Cars probably in the garage. What if the kids and wife are home? Wouldn't be right. It's not my night. I've got to figure out what happened to that church and what they know.

For all Seraj knew, the police could be perched outside of his home in Apopka but he knew the way and wanted to gather just a couple more hours of sleep before heading back out to Sarasota to inspect his work at Saint Florian's.

When he arrived home, he woke his father who had fallen asleep on the couch.

"Seraj is that you?!" he asked with a rolled up newspaper in his hand. "The police have been looking for you. Where you go?"

"Out."

"That's not a good answer. You answer me, boy."

"What the fuck you gonna do with that newspaper? The only place that newspaper is going to end up is up your ass, old man."

"Did I raise a monster?"

"I'm not there, yet."

"My God, what did prison make my boy?"

"Don't worry it will all be over soon. Too bad, you'll be left alone in this shit sty washing dishes for that greaseball."

"How can this be? You're all I have left and now you're saying these things. I don't understand."

"Well, since I ain't coming back here, I mine as well tell you that the two people who put an innocent man behind bars are living a stone's throw from your door."

"Stone's throw?"

"Fuck dad, you didn't really learn shit for English in the last twenty years. They live close to you."

"And so you mean to hurt these men?"

"To put it mildly."

"Why can't you rebuild your life?"

"Where? In this fucking dump? In a motel?

"You're a handsome boy and you have a college education. You have a future."

"That's where you're wrong dad? My future was taken from me. It might only seem like eight years but it's enough time to make me into something that I wouldn't want to be for the next thirty years. Maybe you're right. Maybe I've become a monster."

"You can change. I worked hard for you to become something, not to become a criminal."

"You're a fucking sandnigger, dad. Your people are the most bloodthirsty revenge seeking savages on the planet. They'll stone a bitch to death for showing some fucking ankle. That ain't justice. What I'm going to do is fucking justice."

"Just let it go and no, this is not my religion."

"I can't do that. You talk foolishly, old man. You make it seem like someone insulted my shoes. Men conspired to end my life and they are walking freely, playing with their kids and living in peace. I cannot let that be."

"Then, talk to the police."

"You really think I'll get justice in a court of law. Because that worked so well the last go round."

"You can try, Seraj!" The wheels did start to turn in his head. Maybe going on the level would be the proper way but how could he trust in a system that buried him?

Wouldn't that be the ultimate justice, seeing those infidels wear the grey uniform I had to wear? But how? What can I prove? Time is of the essence. They're going to find out that I burned that church down.

"So, the police just want to talk to me, dad? They just want to take me out to dinner and ask a few questions? They're probably curious about whether I enjoy long walks on the beach.

"Dad, fuck this; I need to go to bed." The father understood and in his clothes, Seraj slept a troubled sleep. He cranked up the AC unit in his room to the maximum output so that it felt like a heavy wind was blowing. In the morning light, he awoke, a habit of prison, though he desperately wanted to sleep away the morning and the afternoon. He recalled and was disturbed by the final vivid dream of a storm wind blowing him through the open bedroom with his right hand clutching the sill for dear life. A voice from on high called and asked him if he wanted to go to which he replied with a solemn "no."

Fuck, it's true. I'm not ready to die and this bloody quest will surely mean my end. My dad's right; I need a better plan than this but I sure as hell ain't going to walk into the precinct and answer some questions. He decided to call the very detective he insulted the day before.

"Hello, this is Seraj. Am I speaking to Detective Shore?"

"My man, Seraj" Shore answered, surprised by the pleasant tone.

"Ah yeah, this still detective Shore?"

"Hey man, thanks for taking the time to call."

"No problem, I…"

"I know you're usually busy screwing my wife. Better start talking 'fore I take that comment to heart."

"Words of distress, you understand?"

"Man, I ain't gotta wife. Otherwise, you might be one hurting dude."

"… You believe me, right?"

"Of course I do. Shit it's early; I didn't get much sleep last night. Hey Seraj, I'm in Sarasota but I'd love to come meet you this afternoon. You want to go to Cici's, grab a cheap slice of buff chick pizza and talk about what these guys did to you?"

"I'm not certain why we need to meet face to face."

"Man, don't you think it's better to meet face to face?"

"Can't you see how a man that spent eight years behind bars for a crime he didn't commit wouldn't want to grab some slices with a man who has the power to do that to me again?"

"That's fair, Seraj, but don't you want to see some justice done? We can get this thing done if you can do me a solid and come down to the station."

"Knock it off. I'm not going to put myself in police custody that easily."

"Well, that's one more day the people that did this to you walk free."

"Make sure you check out Eckhart and Father Gilbey? Them the two dudes that put me here. I gotta PI already on them but I want as many eyes on these crooked bitches as possible."

⟞⟝

"King, weren't you saying that there was something off about Father Gilbey?" Shore asked.

"I just suggested, even to him, that he is different" King replied. "What's up?"

"I don't know what to make of it. Seraj believes that not only did Michael Gilbey frame him for the murder, he burnt down his own church."

"Sounds cool but we followed that rabbit hole and the motel register in Tampa checked out."

"He could have paid someone to do it."

"For what purpose?"

"To set up Seraj."

"You believe that?"

"I'm entertaining the idea. We need to figure out why this dude was exculpated in Korea."

"You speak Korean?"

"Of course not, but we can get a translator."

"Yeah, that's really going to fly with the captain. Translators cost money, probably fifty bucks an hour and if you need one great but do you really want to tell Rowan that we're spending all this money to chase a kind of bizarre lead."

"Well, this entire case is bizarre. How long and how much money do you think it would take to dig into Seraj's claims?"

"More than I care to invest. Our mission is to find Seraj and put him under the light and ask him hard questions, not dig up conspiracy theories."

"Guilty or innocent, this kid has been hardened by life in a Korean slammer and we've got nothing on him. He's not going to talk if he burnt down that church. I'm going up to Tampa to some Korean BBQ joint to find a translator."

"What are you going to tell the captain?!"

"That the unit's best is out in the field."

"Fuck yes, Arirang" Detective Shore said, rejoicing at the spread of Banchan before him. "I don't even know what these red squares are but they are rocking my miniature world."

"You like?" The middle aged Korean waitress asked.

"I love it" Shore assured her. He devoured his Dolsot Bibimbap like a champ, wiped his mouth and made the final proposition to the waitress who was possibly the owner.

She goes a little heavy on the green eye shadow but she's just thick enough in the thighs for an Asian chick to be my type.

When detective Shore made his proposition, the lady squinted even though the sun was not in her eyes, calling into question her English proficiency.

"I'm not a translator" she said "but I can give you a number."

"The problem is that I can't go with a professional because I need a really good rate."

"My niece will give you a good rate. She's busy. She's a pharmacy student at The University of South Florida."

"Smart family.

"I guess. Anyway, call her number. What you need translation for?"

"I need to contact someone overseas."

Kim Min-Hee was much cuter than Detective Shore expected but as the middle aged adult, he made sure to keep his eyes from admiring her full rounded cheekbones. Like her aunt, she had a curvier figure than most of her compatriots.

Detective Shore sat her down at his desk and caught the stink-eye from Detective King.

"Alright, so firstly congratulations" Shore said. "You've been on the clock since you got here. Now, you'll also get paid for the time it takes me to explain this job."

"Yes."

"Detective King and I are trying to work with law enforcement in South Korea to find out some information."

"Ok."

"Have you done this before?"

"A little bit."

"That's fine. I didn't expect you to be completely polished. We understand that that comes with the territory of paying a lower rate."

"That's fine. This is much more than I can make at work study."

"The first thing I need to tell you is that the work we do here is confidential. Don't come back home with your 100$ in hand and tell your family the story of everything interesting that you heard; understood?"

"Of course."

"So, this case is really unique and begins in your country. Actually, were you born in Korea?"

"Yes."

"Okay. Well, there was a murder in your country when you were a teenager, involving a couple that had just gotten married. A foreigner, a man from Florida, was put in jail for that crime and has since been released and is now back in Florida. He now claims that two other men, not from Florida, but currently residing in different cities Florida, framed him for the murder. Do you understand 'framed?'"

"No, sorry."

"They may have committed the murder and made it look like this other man did it. That's what he claims anyhow, so now for what I need you to do: We need to get all the relevant files and other pertinent information from law enforcement in your country so I've gone ahead and got the number for the police department in a city called Daejeon, where the murder occurred. I need you to translate for me. Firstly, as you know, I'm trying to obtain records involving the case including forensic files, court records and things like that. What I really need to know is why the court of appeals overturned Seraj Mukhtari's murder conviction and what the case files say about two other foreigner, James Eckhart and Michael Gilbey." The whole time Min-Hee had been jotting down notes.

Sitting at her desk sifting through reports, Hye-jeong was surprised to hear her secretary announce that she was receiving a call from a translator in Florida regarding an old murder case. Without much consideration, she answered.

"Hello?"

"Hello, this is Kim Min-Hee. I am a university student and translator. I have been hired by the police department of Sarasota to obtain records involving the case of the murder of Ji-Sung Jung, also known as Jacob Jung."

"Sure, do you have a fax number or E-mail?" Kim Min-Hee gave the fax number that Detective Shore instructed her to provide.

"Is there anything else?"

"Yes, Detective Shore wanted to know if there was any information that was not in the reports."

"It was the strangest, most high-profile case I've ever investigated, so I don't really know where to begin. The person you really should talk to, though I would hate to inspire him, is detective Woo-jin. He's down in Boseong for a Holiday but I can put him in touch with you. He investigated the case with me and to say the least, he retains a keen interest in it, though it is officially closed."

"My detective wants to know why Seraj Mukhtari was let go."

"It's in the report but we personally don't feel that he should have been. A jury eventually found that the forensic evidence or lack thereof was in the favor of the foreigner. We know that a murder has been committed because the skull fractures are consistent with blunt force trauma but our forensics team did a poor job and we weren't able to find any evidence that Seraj had been to the mountain that day. An overzealous officer probably planted evidence, which made it look like a set up and that obviously played a part."

"But you still think he did it?"

"He maybe wasn't on the mountain that day. I believe he was, but we believe that several individuals, including his own wife, conspired to have him murdered for the insurance payout."

"Why was she never prosecuted for murder, just the lesser charges?"

"Beauty can save us from nearly everything, even jail. Also, once again, there wasn't enough evidence linking her to the murder. She went to trial and there was a large public outcry against her but ultimately she went free after serving such little time because the evidence was circumstantial at best."

"What can you say about James Eckhart and Father Gilbey?"

"Father? Is he a priest?" Hye-jeong asked. After consulting Shore, Kim Min-Hee confirmed that he had been recently ordained and that his parish had just burnt down.

"Recently ordained."

"He was an interesting individual. We believe that he was somehow involved in the murder of Jacob Jung because he was constantly in touch with the widow and the convicted via cell phone calls and text messages. Ultimately, what set us back was that we could find no real motive for Gilbey. We tried the jealousy angle but the kid was so rough around the edges and so unwilling to appear fashionable that he seemed completely unmoved by thoughts of romance. We did not charge him nor did we charge his friend, Eckhart, who seemed to be a genuinely good guy. Eckhart was romantically involved with the widow before the murder but they had gone their separate ways. At least, we couldn't prove otherwise. If he did anything, he was sucked in but if he did play a part and was complicit, then he too deserved some hard time in the slammer, maybe not as much as the ringleader but punished nonetheless.

"Are there any other questions?"

"Detective Shore wants to know if he could obtain a criminal record for the widow and the two foreigners prior to the murder."

"That's the strange thing about the case. None had any priors the night of the incident, which is probably part of the reason they got acquitted."

"Alright, well if you could just fax or e-mail everything over, that would be great."

"And please understand that this case has thousands of pages of files. Luckily, because of its high profile nature and the period in which it happened, most of what we have has been digitized to PDF format."

What Detective Shore would not be told was that the bulk of documents were in Hangul and remained untranslated. He would need Kim-Min Hee further.

Woo-jin couldn't just show up at the Lee or Jee family farm and ask questions. He needed plenty of liquid courage and a designated driver for that so he went to Boseong police station and flashed his badge.

An older detective, Min-hwang Jeong, invited him to a spot of tea in a corner office.

"How may we be of service to you?" the older man asked with sincere kindness in his eyes.

"I was one of the original investigators in the Jacob Jung death case."

"Oh yes. It was quite sad what happened to that boy. You must be troubled by the fact that whoever did this is walking free right now."

"Yes, it's occupied a large part of my mind for the last seven years but we just didn't have a whole lot of evidence. There was no weapon and no DNA at the mountainside save for that of the deceased."

"So, you must be here for the young widow who has gone to her family farm."

"Of course."

"She's got the whole town stirred up. Well, this time it's not her fault. I have to be careful what I say here even to a fellow officer as there have been some recent developments that are extremely sensitive. She's just been married off to a man, presumably because she was to bear his child."

"Glad you guys are keeping tabs. I worry that this girl could bite the head off of another mate."

"I hardly call what we're doing keeping tabs. This is a small town. We have some tourism related incidents that require some investigation but most of these tourists have come to look at lush plains, reeds and fields of tea. Mostly, this little thriving town of ours relies on order and this force not upsetting the balance.

"I don't see the presence of a dainty thirty year old girl as having a killer on the loose. Her lover, a good boy in his own right has made a grave mistake in my opinion by impregnating her, but he knows what she is.

"Can I ask you, have you been sent on official police business?"

"I'm on vacation."

"You come to police stations on vacation. I'm sorry we have no postcards." The old man laughed and expected Woo-jin to join him but he did not. "Is there any way an old man with a satisfied mind can convince you to put the past away?"

"This case is all I've got left. Once it's said and done, I can rest in peace." Sympathizing with the overt sullenness in Woo-jin's eyes, the old man tried to offer some comfort.

"Be careful what you wish for." The old man took on the air of a thin Buddha. "If the case is all you have left, don't be so eager to finish because when the book closes, you will have nothing and you will only have the final work of dying, which is the worst labor of all.

"My work is never finished. Irresolution is the key to my vitality. I have my own pathetic tea garden that I tend to and there are my grandchildren. At some point, I will stop watching them grow and helping them develop because one way or another, I won't be able to anymore.

"Don't you have some hobbies? Don't you get some joy from sitting back with the bros, knocking back sojus, reminiscing about the old times?"

"Sorry sir, but thinking about the old times just plunges me into despondency because I think of everything I let slip through my hands."

"You're rather neurotic for a detective. You must be nearing your time. I'm sorry that life hasn't turned out for you the way you wanted it to. I guess I should be grateful that things fell into the right place for me.

"I shouldn't do this but I'm going to help you out, today. I will warn you that if you disgrace me, I will see to it that your star falls just the same, though by your scruffy look, you seem to be someone who doesn't have much to lose. I suppose I shouldn't threaten but I would say that if you handle this sensitive information in the wrong way, you will be worthy of the miserable lot you have earned in life."

"You have my word; it's all I have left."

"I thought this case was all you had left."

"Touché."

"Well, honestly, I'm not telling you for your edification. I've already explained our ways and I don't believe we have the will, skill or manpower to solve this one and let me emphasize, we are not counting on you to be a cowboy and solve this for us. We just need every pair of eyes we can get. Also, soon enough this information will become public, inevitably, through some leak to the media if the country still cares, so time is of the essence because in my long distance studies, once the media gets its hands on something, it spoils it rotten."

"Well, what is it?" Woo-jin's eyes had lost their sadness and he now had the gleam of a playful puppy waiting for the tennis ball to be thrown.

"A few of our officers were called to the local hospital last night to investigate the miscarriage of Bo-kyung Jee. Of course, the investigating officers were interested, knowing her history and wondering whether the White Oleander had another trick up her sleeve but in light of the heaviness of the tragedy, they probably wanted to skirt out of there as fast as possible after offering some cheap condolence.

"You'll have to forgive me; I'm an old man and talk in circles around company. I was almost thirty when I went to the academy and so I must wait just a little longer in order to collect my pension and be on my way. I am of little use to this department. I was never full of piss and vinegar and never would have survived a post in a bustling city but my digressions continue farther. I need to get to the point before I croak and leave my eager guest hanging.

"The attending physician determined that certain abortion drugs – I forget the names – were in the system of Bo-kyung Lee and so now the flower thought to be poisonous has been poisoned.

"We have no real leads. Any person in the Jee family could have done this. They had a lot to lose through this deal. It's a small town and everyone knows that the Jees had been counting on their youngest and brightest star to marry into a family of import, to save the farm and let some of the old hands relax. This pregnancy eradicated the certain hope of that and so by terminating the pregnancy, a Jee would have rekindled the hope that the marriage would be annulled and Jin-hee Jee would marry the first intended and they would push the ghost of Bo-kyung and the unborn back into the closest and live happily ever after.

"So, that is a very good place to start. Of course, you can always have the vacation that a normal person would indulge in and visit the green tea fields and sample some of the finest tea in the world but if I were a betting man, I'd say that you'll do nothing like that. You'll go straightaway to the farm and investigate but whatever you do, one thing is for certain, I didn't tell you shit.

"Another cup?"

CHAPTER 7
ROUND HERE

"The sun is drowning in the flood"

- ("Say It Ain't So") Weezer

There was fog in the low valley that night and when Woo-jin happened upon the Jee farm, he felt as though he were entering the threshold of a ghost tale. Through the fields he walked and in the thin fog, his own ghosts seemed to rise up in his memory but when he tried to hold onto the good moments like the vivid image of him tossing his infant daughter in the air, the joy vanished into a nightmarish recollection of equal impression like the revelation that his wife loved him no more or that the bottle had caused his life to simply pass him by.

Travelling up the front steps, Woo-jin left the ghosts brooding behind him in the foggy fields. He sighed and thought of turning back, but to what? Another bottle? Another chance at meeting a replacement for the love he lost some years ago? A date with the motel bedroom and the array of softcore pornography he could cycle through until he was gratified enough to lament the ghosts until sleep passed over him?

He knocked on the sturdy wooden door of the main house and finally began to ask himself whether the fog was the only reason no one could be seen working in the fields during Ujeon, the peak tea gathering season.

An old lady answered the door and scowled at Woo-jin. When he informed her that he was a detective, the scowl only grew in intensity to the point that Woo-jin had to turn around to make sure that the sun hadn't dried out the fog.

"We're not killers here" the old lady said. "We did everything we could to support that reckless girl, even paid for most of the wedding and now the talk of the town is slanderous. If you want to know what happened, the bitch really went off the deep end and poisoned herself. She was already nuts and prison can turn you worse, so you just go on and ask your questions and leave."

"So, you're saying she was poisoned?"

"No, I'm saying she poisoned herself."

"Is that something you believe or is that a point of fact?"

"Stop putting words in my mouth. I'm just guessing what happened is all. Jin-hee told me that she miscarried and had abortion drugs in her."

"That's the husband?"

"Where are you from?"

"Daejeon."

"Why the hell did the send some city cop from hundreds of kilometers away to investigate us like we're Ji-Jeon Pa? Are you from the NIS?"

"When you come down from your hysteria lady, I'm going to need you to find Jin-hee for me."

"You think he did this to his own wife?! You're sicker than the perpetrator."

"Lady, you're starting to get on my nerves. I didn't say that. Stop putting words in *my* mouth. I only want to see the boy and what I want to ask him is none of your business, so I would prefer if you would just run along and fetch Jin-hee."

The car would have to serve as the interview room with Woo-jin in the driver seat and Jin-hee in the passenger.

"This is the best you could do?" Jin-hee asked.

"Well, you've got acres of space and not an inch of privacy on this farm. This car has served me well in conducting my private interviews out in the field."

"Well, it smells like a cigarette factory."

"I forget. You farm people are used to that fresh air. It's a good life. Country ajummas die in their sleep in their nineties. City ajummas have soot in their lungs and die with a mop in their hands. They should bury them clutching that mop like soldiers who are buried with their rifles."

"You're not a suspect, Jin-hee, not yet anyhow but I'm hoping you can point me in the right direction." Woo-jin was trying to look tough by playing with the toothpick in his mouth.

"I don't know. Why are my family automatically the suspects?"

"Because nobody in the Lee family has a motive. That baby was their payday."

"We're not getting divorced, by the way."

"And why is that Jin? Are you in love?"

"Because I'm a man of principle like my grandfather before me."

"I appreciate the candor and I'm sure others do as well but in my humble opinion, you're much too young to know what kind of man you are. I've expressed a lot of rage in my day; it helped me in my job. However, rage never carries the day. You think anger is going to propel you to do great things and that you're going to blow past all the calm people in life but you end up just burning yourself into utter exhaustion."

"I never said anything about anger. I'm talking about principle here. I'm determined to do the right thing, here and now. Are you telling me I should just leave her? Man, absolutely nobody believes the two of us should be together."

"I don't have an opinion either way. As a fellow male, who has had his share of women problems, believe me, and parental problems, I try to look out for my brethren. You're not some tyrant of a man who goes storming around looking for fights and loose women. Good men shouldn't be lost on things as abstract as principle.

"But, if you really want to be a man of principle, as you claim, then you'll find out who created the chasm in your life but really though, from a personal standpoint, really ask yourself, do you want to be with this woman forever?

"Sorry for taking it to story mode, but when I was young, I wanted to live the life of a bachelor. I was a rootless thing and I never really thought much of it but the older I got, the more people prodded me about not having a wife or wife to be, as though I were openly living in sin or driving on the wrong side of the road. Finally, I succumbed to pressure and married a schoolteacher. I mean she was decent girl, but whenever I went wayward, she scolded me like a child and what did I expect? I never loved this woman. I loved the idea of satisfying my mother and being rooted to a spot and having people who relied on me but marriage in the modern world really isn't for people who want to take half-measures. Are you willing to give your life to this woman? Are you willing to have your whole family hate you for it?"

"What the hell is she doing?" Jin-hee asked.

Ji-hyun Do took a solitary spot out in the field and closed her eyes under the brilliance of the sun. Titling her head back, she stretched her arms out like a scarecrow and yawped.

"I don't know" Woo-jin said. It's your whacky family; you tell me."

"I've never seen her do this before. She's one of the normal ones."

"That's saying a lot." Woo-jin rolled his eyes. "Let's get her attention."

"I would but I feel like I'm interrupting something important."

"I'm not sure if she's praying or breaking down. Do you mind if I smoke?"

"Yes, I mind. Being in this car already makes me feel like I'm smoking a cig. You know what, while you're at it, roll a window down so a man can breathe."

"I resent being told how to treat my own car."

"I didn't ask to be here."

"I'm not selling you vacuum cleaner attachments. I'm trying to solve this crime for you and the wife that you're trying to stay with."

"Do it with cleaner lungs. Might clear your mind." They stopped their quarrelling to observe the remainder of Ji-hyun Do's religious performance. She knelt in the field and began to pray, presumably trying to cover herself in the fog,

"Blow winds!" she cried but the winds remained quiet. Woo-jin and Jin-hee watched the show for a little while longer but the prayer turned to sobbing and when the sobbing became uncontrollable, Woo-jin and Jin-hee joined the shrieker in the field. They stood over her, not certain that he knew they were around him. Jin-hee touched her consolingly on the shoulder. The woman clasped his hand, which remained on her shoulder, and she got up slowly as though a demon had been exorcised through all that wailing.

"How could they do this?" she said. Woo-jin took keen interest. "You guys were entering the prime of your life and like Rumpelstiltskin, they snatched your baby from you."

"Who's they?" Woo-jin asked.

"Who are you?" she asked Woo-jin.

"Detective Woo-jin."

"The mighty star of this family has fallen and my pitiful husband is to blame."

"What are you saying, exactly?" Jin-hee asked.

"I found a small package in the trash bin of our bedroom that was strangely sealed. I opened its contents and found empty bottles of medicine with instructions for usage; they were abortion drugs. My husband must have ordered them and administered them to your lovely wife somehow." Jin-hee took off like a prized horse for the glory of the winner's circle, scraping past the camellia sinensis as he went. Woo-jin was too old and out of shape to keep pace with such a brawny youth but try he did. The wooden door to Jung-hae's tiny farmhouse swung violently behind Jin-hee to its ajar position.

By the time Woo-jin entered the cabin's raised threshold over the foundation of fortified logs, he could hear loud banging inside.

He's going to kill the bastard. Perhaps, I should let him.

To the best of his ability, Woo-jin carried himself through the house and was panting heavily now. Hard objects like pots and pans were flying through the air and Jung-hae, whom Woo-jin had never seen before was running from spot to spot like a cornered squirrel.

"Order!" Woo-jin called, something that instantly would have reminded him of his schoolteacher ex-wife. Jin-hee did not heed his call and finally cut off the old man in the corner of the bedroom to begin flailing at him wildly.

"I'm innocent!" Jung-hae cried as he received the blow.

Woo-jin allowed a shot or two to get in but then pulled back the assailant to end the reign of domestic madness.

"The man deserves to be heard out" Woo-jin said. The sound of a door being opened could be heard again. This time the shrieker, Ji-hyun, came in and like Woo-jin, pleaded for Jin-hee to have mercy on her husband.

Jin-hee stopped his attack, mostly because Woo-jin had him in a bear-hug but he commanded his uncle to stay down and the man obeyed. Woo-jin took a deep breath and spoke to Ji-hyun who was shrieking again.

"Where did you find the medicine?"

"It's in the trash by the basin."

"It's high time we call in the local police. Don't touch anything. We all need to get out of this house. We've already contaminated the crime scene. Ahjussi, wait in the car with me."

As Woo-jin went to leave with his suspect, he noticed that a small gathering of Jees through the bedroom window. They had come together to see what the ruckus was about. Even the elder with his sullen head hung low came out to join his clan in what was a historic moment for it. They didn't spit on Jung-hae or yell, or ask him if it was true. They merely looked away as a sign of judgment that he was no longer a Jee.

Feeling the absurdity of clan justice, that one is guilty until proven innocent by the law of suspicion, Jung-hae shouted vigorously to be heard but not even the youngest among him moved her eyes to see or her ears to listen.

In the car, Woo-jin did more contextualizing of the situation in his mind's eye than honest to God police work.

Is this how my book ends? I've got the suspect in the back of my car, the very person who spoiled the dreams of the White Oleander. I don't even need to talk to this piece of shit. I can make up anything and the public will believe me. I can say that he confessed to me...

"They're going to fry me for this" Jung-hae said. "I married a monster. You, you have to help me."

"Well, if you want me on your side. You'd better talk before the local police get here."

"Before the wedding, my wife was beside herself. She swore that if this marriage and the birth of Jin-hee and Bo-kyung's child succeeded, she would kill herself. With nothing to lose, she promised to kill Bo-kyung's child so that we might have life. I told her that this is not our way but she wouldn't listen.

"She's the one you want. She acquired the abortion drugs."

"How?"

"You'll have to ask her. My only crime was silence. Once I heard about the miscarriage, I knew it was my wife but goddamn it, I wanted to save the reputation of our family so I kept quiet. I should have known that this sorceress would crack and try to suck me under in the process.

"Can't you see what she's doing? She can't live with the guilt so she's pinning it on me because if I go to prison, she won't have to worry about some policeman knocking on the door and arresting her."

"I'm sure you'll have plenty of time to get your story right" Woo-jin said. "Let's just sit here and wait for the police to come."

Sitting in the back of Detective Jang's car, Woo-jin was not used to being on the other end of interrogatory questions. They had driven away from the farm and the fog and were on a quiet dirt road that led to more frequented thoroughfares.

"What were you doing on that farm?" Detective Jang asked

"I got a lead."

"But you're Daejeon police. Did they send you down here?"

"The White Oleander Murder case, that was me. A prime suspect in that case has since moved here."

"But, excuse me, detective sir, you didn't answer my question. Are you some kind of vigilante? Is this something your captain would have your ass over a barrel for?"

"I'm at the end of my career, sir. I remember when I was just like you: young dumb and full of cum. There's so much to gain, so much of the ladder to climb. The illusion is that you think you are in the prime of life but really, of the two of us, I am the only one who's free. There are no more rungs for me, I can free fall out into nothing and relish in my own weightlessness.

"In short, there is no barrel I can be held over because gravity doesn't fucking apply. Before you let me walk free as that wingless bird I claim to be, let me give you a little advice. I don't know what this profession is coming to…"

"Great another lecture. I haven't been receiving these my whole life. Why don't you get to it old man?"

"What's wrong with you? I have information to tell you that's useful to your case."

"We have your number. We'll contact you if we need you but we have our man so we're just going to drive you to your hotel to get your belongings and then drive you to the bus depot so that you can be on your way."

"But, I was the first to respond. How can you proceed without me?"

"We're going to try to make you a footnote in the report. If you want to do us a favor, stay out of our way."

"But the wife, aren't you going to investigate her?"

"Woo-jin, I've already taken down everything you told me. This is a closed investigation. Go read about it from the fucking papers."

"I should have known that you would butt in" Hye-jeong told Woo-jin over the phone. Woo was in his hotel room sipping his complimentary cold coffee drink trying to wade through all the bureaucratic criticism. "I have no choice but to call you back from your vacation before you do any harm. I regret to inform you that we will have to have a formal meeting on Monday regarding your appalling conduct."

"Appalling?

"This case is my life, Hye-jeong! Now, I'm not going anywhere. Dismiss me, suspend me or fire me. The action is here and I'm staying here. There's nothing for me back in Daejeon but maddening silence often interrupted by a pool ball rolling across my desk. You'll need force and not words, to stop me.

"So go back to your desk and your paperwork. Go play with your grandkids. Eat, drink and be light. Only gravity can fucking hold me now."

The Bradenton police found no evidence with which to convict Seraj and with Detective Shore's sympathy, he found himself free once more, from the law at least. For six weeks, he kept himself clean by going to his shifts at Ali Baba, keeping his nose to the grindstone and plotting his revenge in silence.

"What's to stop him from attacking again?" Eckhart asked Father Gilbey. They were consuming fajitas and brew at Casa Ramos in North Tampa because Tampa was equidistant from their respective abodes.

"Maybe he went straight."

"That's your plan, Gilbey?! Hoping that this psycho finally just got too tired to kill."

"From what we know, he's no killer. Ok, maybe he wants to tear you and I limb from limb but the specter of spending the rest of one's life behind bars after getting a seven or eight year taste of it is quite a deterrent."

"Listen Gilbey, I travelled 72 hours back to Korea scared as fuck that I was going to be arrested for our crime and locked away with the key thrown away but I went to Cheonan prison and I looked into Seraj's eyes and I saw something that was not there before. I

don't think a stint washing dishes at a hookah bar & restaurant are
going to stall his march toward vengeance."

"Then, why did he stop?"

"To give us a false sense of security, to toy with us. God, it's just
like it was with Richard Wallace. We are at the mercy of another
monster who means to do us harm."

"I defeated Wallace and I can defeat this raghead as well. I out-
last them and out-think them in the end. It's a good thing you're
on my side." Gilbey winked. "Let's bring the fireworks to that little
shanty round your neck of the woods."

"We going to take out his father too?"

"What the fuck has he ever amounted to? He just waits tables at
the same restaurant as Seraj. We should two kill two birds with one
stone and send that bungalow up in smoke. They won't begrudge
us that. They'll be too busy fighting over the 144 virgins between
them."

"Every time I think you turn a corner, you show your coldness
but I'm done being a moralist. Nothing will sway you. I will say this
and it may seem sheepish but I think it's fair. You got us into this
mess and time and time again, you dug us deeper and so I think
you owe it to me for the shit you got us into in Korea, for beloved
Nora, for turning my home in South Dakota into a bullet riddled
nightmare, for all the other unspeakable horrors which I've forgotten. This is a solo mission."

"I understand that you're thinking in your best interests and
the best interests of your family but I think it bodes well for both
of us if you don't leave the whole thing up to me."

"What happens if Seraj guns me down in a showdown? Then,
you'll have to tackle him all by yourself."

"What did you have in mind?

"It's hard man because our private investigator knows that
we've been keeping tabs on this dude. If he ends up with a bullet in

his brain base, Swift is bound to drop a dime on us and then police from several counties have warrants and going through our trunks and closets and you've got to explain to your wife and kids why very official looking men are combing through your personals.

"I've watched enough episodes of *Forensic Files* to be skeptical of our ability to get away with murder. We did it once before but that was in Korea and on a mountainside where the rain washed everything away."

"Gilbey, I can't live with this shadow over me. How can I sleep when I know that just twenty miles away is some man who means to torture and/or kill me? We moved here in the event that Seraj might be freed and might come back to his father's house and now he's here. The plan was to ambush him on his return so I'm basically seeing that there was no reason for me to move to this hot ass place with Chick-Fil-A as its only claim to civilization.

"I'm starting to think that it would have been better for me to move somewhere far away and let you keep watch alone for Seraj's return. In fact, I'm inclined to tell my wife that we should look to move."

"Not such an easy thing to do, drop everything, pack everything and fly with the wind."

"Look who you're talking to, Gilbey. We fit everything we owned in two suitcases and when I went to China, I found that to be too complex, so I fit it all into one."

"Yeah, but you've got a wife and kids now. You remember when we walked those lonely streets in the wee hours of the morning and we agreed long before there was any death of Jacob Jung that a wife and kids would be an anchor. My character is questionable, my crimes many, the path I walk dark and bloody but I was man enough to face the darkness every day of my life.

"You couldn't stomach the lonely lights so you planted your seed and now you've gone and tied an anchor around your neck like a millstone and thrown yourself into the ocean."

"This is what eventually happens to those of us who have enough game to see chicks naked. There was never any chance of you ever getting any pussy so yeah, becoming a priest was a good option for you.

"I mean, what was I to do? Rent out a studio apartment for the rest of my life, keep a snub nose in the glove compartment and sleep with a magnum under my pillow and hope the tooth fairy doesn't take it. That ain't living."

"It's life and as shitty as it gets, we must preserve it at all costs. How many times have I told you that survival is a kind of revenge? If Seraj kills us, even with those eight years in the slammer, he wins. You must live at all costs, live in spite of being condemned to a subterranean existence.

"Since you're adamant that I've shepherded you from a life of wholesome Midwesternness to a life of sin, I'm going to take care of Seraj for you. You know, I really am sorry about Nora. That shit bothers me to this day." Eckhart gritted his teeth. "And though it may not seem that way, I always wished happiness for you. I've told you that and I'm sorry for all the demons I invited into your life. I fear that no matter happens, I will be remembered by you as some kind of monster. If I take care of this problem for you, and let you get on with your life, can you promise me that you will try to see me as a human being, just like you?"

"Whatever; get it done. You owe me dude and then we can part ways and I can finally sleep at night."

CHAPTER 8
BULLET WITH BUTTERFLY WINGS

"...but the rain
Is full of ghosts tonight, that tap and sigh
Upon the glass and listen for reply."

- ("Sonnet XLIII) Edna Saint Vincent Millay

Woo-jin lost his appeal and his badge and the glue that held him to this world of the living. His lone saving grace was a document that he filched from the desk of Captain Hye-jeong containing the specifics of a phone call from Florida from a Detective Shore. Woo-jin devoured the report and vowed to go to Sarasota if given the chance so once the job went away, he went away with it.

Taking no time to dwell, Woo-jin booked the cheapest flight he could find, which was a 600$ ticket through Air China and United Airlines.

Twenty-one hours later, he landed at Tampa International Airport after stopovers in Beijing and Chicago. The first thing he did when got off the plane was get a room at the airport Marriot and sleep eleven hours. He took one hell of a piss and set his mind to renting a car and getting to Sarasota to check up on the old haunts occupying new dwellings.

It felt good to leave seven Celsius behind for a temperature in the low twenties. Woo-jin hadn't seen such tropical vegetation since his visit to the Philippines with his ex-wife. This was better than that because it was sweltering in the middle of March on that trip and Woo-jin ate something that gave him his worst ever bout of diarrhea and vomiting. He still claims to have lost five pounds on that trip. Here though, the food and the implements used to cook it and eat it were sterile. He would pay more for it but for the first time in thirty years, there was little consideration of the future because the only hues he could paint it with were bleak and dull.

For that reason, he kept his mind away from the phantoms of the past and the demons of the future and instead fixed his mind's eye on the sea breeze when he got off of 75 and rolled his window down. His was mood was calm and his contentment so great that he had to persuade himself to carry on with his business and not go off and rest in the sunshine. He had heard about the world-class beaches and all of the other attractions.

Maybe the local girls would find a foreign guy like me to be exotic. Who do I think I am kidding? I'm a fifty year old perv. The only time we'll lock arms is if they help walk me across the street. Still, I'm grateful for this parting gift. I didn't know that I could still live but to this final bit of business I must attend.

Woo-jin had been in contact with Detective Shore via Skype for several weeks and so Woo was an expected guest at the local precinct.

"Welcome" Detective Shore said and tried to bow because YouTube told him how to greet Koreans. Woo-jin bowed back and they shook hands American style.

"Well, I am impressed!" Detective Shore said emphatically. "Must've been one hell of a case for Korea to send someone all the way to our little town." What Shore was oblivious of was the fact that while he was still employed, Woo-jin's claim that he would come to act in Sarasota as the Daejeon's police forces personal plenipotentiary was an utter lie.

"It was serious public drama" Woo-jin said.

"Do you have plans to extradite anybody, bring anybody back to Korea?"

"We can't. Case closed."

"But there's always the chance."

"That's right."

"What did you think of the characters involved: Michael Gilbey, James Eckhart and Seraj Mukhtari?"

"I hate them but in my country, justice system is different: less crime, murders and shorter prison time."

"Even in a murder case?"

"Sometimes prison for life but depends, sometimes like 25 years."

"Do you think Seraj could have been a scapegoat? Sorry. Let me phrase that another way. Was Seraj selected so that the case could be finished?"

"Possibly."

"Why not the other foreigners? This James Eckhart also had a relationship with Bo-kyung Lee. Was it just easier to pick the Arab?"

"Maybe." Woo-jin giggled following his short reply.

"What would it take for your country to reopen the investigation into James Eckhart and Michael Gilbey and the widow as well?"

"New evidence. Have they done anything here?"

"Well, let me catch you up to speed. Michael Gilbey has become a priest."

"Oh really. Maybe not too surprising."

"Why? Was he very religious?"

"No. When we asked him if he was also romantically involved with Bo-kyung Lee, he said he never had sex or even kissed a girl."

"Yeah, I once had a psycho ex-girlfriend claim that she was a virgin but she never bled, lyin' ass. Anyhow, what's your point? Did you believe him?"

"Of course. I don't think he was a virgin because of religion. He was virgin because even if he was a millionaire, it would be hard for him to get a basic girl."

"He was a friend zone kind of guy?"

"Girls didn't even really want to be his friend."

"Well, he's not the most attractive guy in the world and he wasn't then."

"And he had no fashion. That's a big deal in Korea."

"You know 'big deal.' You're English ain't so bad after all."

"Thank you. What job do you do if you can't kiss girls?"

"Become a priest or monk." Woo-jin pressed his hands together in mock prayer.

"Yes."

"Interesting. So because he can't have sex with women, he became priest. Not evil though."

"Doesn't make him a bad priest either" Detective King interrupted. He slid his large frame into the room gracefully and was unnoticed until he spoke. "He's better than some of the deviants that fill the ranks. To his credit, no child has made even a hint of an accusation."

"That's a totally different kind of crime, King" Shore said.

"Let's put it to our Korean friend. What's your name?"

"Woo-jin."

"Can I call you Woo?" King asked.

"No problem."

"We've already established that Jacob Jung was murdered. I know that from the forensic files Shore showed me that said that all reports were consistent with repeated blunt force trauma."

"Yes. It is very probably that someone murdered him" Woo-jin said. King flinched at the poor English but tried to still his countenance.

"And so who would you pick as the killer?" King asked.

"I would pick number one probably, so I say it's Seraj. He also had the most desire for murder. Very jealous guy I think."

"There you go" King said.

"Wait, this thing is not settled" Shore rebutted. "Gilbey is no small dude. He was almost 200 pounds at the time."

"I don't know pounds" Woo-jin said.

"It's like 100 kilograms" Shore said.

"Well, yeah, that's a lot. Like your size" Woo-jin admitted.

"You see!" Shore said.

"Ok, he didn't change his pick" King said. "He just said it's possible."

"By the way, have you ever felt Gilbey's hands?" Woo-jin asked. "My mom's hands are harder. He has woman hands."

"So she had some blue collar hands" Shore interrupted. "And yeah, we never said Jacob Jung was killed with someone's bare hands. I think we can all agree that a blunt force object was used. A fourteen year old girl 110 pounds soaking wet could kill a giant on a mountainside if she hit him right." Woo-jin nodded in agreement. "And here's what we're trying to figure out, Woo. Recently, Father Gilbey's church burnt to the ground."

"Wow, burn? Fire?" Woo-jin expanded his hands to show a flame rising out of nothing.

"Yeah anyway, this burning has coincided with Seraj's return to Florida" King said. "But, we have no evidence. We just know that the fire was started with an accelerant. I'm amazed at how few places have cameras in the 21st century. That church has an f'ing camera in the basement, case solved. As soon as one of those fuckers is looking at thirty years in the slammer, they'll talk."

"We have another question for you" Shore said. "Seraj is from Florida so his return makes sense but why the fuck would a Midwestern farm boy and a city kid from the northeast come to live in Florida before their hairs turn grey?" Woo-jin only shrugged. The detectives weren't sure whether it was because the question was too loaded or whether he didn't command enough English to understand.

"Isn't it obvious?" Shore asked after some silence. "Okay, maybe it's not obvious but this is my theory: Eckhart and Gilbey did Seraj dirt cheap like the AC/DC song says and they had the expectation that he would be put there forever like the man in the iron mask."

"Just curious, Shore" King interjected.

"Yeah."

"How many references does this theory have?"

"I like references. My favorite rappers use a lot of references."

"Fine. Just continue."

"Eckhart and Gilbey moved to Florida in the event that Seraj would be freed via appeal, which he was, eight fucking years too late if you ask me but freed nonetheless."

"Doesn't make sense" King said. "If I wronged a man and drove him to vengeance, I wouldn't be barbecuing a wild boar in his backyard for his homecoming."

"Maybe they're afraid of extradition or some other form of legal retribution" Shore said. "If they can stay close enough to the flame, Seraj will be tempted by the sweetness of revenge instead of the rightness of justice. They want the boy to walk into the trap so that they can kill him in what looks like self-defense." Detective King sighed.

"Woo brother," Detective King said. "There's a reason we don't clear any cases. I think my partner is in the wrong profession; he should be writing scripts for TV shows. What a creative type, making theories with no evidence."

"Well, if we could tail one of these guys, we could find out a thing or two" Detective Shore said.

"You mean, you just let these bad guys walk around?" Woo-jin asked with wonder.

"We're kind of understaffed here" Detective King admitted. "We can do a little surveillance but nothing more than a couple of hours at a time. It's a small department with few serious crimes."

"If you give me the locations, I can watch them." The two detectives looked at each other.

"We appreciate you coming all the way to Florida, Woo" Detective King said. "But, we would be in a very difficult situation if you got in the thick of things and all of a sudden we had to explain your presence. I hope you weren't misled by your superiors. You can still be of great use to us, but as a consultant on this highly complex and sensitive case."

"Of course. I understand. I'm mostly here to enjoy the hot sun. My department is paying for this trip."

"Damn, you get it nice over there" Detective King said. "How much they pay you?"

The conversation ended with the three men doing their best to convert the salary of 2.7 million won into US dollars.

When Woo-jin walked out into the sunshine discouraged by his lack of involvement in the case, a hurrying Detective Shore followed and slipped the Korean a piece of paper with the addresses of Eckhart, Gilbey and Seraj. Woo-jin nodded and looked into Shore's eyes with deep understanding and compassion.

In the motel room with a bottle of Southern Comfort to ease the demons, Woo-jin thought of whom he would pay a visit to first.

"God, Jacob Jung was a bastard, wasn't he? Why the hell was I so hell bent on solving this case? Hye-jeong had the right idea by living her life and not letting this case become her. At the end of the day, what obligation did I have to Jung Sr. He had other children but what about me? What about Woo-jin? Jung Sr. lost a son but I lost everything and everyone.

"Jung Sr. is an old man now but he moved on; I know he did. CEOs are not men who dwell and so now he can...

"Man, the thoughts that the bottle leads me to. I've got to focus on the book, do what's best for the book. Whom to interview first? The priest, logically. That chubby fuck is the only one who's going to open his mouth; better rattle his cage first."

Woo-jin walked to the outdoor range of the Sarasota Archery Club where he found his mark, Father Gilbey, controlling his breathing and aiming his arrow at the bullseye.

"Shooting priest?!" Woo-jin called from beyond, causing the arrow to fly astray and hit the upper rung of the target. Father Gilbey quickly turned his head to see the familiar foe. "Why not golf next door? I think it's more common for priest."

"I prefer to be left alone."

"Honja. In Korea, this is a word for sad people that eat lonely. Come old ghost, have a maekchu hana (one beer) with me. I'm trying to write a book."

"You mean to tell me you flew 8,000 miles to ask me a few questions for a book. Aren't you still police?"

"Discharged. They took my pension, bastards. I'm hoping that I can be famous from this book because it's still a drama case."

"Well, I've got some questions for you as well. I think that's a fair exchange. You eat Cuban food?"

"Sure." Woo-jin had never had Cuban food before.

Sitting at the squared wooden table in blue chairs with gold frames, Woo-jin ate, drank and conversed.

"I have to say you scared the shit out of me" Father Gilbey admitted. "I'll have to talk to the people at the range. You could have been seriously hurt. When I started at this archery business, I couldn't hit the damn target. Now, I've got a precise shot. Even I can learn things as I go.

"Shit, when last we spoke you were trying to seal me in a narrow jail cell but now we can eat together like civil Christian gentlemen." The waiter brought the entrees and Woo-jin was surprised by the reverence shown for Gilbey by the Cuban-American waiter.

Don't they know who he is? Must've flocked to the church for this little respect these people give him.

"So, why'd you get discharged?" Gilbey asked, eating his steak sandwich with all the primality that he had shown before.

"I've never seen anyone eat like that before" Woo-jin replied. "Well, except my sister. She could eat more than a small army." And then Woo-jin thought of how he was estranged from her as well. "I defied orders. I was too obsessed with the Jung case. Tell me, do you still think about it?"

"All the time. By the way, I heard Seraj got out on some kind of forensic technicality."

"Yes. Many people are angry because it opened a wound in the nation. Koreans think that foreign men just come here to fuck our women."

"Well, if the shoe fits." Woo-jin looked down at his loafers. "I'm pretty sure a lot of my fellow expats made the 8,000 mile trek for some cute Asian girls."

"Yes, so our feeling is correct. We finally extradited an army kid for the 1997 murder at a Burger King."

"I suspect the people are calling for one more body or two with a little bit more blood on their tongues."

"Can you speak more slowly? I think I understand what you're saying."

"I'm guessing that the Burger King murderer isn't enough of a distraction. The people really want to find Jacob Jung's killer. I couldn't remember what your theory on that was. Can you refresh my memory?"

"That's what I came here to ask you."

"Well, I suppose you did travel 8,000 miles to pay me a visit, in a way anyhow. I mine as well be courteous.

"I think that that wretched widow, Seraj and that motel gangster were to blame."

"Ah, Tae-woo not a gangster, just a motel clerk who helped some gangsters."

"It's anyone's guess though, right? Because from what I've heard, no meaningful evidence was collected at the mountainside. Could've been you for all the public knows but I suppose this chick was intimately involved with a lot of foreigners, so it's convenient to believe that a foreigner beat the piss out of that spoiled little brat."

"Did you feel sad when Jacob Jung died?"

"Do you want me to answer that?"

"I want you to answer all for the book...Why'd you do it?"

"Why did I become a priest? Because I have been touched by the Holy Spirit and now I have a special devotion to Mary."

"Don't be stupid. I know you killed him."

"Kill? Feel my soft hands once more." Gilbey reached out his hand palm first; he could never keep his fingers from trembling. He blamed his condition on the duress he underwent in Korea but admitted that this had no effect on his quality of life.

Woo-jin obliged and reached out like Michelangelo's David and felt the smoothness of his palms. The softness was a compelling argument but anyone with a will could've committed that murder.

"And what of that bloody rock in Seraj's room?" Gilbey asked. "Wasn't that the smoking gun?"

"You didn't hear. The blood belonged to a pig and the rock didn't match the wounds. That's why Seraj become free after eight years. Don't play stupid; the man who killed Jung might have done it – maybe it was you – but someone wanted to punish Seraj. I heard you two weren't the best of friends."

"I disapproved of the immorality of the affair between Seraj and Bo-kyung but it's not my nature to fight evil with evil. I fight evil with the goodness of Goodness itself in the person of Jesus Christ."

"Whatever. I was born Buddhist. I don't believe in that either but at least we don't talk like that. I have one more question: Why did you move to Florida? You could've gone anywhere but you decided to become a priest in a state where you had no connection."

"I had family in Miami."

"So that's why you moved down here? For family? What family? I told you all I see is honja. I'm going to ask Eckhart, too."

"I doubt he's as chatty as me but if you want to know, he moved down here to setup an air conditioning business."

"You, Eckhart and Seraj here is not coincidence. I don't know what you're doing, Michael Gilbey, but I don't believe you. My advice is to go outside and smell that fresh air because pretty soon police come with cage for you like an animal."

"Ha! Despite all my rage, I'm still just a rat in a cage. It's an old song. I'm an innocent man I assure you. Anyhow, it was so nice to catch up. I hope you enjoy your stay. Tell me, for how much longer are you in town?"

"I'll be here until I see everything I want to see."

"Well, good luck with your book. That's what you're here for, right?"

⊨+ +⊨

Gilbey and Eckhart met halfway once more, this time at EATS! American Grill.

"I better relish these buffalo wings, James, because they're bearing down on us."

"Stop acting like a little bitch, Gilbey. You've got the protection of the Church. They've aided and abetted child rapists. They're going to do what they can to stop a foreign country from extraditing you. I, on the other hand, would make a nice scape goat."

"You once told me to stop crying and get on with my life because I was ruminating on a past that you made dreadful. Well, in the light of everything, it's stupid fucking advice. Where or when exactly was I supposed to move on with my life? Should I have done it when Wallace was crushing my fiancé's skull and trying to cut my dick off? Or should I do it now that I've got another dude gunning for my life?"

"Yeah, well right back at you, brother. It's time for you to stop crying and heed your own damn advice. You've been stringing me along, promising me that you would take action, but so far you've hidden behind that collar."

"Well, if you want to discuss particulars, we'll have to do it in the car."

The conversation carried on in the Sebring.

"I understand that you're upset that Seraj is only a stone's throw away and could huff puff and blow your house down at any moment" Gilbey said. "I'll be the first to raise my hand and say that the Florida plan was not the best."

"Not the best?! It's like you said about them banging down our door. Even Detective Woo-jin is here trying to shackle us."

"He's trying to write a book."

"Potentially."

"Look James, it's like chess. We can't just rush in or they'll take our queen and eventually capture our King. You're the one with a sure shot, but if I go in like John Woo with two, I'll either get gunned down, and boy would that make a story, or we won't be able to use the stand your ground law that let George Zimmerman go free. Plus, unlike the murder at the mountains, there'll be a shitload of evidence to damn us.

"I suggest you go with your original plan and move your family away from all of this."

"How can I explain this to my wife? 'Hey Honey, I know we are very well off here and live very well here and I know my business is thriving here and we're on our way to sending our kids through college debt free but let's move.'"

"Your woman and family problems are not for me to figure out. I've never had a woman to love me."

"You've never even been kissed."

"Fair enough. I wasn't made to love and so being deprived of the joys of romance of intimacy, I am also free of the burdens." Gilbey then changed his tone in order to attempt the best sardonic impression of Gilbey he could muster. "'Wow Gilbey, what a brave man you are. You could live anywhere but you choose to live right under Seraj's nose.' Yes James, and I do that and though I am protected by the collar, I still live under the gun every day to protect us from the madman and when the time is right, I will strike him down, and we will be freed and all the wrongs I've done will be righted."

"Seraj isn't the only one who's lost ten years of his life."

"Now who's being the drama queen? Because of what I accomplished, that animal was locked up."

"Animal? He was a party boy who didn't follow social rules. You think because he fucked someone's wife, he deserved what he got. You made him an animal!"

"In previous generations, men were castrated for such trespasses. Heck, in Africa they probably still are. Whatever you do, don't point your finger at me like I'm the Frankenstein who created this monster."

"That's exactly what I'm doing. Way back in that alleyway out in TimeWorld, I told you, but you just wouldn't listen, would you? I told you not to meddle so that you could get along. I actually liked you and wanted you to make it in Korea because Max told me that you had problems adjusting. I also didn't want you to get your head kicked in."

"You were also protecting your boy."

"Yeah, he was my friend and I follow the bro code."

"The Bro code?! You say that I am immature but you sound like a seventeen year old. You want me to take you to Hot Topic to buy a green lantern shirt? We can listen to Blink 182. Whaddaya say?

"I don't know what to tell you, James. I am grateful for your friendship. You might call it something else. You might say that your association with me is merely a matter of survival and that you are too paranoid to leave me to my own devices and that you are only so close to me because of some half-cocked plan on mine to take out Seraj."

"At least, you're admitting that you have no real strategy."

"But the thing is that you don't sound very surprised. For all your bravado, James, you don't have a whole lot of friends or ideas of your own."

"More than you."

"Look where your travels took you and what have you taken with you? You met a blonde girl in China. That is quite impressive; I'm not gonna lie and you belonged to that little 'Knights of the Round Table' clique whose sole stated purpose was to drink beer and fuck women. I'm the only real friend, as flawed as I am, that you've ever really had.

"It's been six months and Seraj hasn't so much as threatened to lay a finger on us so am I really the one who's acting like a pussy?

If you're really so afraid, move to fucking Arizona. It's a fucking desert out there. It's hard to imagine anything hotter than this giant massive heat stroke waiting to happen but Arizona might be. Design air conditioning systems there. Shit, be an innovator. I don't know. I'm not a businessman. You know what to do."

"Actually, I don't. I've been here for five plus years and built my fucking business here and have all my clients here. I'm not going anywhere and I'm not living near Seraj so we are at an impasse that I expect you to solve. Asking you to fix this problem has become tiresome. Now you're asking me to move to Arizona. You suck."

"What's really here for you besides this business? Do you need to have such massive means? Isn't it okay if your kids go to community college or state school and have to bust their asses like the rest of us? Central Florida is the cesspool of human civilization. Why don't you go somewhere that has more to offer?

"In any event. I have no plans to rush into that sorry excuse for a bungalow and waste Seraj and potentially, his father. As my old man used to say, if you want it done, do it yourself."

CHAPTER 9

THE FINAL ACT

"Insanity's horse
Adorns the sky;
Can't seem to find the right lie."

("I Can't See Your Face in My Mind") The Doors

Disconsolate, Eckhart returned to his home and his family to whom he assured complete safety He kissed his wife, who coiled back a bit and hugged his kids, but if you could only see his eyes, you would know that his mind was on other matters.

"Now that the worst is over, you'll have to tell me what really happened in Korea" Myra Eckhart said, noting the weariness on her husband's face. "I feel like a stranger, that there's so much of you that's a mystery to me. I always worried that you wouldn't let me in."

"I love you" Eckhart said with little conviction.

"I love you too." She grasped his hand firmly, suggesting that this newly discovered enigmatic side of her husband turned her on.

After dinner, Eckhart lay in bed and stared at the ceiling. He was exhausted but couldn't sleep, so he got out of bed and went to his study. His head was pounding; he took an aspirin.

If you want something done right, do it yourself. When Seraj gets out of the picture, I can live in peace once and for all. If only there were some way to kill two birds with one stone.

And so, not too late into the night, Eckhart went out to the car and using the burner he purchased with sixty minutes on it; dialed Seraj. The latter man woke up in a daze.

"Hello. Who is this?" Seraj asked.

"I thought you would have killed me by now or at least, Gilbey."

"Ah James, it's been so long since I've heard your voice. Tell me, how are you?"

"What?" He expected rage. "Have you found God or something?" Seraj roared with maniacal laughter at a high pitch.

"What would make you say that? In that dark and lonesome cell, I stared into the abyss until I could see that blackness radiates just like light and there was no God."

"Why then, peace? Why let Gilbey live freely for another day?"

"Peace, is that what my life has? The last time I had peace was back before you and that scoundrel pried my freedom from me."

"Me?"

"Go on and protest your innocence in the hopes that you'll be spared. I don't want you to think for a New York second that I spared either of you for mercy or peace because I haven't. I know it hurts more if you have to wait. I'm going to let it burn slowly."

"Listen," Eckhart was calm and composed. "I suffered too from Gilbey. Because of him, I had to watch my fiancé die and I almost was castrated myself that night. Haven't I paid my dues? Why should I suffer? I didn't kill Jacob Jung; Gilbey did. He's the one you want."

Seraj hung up.

Eckhart destroyed the burner and stroked his chin deep in thought.

I'm going to have to confront him. Gilbey won't do it. He's just going to hide behind his collar. I have to see what happens if I show up to his home or his work. Wouldn't that be the fucking outcome? I get one right between the eyes, Seraj goes back in the slammer, this time for good and Gilbey gets to live out the rest of his years in relative prosperity. Is there a way I can get Seraj to kill Gilbey or vice versa? Should I just move the fuck to 'Zona? Am I playing with fire? No, so long as these two suckers are alive, especially Seraj, I cannot rest. Looking over my shoulder for the rest of my life is no way to live. But how? I should just off him in the parking lot of Al Wadi. Now, is there a way I can frame Gilbey for it? I could plant the gun on him after the fact.

⋈ ⋈

At around 3 in the morning, Eckhart had to shake himself from sleep on the road to Apopka. The previous three hours were spent working up the courage to do the deed and figure out what to do once the deed was done.

For Family.

Eckhart went 'round the back of the house whose roof was so slanted that for a half-second he thought he could just wait for the roof to cave in on the occupants. Using a crowbar, Eckhart was able to jimmy the hatch to the basement. He used the flashlight on his phone to light the way through the darkness.

I feel like I'm in Texas Chainsaw Massacre.

His heart started pounding and he just stood there paralyzed, knowing that he stood at a monumental threshold. This was his last chance to turn back, to jolt back up the steps, and go back home to work out a more thorough plan but he had been through all that and had decided that this was his fate. For so long, he lived in limbo, relying on the inactive Michael Gilbey to finish what he could only make worse. By walking up the basement steps, Eckhart had deemed that living in limbo was no longer tolerable. He'd dwell in purgatory or walk through the fires of hell but no longer could he wait for the ominous ring of a bell.

All or nothing.

The stairs creaked as he ascended slowly. He could not keep still his heartbeat. Nothing could prepare him this, not being investigated by the Korean police for murder, not being helpless as gangsters raped and beat his fiancé. Finally, Eckhart was succumbing to the violence. This time when the shot rang out, there could be no appeals of self-defense, no justifiable homicides, just the taking of a life for his own gain.

He opened the door into the darkness of the kitchen and stood in the cool air, trying to appreciate the burdens he had felt that he would set free once he put to bed this loose end. As he groped his way through the kitchen, he could hear sonorous breathing, hoping that it belonged to Seraj. With his right hand clutching the pistol, Eckhart felt along the wall and moved slowly towards the breathing. When he got so close that he was nearly on top of the sound, he shined his light, which jerked the old man from his sleep so that he sat face up.

"Don't scream" Eckhart ordered.

"We have no money in this house." Eckhart paused, looking less for a strategy and more of a response to the old man's robbery concerns.

"Do you have any prescription pills?"

"Just my heart medication. You don't want that."

"No, I don't." Eckhart grabbed the head pillow that Saeed vacated, raised it, put the pistol to it, cocked it back and let it go. On the one hand, Eckhart was impressed with the efficacy of the pillow in the matter of suppressing the gun blast, but on the other was revolted by the blood that sprayed him. It was a clean headshot. Abu Seraj was dead.

Eckhart carried on, silencing his inner thoughts, for he had already crossed over to the other side. One last set of stairs to ascend and he would climb them like rungs to Shamayim. The pistol wrapped tightly in his glove became him and when he got to the top of the stairs, he absorbed the silence again. For the first time in a long time, time was on his side or was it?

The three round burst reverberated throughout the house. It was loud enough to wake the neighbors. Fresh holes were in one of the bedroom doors and light funneled in. Eckhart looked to his side and saw that the bullet was embedded in the bannister.

"Stay the fuck back, Gilbey!" Seraj shouted through the door. The hole seemed to amplify the sound. "I've got an assault rifle on the other side of this thing."

"It's not Gilbey...It's Eckhart."

"Papa!" Seraj cried. "What was that sound just now?! Did you shoot my father?"

"Yes. I sent him to his God."

"Goddamnit Eckhart, I was supposed to take from you, not the other way around."

"I know" Eckhart said in a strained and shaken tone. "It's not about justice. Gilbey taught me to stop believing in that sort of thing a long time ago."

"Father, can you hear me!?...So, Gilbey is your master."

"To be honest, I was hoping to pin your murder on him."

"So, you were just going to kill me and blame it on that fat clown. He really has become your mentor."

Seraj shot through the door with another three round burst. Eckhart took cover but not before one of the bullets grazed his arm. He grimaced in pain, though it was only a flesh wound.

"I was going to save you for last. No, I was going to rape your wife in front of you and kill your whole family while you watched, but that was to be after I cut off Gilbey's ears and nuts.

"Are you listening to me?"

"You could have done whatever you wanted to Gilbey." Eckhart had to shout as he was using the bathroom as cover. "I only came here tonight because I had to protect my family. You gave me an answer tonight and it's not what I was seeking. It didn't have to come to this."

"Maybe I'm too stupid to live, Eckhart. A real murderer would have played nice and gotten close and done all the things that I just said I was gonna do. Maybe I could have gotten away with it. You know what the shameful thing is. One of us is going to die and whoever lives is going to spend the rest of his life in prison while that rat…"

"That's what I'm trying to tell you; we can get proper revenge."

"Bullshit. How do you figure? You just killed my father! There is no turning back and don't think you're any better than Gilbey either. I hate you just the same."

"Come on! We both know that's not true. If that were the case, you would have fired more than six shots just now. Admit it, the wheels are turning. You want both of us but you'd prefer to torture and kill Gilbey over me. We have memories together, a shared past."

"Man, you turned your back on all that shit. As far as I'm concerned, you chose that dweeb over me. You're just one spirit dwelling in two bodies and so your fate should be the same."

"You have to admit that one of us dying, one of us rotting in a cell for the rest of our natural born life and Gilbey living on is the worst of all possible worlds. Your father might still be alive. Maybe we can save him, put him back together again and go after Gilbey together."

"You must take me for a fool. Do you think I left all of my sanity and logic behind in Cheonan? It doesn't matter with me now Gilbey. Do you know why?" Eckhart readied his pistol, knowing that when men run out of words, they draw their swords. "Because it's Florida, baby! Castle law!"

As Seraj spoke these final words, he kicked the door open and began firing towards the bathroom. He got off maybe nine rounds.

"I saw you through the peephole, Eckhart. I know you're in the bathroom. Are you powdering your nose in there, Susan?" Seraj was laughing now. "The last thing you'll hear, Eckhart, is this laughter and the sounds of hell's bells. Any final words? They will be lost on my ears anyhow. Do you want to die like fish in a barrel or do you want to come out here and kiss my feet and beg for my forgiveness?"

Eckhart breathed in deeply and raised his gun, pointing it toward the sound and then fired one solitary shot. It ricocheted off a tile, went through the door and the splintering wood caused it to change direction and embed itself in Seraj's heart. He gave a quick gasp before his life ceased. Eckhart kicked the door open and shot once more indiscriminately for he knew not that Seraj was dead until he saw his wide wild green eyes wider than a river's mouth pointing heavenward and his arms still clutching the assault rifle.

Eckhart stood over his work and time started to do something that seemed unfair. He had to clean up this mess, but how? He had to dispose of two bodies. Had the neighbors heard all the commotion? They had to have.

Even if I get the bodies out of here, this place is soaked in blood. I'm no professional. If I were, I wouldn't do a job like this. I wouldn't even have tried it like this. Gilbey was right; this didn't require such a desperation maneuver and would you know it, he's going to be a free man. What God can there be in a world where Gilbeys reign and Eckharts must be locked away? There's still a way out. I'm wearing gloves. Maybe they won't find my DNA. First, I need to get that old Rag to the fucking trunk.

A world of blue and red fluorescence suddenly illuminated the whole house. The police had arrived and there was little means of escape now. Eckhart plopped to the floor, took the cellphone out of his pocket and called Gilbey. Normally, Gilbey wouldn't bother to answer the phone at such an ungodly hour but he had woken up to take a leak and saw his phone vibrating on his nightstand so he answered it on his way to the restroom.

"Eckhart, you truly have a troubled mind or are you calling to say goodbye as you roll towards the deserts of Arizona?" Gilbey emptied his bladder awaiting the response.

"It's over, Gilbey. Somehow someway, you've won."

"What, should we be talking over the...?"

"These will be my last words and sadly they will be spoken to you. Why not my wife? I guess I never loved her. So, what does that mean? I guess I must love you instead in some sick way." Eckhart laughed more at the absurdity of his own situation than his attempt at humor.

"I love you too, Eckhart" his friend said sincerely. The police were shouting something over the loudspeaker as they had when Richard Wallace had Eckhart, Nora and Gilbey tied up in the basement of the Tauler homestead.

"Goddamnit, it's not a profession of love. I must definitely have...I don't have time for this."

"What *do* you have time for Eckhart?"

"This can't be happening." The muffled voice carried louder. Eckhart heard the words "surrender" and "harm."

"Seriously, Eck." Gilbey had never called him by this before. "You mean everything to me; you always have. No matter what happens, I will always see myself in your shadow. You just couldn't see it though. You always had this life that I just liked to see on display. No matter how much I ruined your life, you would come back sleeker and I wanted to have what you have. I think I might have traded my best years to experience for a moment what comes easy to see you, to see a female losing herself gazing at you.

"What's going on, anyhow? Where are you?"

"I've shot Seraj and his father."

"Where? Please tell…no, not in their…"

"Yes."

"You have to get out of there!"

"Boys in blue all around me."

"C'mon Eckhart, try something! Can't you make this look some kind of self-defense?"

"I shot Seraj's father at point blank range, using the pillow as a suppressor."

"Jesus. Make it look like Seraj did it."

"I bought the gun, Gilbey."

"We'll fight it in court. You'll go on trial but seeing what a handsome upstanding man you are, they'll acquit you even if by jury nullification."

"I don't have enough to run this race. I can't live with the ghost of this sensational case and what it will do to my family, to see their eyes when they learn…"

"But they won't learn because we're two clever foxes and you're just going to walk off Scott Free. Then, we'll have a beer and laugh about it."

"Easy for you to say; you have a stonewall alibi. You know, that was the difference between you and your father; he knew when the game was up."

"I still don't know why I called you instead of my wife. I'm not sure I ever loved her. I can't even see her face in my mind. All I can see is yours, haunting my steps as I went from Daejeon to Beijing to Dakota to Florida. My only consolation is that you're going to be left alone. I'm going to die but you'll be dying from here on out. You're just going to rot away for the next thirty years. Alone. If that is victory, you can have it. Now, I need this final moment to make what peace I can."

"Eckhart, what are you talking about? They'll never convict you! You're a good ol' country boy. You're the white OJ Simpson. We'll get you the best legal defense money can buy."\

"Living means spending the rest of my natural life in a narrow jail cell; you know that. You also know that my death is a certain defeat for you. I'm all you ever had."

"I can visit you in jail."

"Ha, but you'd get to go home and walk under the palms with the cool breeze at your back. I'd go back to staring at a sterile wall."

"There's...Eckhart, I love you! You're my fucking pristine Aryan god. You have to live, for your family, for me!"

"You never did learn how to say goodbye." Eckhart hung up the phone. He just sat there looking at Seraj, who was no more alive than the shaggy carpet upon which his supine corpse lay. Closing his eyes. Eckhart thought of how things could have turned out differently. He envisioned Nora and himself walking through the black hills without the fear of the invasion of demons that torment.

There was some meat on the grill, marinated in kalbi sauce the way he liked it back in Korea. His two blonde children were running around the yard as carefree as birds in flight but in this vision, time assailed him once again and the hours turned to minutes and in the backyard with his contented face, Eckhart looked to a high hill and there on the sad height was Gilbey in his frock with a bloody rock in his hand. The priest's face was sullen as he tapped the rock twice and blood shot forth from the rock. Father Gilbey then bathed in the blood.

When the thought ended, Eckhart smirked wistfully, put the revolver in his mouth and pulled the trigger.

EPILOGUE

**"What are the roots that clutch, what branches grow
Out of this stony rubbish? Son of man,"**

- ("The Wasteland") T.S. Eliot

For those seeking to know how Gilbey fared in the aftermath of the James Eckhart murder-suicide, I apologize that I must save that tale for another day but "knowing how way leads on to way, I doubt I shall ever come back" to the forlorn crownless King Nothing.

Somewhere out in Boseong, Woo-jin was putting the final touches on his book that was surely destined for greatness now that he had the Florida bits. It bothered him that Gilbey served not a single day in jail for any of his criminal activity. He didn't dwell on it though because at 46 years old, life was beginning to show some promise because he believed wholeheartedly that his book, which he had yet to publish, would launch him into stardom and he could get a place in Gangnam, and brush shoulders with the cute little starlets from KBS dramas and one of them, despite being half his age, would share a bed with him. She would make him feel younger and in all the excitement of a brave new life full of so much zest, he would be born again.

The Boseong police eventually discovered that Ji-hyun Jee was the one who ordered the abortion drugs that were used on Bo-kyung. Rather than plead to a lesser charge, her husband fought the law in court and with their being little sympathy for the victim because of past transgressions, he was let off but as soon as he was released, he packed his bags and headed for Pohang. He would stay in a goshiwon and the elder Jee would set up some menial work for him and that's how he was doomed to spend the remainder of his years.

As for the lovers themselves, Jin-hee took the opportunity to continue the honor of the Jee name by severing the relationship through annulment. Bo-kyung pleaded with Jin-hee that their love should endure the miscarriage. Although moved, Jin-hee refused to yield to her pleas, knowing that the door to exit was only open for a short time like in *Stargate*. Whether he loved her or not, only Jin-hee's heart can know but certainly, the family silently rejoiced when it was announced that the original bride was once again the betrothed.

Jin-hee stood out with his palsy-ridden elder (Jong Suk Jee) surveying the fields of green tea.

"We didn't quite have the tea season that we wanted to have, hal-abeoji [grandfather]. The winter was too warm." With all of his strength, the elder lifted his cane in his trembling hand and pointed toward the fields,

"Soon, I will be returning to this. The birds of the air peck at my corpse and worms dig through me."

"I don't want to think about that, hal-abeoji."

"Well, you must! You were dumb enough to almost ruin this family. Do you think I am immortal? I can only pray that one day you will be standing at this field with your own grandson, telling him what he seeks to inherit."

"Yes, sir."

"Let's go now; the twilight is calling us in."

AUTHOR BIOGRAPHY

R. W. Kennedy is an adjunct professor of writing and composition at two colleges in Boston, Massachusetts, having received both his bachelor's and his master's degree in English from Providence College and the University of Massachusetts (Boston), respectively

The setting for Kennedy's crime thriller, *The Truth the Dead Know*, was inspired by his impressions and experiences during the time he spent teaching English in South Korea and other locations.

41790436R00169

Made in the USA
Middletown, DE
22 March 2017